T0158527

PRAISE FOR *BLACK HEARTS*

'A new outing for the Skelfs deserves dancing in the streets of Edinburgh' Val McDermid

'A total delight to be returned to the dark, funny, compulsive world of the Skelfs ... Johnstone never fails to entertain while packing a serious emotional punch. Brilliant!' Gytha Lodge

'The Skelfs keep getting better and better. Compelling and compassionate characters, with a dash of physics and philosophy thrown in' Ambrose Parry

'Doug Johnstone does it again. Expertly written, with poise, insight and compassion, this poignant reflection on grief and what it means to live after death is a welcome addition to a unique series. How wonderful to be immersed once more in the world of the Skelfs, three generations of indomitable women who light up Edinburgh's literary pantheon, in this visceral yet tender read' Mary Paulson-Ellis

'Dynamic and poignant ... Johnstone balances the cosmos, music, death and life, and wraps it all in a compelling mystery' Marni Graff

'A gritty mystery full of crime, betrayal and fear – but it's also a remarkably told tale about the subtle and chaotic effects of grief and loss' B.S. Casey

'A symphony of tension, tenderness, despair, healing and hope ... it's difficult to come away from *Black Hearts* without feeling inspired, uplifted and in a way spiritually laundered' Café Thinking

'Just when you thought you couldn't love the Skelfs more, Doug Johnstone finds a way to turn up the heat' Live & Deadly

'A study in humanity from the darkest of corners' Sarah Sultoon

'This whole series has this unique combination of mystery, thrills, drama, science and humour ... *Black Hearts* is a fantastic addition' From Belgium with Book Love

'From moments of tension, to moments of quiet reflection, the ebb and flow of this book is pitched perfectly and I absolutely ate it up' Jen Med's Book Reviews

PRAISE FOR THE SKELFS SERIES

SHORTLISTED for the McIlvanney Prize for Best Scottish Crime Book of the Year
LONGLISTED for Theakston's Old Peculier Crime Novel of the Year
SHORTLISTED for Amazon Publishing Capital Crime Thriller of the Year

'An engrossing and beautifully written tale that bears all the Doug Johnstone hallmarks in its warmth and darkly comic undertones' *Herald Scotland*

'Gripping and blackly humorous' *Observer*

'A tense ride with strong, believable characters' Kerry Hudson, *Big Issue*

'The power of this book, though, lies in the warm personalities and dark humour of the Skelfs, and by the end readers will be just as interested in their relationships with each other as the mysteries they are trying to solve' *Scotsman*

'Remarkable' *Sunday Times*

'This enjoyable mystery is also a touching and often funny portrayal of grief ... more, please' *Guardian*

'Wonderful characters: flawed, funny and brave' *Sunday Times*

'Exceptional ... a must for those seeking strong, authentic, intelligent female protagonists' *Publishers Weekly*

'Keeps you hungry from page to page. A crime reader can't ask anything more' *The Sun*

'If you loved Iain Banks, you'll devour the Skelfs series' Erin Kelly

BLACK HEARTS

ABOUT THE AUTHOR

Doug Johnstone is the author of thirteen previous novels, most recently *The Great Silence* (2021). *The Big Chill* (2020) was long-listed for the Theakston Crime Novel of the Year and three of his books, *A Dark Matter* (2020), *Breakers* (2019) and *The Jump* (2015), have been shortlisted for the McIlvanney Prize for Scottish Crime Novel of the Year. He's taught creative writing and been writer in residence at various institutions over the last decade, and has been an arts journalist for over twenty years. Doug is a songwriter and musician with six albums and three EPs released, and he plays drums for the Fun Lovin' Crime Writers, a band of crime writers. He's also co-founder of the Scotland Writers Football Club.

Follow Doug on Twitter @doug_johnstone and visit his website: dougjohnstone.com.

The Skelfs Series
A Dark Matter
The Big Chill
The Great Silence
Black Hearts

**Other titles by Doug Johnstone,
available from Orenda Books**
Fault Lines
Breakers

BLACK HEARTS

DOUG JOHNSTONE

**ORENDA
BOOKS**

Orenda Books
16 Carson Road
West Dulwich
London SE21 8HU
www.orendabooks.co.uk

First published in the United Kingdom by Orenda Books, 2022
Copyright © Doug Johnstone, 2022

A catalogue record for this book is available from the British Library.

ISBN 978-1-914585-29-6
eISBN 978-1-914585-30-2

Typeset in Garamond by typesetter.org.uk

Printed and bound by CPI Group (UK) Ltd, Croydon CR0 4YY

For sales and distribution, please contact info@orendabooks.co.uk or visit
www.orendabooks.co.uk.

For Tricia, Aidan and Amber

1

DOROTHY

The atmosphere in Liberton Cemetery was off. Dorothy pulled at her cuffs as she walked behind the four pallbearers carrying Kathleen Frame to her last resting place. The starchy Church of Scotland minister had just finished an awkward service in the kirk behind them, and that energy followed them out to the graveyard. With the stone steps and rough tarmac here, they couldn't use the wheel bier. It wasn't good to have the coffin rattling its way to the grave, mourners imagining the body being tossed around inside.

Archie was front left of the coffin, holding a handle at waist height. Across from him was Mike, Kathleen's brother-in-law, mouth turned down. Back left was Kathleen's son Danny, gripping his handle so tight his knuckles looked fit to burst. He glowered at Mike's back like he was trying to burn a hole through him.

Grief came in infinite forms, there were as many different ways to mourn as there were people, and Dorothy had learned never to be surprised. Some wailed and gnashed their teeth, others quietly sobbed, laughed nervously or openly, stood like statues, simmered like pressure cookers.

They passed a row of old, fallen gravestones, no living relatives to pay for restoration. They walked past a gathering of smaller graves for stillborn babies, all from the early seventies. She thought about the lost possibilities. They would be late forties now, her daughter's age.

The pallbearers walked through a passageway in the wall separating the old kirkyard from the newer cemetery. The view from Liberton Brae filled Dorothy's heart, Arthur's Seat and Salisbury Crags towering over the city like ancient sentinels. She could see the observatory on Blackford Hill where Hannah's post-grad office was, and Braid Hills further left, large expanses of grass and gorse.

The sky was mottled salmon skin, the leaves on the cherry and yew trees wet to touch as Dorothy passed. She felt the freshness on her fingers, touched them to her forehead. Up ahead, Danny was still trying to crush his coffin handle, staring at Mike's back. The fourth pallbearer was a friend of Danny's called Evan, clearly uncomfortable in a black suit too small for his lanky frame. He'd accompanied Danny to the Skelf house to arrange the funeral. Danny didn't mention his dad throughout the whole process.

As they came over the rise, the view of the city expanded. Dorothy thought about her family's relationship with Edinburgh. She pictured the city as a biodome, a complex and interconnected group of organisms, autonomous yet part of a greater self. She imagined herself, Jenny, Hannah and Indy as miniscule bacteria, working to help other parts of the whole, scurrying from their funeral-director home to hospitals, care homes, hospices, the mortuary, churches, mosques, synagogues, crematoriums, cemeteries, graveyards, memorial gardens, wakes. Helping people transition from life to death.

She looked around. There were thirty mourners, mostly middle-aged, a handful of Danny's friends, wide-eyed at being confronted by mortality. Graveyards were no place for the young.

They walked past a noticeboard at the Liberton Brae entrance. Pinned on it was a council warning not to misbehave, sixteen bullet points written in constipated quasi-legal language: 'No person shall, whilst in a cemetery, wilfully or carelessly use any profane or offensive language, or behave in an offensive, disorderly or insulting manner.'

'Fuck off,' Dorothy said under her breath.

They reached the freshly dug grave and put Kathleen down on a low wooden plinth alongside. Archie joined Dorothy as the mourners gathered at the other side of the grave. The smell of damp earth was strong, and Dorothy thought of planting and rebirth. She was spiritual not religious, didn't follow any doctrine but did believe there were energies in the universe we don't fully understand. Hannah told her that modern physics agreed – the interconnectedness of things, chaos theory, fuzzy logic, quantum entanglement.

She looked at the coffin and the grave. Burial was becoming less common, cremation overtaking. Both were terrible for the environment, but most people they dealt with were old and liked the old ways. Things take time to change.

The minister stood at the head of the grave. Danny glared at his uncle, who stood next to his wife. Mike had a strong jaw and blue eyes, Roxanne had bright-red hair, Jackie O shades and a low-cut black dress.

Dorothy glanced at the adjacent gravestone, worked out the age of William Hush when he died. Sixty-seven. She did this with every grave. Now, at seventy-two, she was older than many she calculated.

The minister's monotone fought with the traffic noise from Liberton Brae. A bus's chugging engine filled the air. Two crows took off from a gravestone and flew into a fir tree. Dorothy felt drops of rain on her face.

'You fucking know.' This was Danny pointing at Mike.

Evan reached for Danny's shoulder but Danny shook him off. The minister stopped.

Danny took two steps towards Mike. 'You know where he is.'

Mike shook his head and took his hands out of his pockets.

'Danny,' he said. 'He's gone.'

'No.' Danny took more steps. 'He faked the whole thing and you know all about it.'

'You're wrong.' Mike's fists were clenched. He shifted his shoulders so that he was now protecting Roxanne.

'You bastard.'

Danny lunged at him. Mike ducked but not quick enough, got

a thunk on the side of his head which knocked him off balance. Danny shoved his chest and kicked his crotch, Mike doubled over. Danny went to punch again but Mike shoulder-charged him, arms around his waist as they staggered towards the open grave. Danny smacked the back of Mike's head then writhed free and spun the pair of them round. Mike's heels hung over the lip of the hole as Danny pummelled him. They lurched backward and for a moment they were suspended over the grave. Mike's feet scrambled until he found footing on the other edge of the grave, Danny gripping his waist, their weight propelling them over the hole and straight into Kathleen's coffin, which slid off the plinth and smacked into William Hush's gravestone. The lid split as the casket fell back from the stone, then it flapped open and Kathleen sprawled onto the grass, her face thumping the ground, skirt riding up her thighs, arms splayed out like she was skydiving.

2

JENNY

She stepped into the water and her breath caught in her chest. She waded deeper, grey swells hitting her thighs and groin. She breathed, tried to get over the shock. Each time she did this, her body acted like it would never recover. Gradually her breathing softened but her skin still burned with cold. She went in up to her chest and turned.

Porty Beach had changed a lot in the few years since she'd lived down here. It was mostly empty back then and no one went wild swimming. She hated that term, it was just swimming. Now groups of women were out in the water, bathing-capped heads bobbing like inquisitive seals along the seafront. Some folk were on paddleboards, kayaks, a rowing boat heading to Musselburgh. The sky reflected the shifting grey of the sea.

She swam straight out. Most other swimmers were in groups, but she wasn't someone who joined in. The dark stretch of Fife lay across the firth as she swam into bigger waves, salty mouthfuls when she timed it wrong, seaweed against her legs. It wouldn't take Freud to work this out. Just over a year since all the shit with Craig on Elie beach – setting fire to him and watching him burn on the boat like it was a Viking funeral. They still hadn't found his body. And here she was, swimming in the same stretch of water to heal herself mentally and physically. And maybe stumble across his charred and bloated corpse so she could be sure.

The waves got bigger as she paused to rest. Swirls tugged at her legs, an undertow she hadn't felt before, despite coming here for the last year. Brandon, her therapist, had his doubts about all this. Dorothy and Hannah pushed her towards therapy because of the night terrors, the alcohol and sleeping pills, the fact she'd destroyed everything with Liam. Fuck, swimming was supposed to stop her thinking.

She pushed into the swells, sea spray on her face. She felt another tug at her legs as a wave swept over her. She flipped, struggled to get upright, eyes stinging from the salt. She saw gloomy daylight for a moment, gulped in air, then another wave crashed on her head, pushing her under like a giant hand, the undertow spinning her until she wasn't sure which way was up. She felt another wave hammering the surface and plunging through to shove her down, her lungs starting to burn, arms and legs frantic, scrambling to get to the surface, whichever way that was, then another wave and she felt energy drain from her limbs.

She saw a figure approach through the murk, then she was spun around by a current. She felt hands on her waist, pushing her up, and she pictured Craig, his gun at her head as he shoved her into the boat and poured petrol over her before she flipped things and sent him to his death. But maybe he had come back, this was his revenge, drag her to the bottom of the ocean with him.

Her head broke the surface and she gasped, swung round and threw a punch, only it wasn't Craig, of course, just some Good Samaritan saving her life, blood now pouring from his nose. A wave broke over her head and she wanted to get sucked into oblivion.

'So that's been my morning,' Jenny laughed. 'Punched a guy for saving my life. What about you, cured any psychos?'

She tilted her head and smiled at Brandon. His office was just big enough for a desk in one corner, a therapy area in the other, two low chairs facing each other. The chairs were uncomfortable and Jenny heaved herself out and walked around. Nervous energy coursed through her every time she came here.

Brandon King was attached to the university's psychology department. He wasn't a qualified psychotherapist yet, which meant he was dirt cheap. His wee office in the new building at the bottom of Chalmers Street was a stone's throw from where Hannah used to attend counselling sessions. Hannah had apparently come to terms with her dad's psychotic behaviour and eventual death. She had Indy for support, a new marriage to a loving wife, two beautiful young things bouncing back from everything life threw at them. Jenny didn't feel like she would ever bounce back from this.

She stared out of the window. The leaves were turning in the Meadows and over on Bruntsfield Links. She could just see their house, three storeys of Gothic Victorian melodrama overlooking the Links from Greenhill Gardens. Funeral directors and private investigators, it was a wonder she hadn't been to therapy before now. And she didn't even believe in therapy. Talking about your feelings was stupid. She'd come here under duress but found Brandon cute and amiable, a daft puppy.

She turned back to him. He still hadn't spoken, classic therapist schtick. He was tall and goofy, a mop of curly black hair, in a plaid shirt and jeans, Converse. He was early thirties, not quite young enough to be her son but not far off.

He stuck his chin out eventually. 'So how did that make you feel?'

Jenny rolled her eyes and tutted at the cliché. 'Fucking great. I'll be lucky if he doesn't sue.'

Brandon nodded. 'Are you sure swimming in the Forth is a good idea?'

He was a hundred-percent right. But imagine a crazy coincidence, if, one time, she found Craig's disintegrating corpse bobbing on the surface, fish nibbling his toes, sucking out his eyeballs, chewing on his rectum. How fucking sweet would that be?

'It's good exercise,' she said.

Brandon frowned. She found his disapproval hilarious. He

knew exactly what she was like yet still managed to be disappointed in her.

'What about the meditation exercises we talked about?'

She went cross-eyed and stuck her thumbs up. 'Just great. Fantastic.'

She was trying to get a rise out of him, part of the playful back and forth.

He shrugged and smiled. It was a cute smile. 'You're paying for these sessions, Jenny. If you don't think they're useful...'

This was part of it too, he pretended he didn't care but he was too nice not to.

'OK.' Jenny put her hands up as if he was pointing a gun. She remembered Craig doing exactly that on Elie beach, lighthouse flashing behind him, the shush of the waves in her ears.

She felt suddenly tired, crashing after the adrenaline from the thing in the sea earlier.

Her phone pinged in her bag, and she went to her chair and took it out. A message from Mum. She read it and lifted her bag from the back of the chair, threw it over her shoulder and stuffed the phone back in.

'Sorry, big guy, I have to pick up a body. You can cure me next time.'

3

HANNAH

Hannah watched Indy walk up Middle Meadow Walk towards Söderberg. Her hair had grown out recently and suited her face, and the dark-turquoise highlights matched her eyes. The curve of her hips in her suit, bracelets on her wrists, henna patterns on her hands. She spotted Hannah and waved. Hannah got up from her seat outside the café and they kissed, once hard then a softer coda.

'How's work?' Hannah said as they sat.

'You know,' Indy said, flicking her hair forward over a shoulder. 'Full of death and grief. You didn't make it into uni yet, then?'

'Not quite.'

Hannah had been excited to start her PhD a year ago, working in the exoplanet research group at Edinburgh University, her own small office at the Royal Observatory. But she was in the middle of it now and felt a little ground down. She was a long way from the initial burst of enthusiasm, but the end point seemed an impossible goal. Her daily routine was number crunching and mathematical modelling, working out the signatures of planets around other stars. But the giant telescopes they needed to detect these things took forever to come online, and it all seemed billions of miles away. Literally.

A waitress took their order, salmon on rye for Hannah, halloumi salad for Indy. They swapped small talk about Indy's work. She still sometimes covered the phones at the Skelf house, but she'd progressed to being a funeral director now, dealing with everything from the bodies to the ceremony, the technicalities to aftercare. It was like being a wedding planner except you had to do everything in a week, at a time when your clients were distraught and fragile.

Hannah helped out between studies, but she preferred to work the PI stuff. At the moment she had plenty of time.

Indy had been talking and she'd drifted off.

'What?'

Indy cricked her neck. 'You weren't listening.'

'Sorry.' Hannah reached for her hand. Her fingers ran over Indy's engagement and wedding rings.

'I said you need to find that spark again,' Indy said. 'Remember how excited you were when you started your postgrad? Kid in a sweet shop.'

Hannah shrugged. 'We all grow up.'

Indy gave her a wide-eyed stare. 'Shit, it's worse than I thought. You're only twenty-three.'

Hannah looked at the path alongside, from the Old Town to the Meadows. An artery full of people, lots of students now that classes were back, fewer tourists since the festival had packed up, and, in between, all the variety that Edinburgh had to offer – young mums, old couples, teenagers bunking school, skateboarders, cyclists, dropouts, office workers. Every one of these people was a newborn baby once. Each of them shaped by countless forces, kind parents and bullies, accidents and bad decisions, good fortune and determination. An infinite interplay that you could never model on a computer. And they would all end up as corpses. The best we could hope for was to live a decent life and that someone might miss us a little when we're gone.

Hannah laughed.

'What?' Indy said.

Hannah shook her head and squeezed Indy's hand. 'Just happy to be alive.'

That was a catchphrase between them, a signal when either of them went dark in their minds. It started as a joke but it felt deeper now.

Their food arrived and they ate. Hannah felt a smirr of rain from the heavy sky, saw the trees sway in the wind.

Indy took a mouthful of salad. 'Hey, Nana called this morning.'

'Everything OK?'

'Just wanted a blether.'

This was Indy's gran, Esha, who'd come over last year from Kolkata with husband Ravi. She liked to keep tabs on Indy and Hannah's exotic lesbian marriage – in an approving manner. Hannah loved that Indy was close to her grandparents, they were all the family she had. She thought about her own mum and gran living together in a house ten minutes from her flat.

A middle-aged woman walked up the lane with an elderly man. He had a cane and waved her away as she fussed over him. Hannah flashed on Dorothy on a metal table in the embalming room and felt her throat tighten. Dark thoughts, just happy to be alive.

'We really should go visit Esha and Ravi,' Hannah said.

Unspoken between them: *before it's too late*.

Indy nodded. 'Kolkata would blow your mind.'

'Hi.'

Hannah turned at the voice behind her, saw a woman her own age, small and thin, hair in a messy bun, hoop earrings, large round glasses and a wide smile. She wore a flouncy white blouse and a hippyish brown leather jacket, leggings and trainers.

'Hi,' Hannah said, a question in her tone.

'Sorry, you must think I'm so rude, interrupting your lunch.' The woman glanced at the plates, then at Indy, then Hannah. 'I'm Laura, we actually met once but you won't remember.'

She left a pause and Hannah tried to think.

Laura shook her head as if reprimanding herself. 'Laura Abbott, I study physics at King's Buildings, final year of undergrad. You did a talk about postgrad opportunities, I asked about mentors.'

That rang a vague bell. 'I remember, hi.'

Laura nodded, making her earrings bump against her jutting collarbone. 'Anyway, I just spotted you, thought I would say hello.'

Laura looked at Indy, who smiled warmly.

Hannah took the hint. 'This is my wife, Indy.'

'Your wife, that's so cool.' Laura seemed surprised she'd said that out loud and raised two fingers to her lips. 'Sorry.'

Indy smiled at Hannah. 'Not at all, it is cool.'

Laura leaned in and glanced over her shoulder like she was about to tell a secret. 'I hope this isn't weird, but I just wanted to say you're a bit of an inspiration.'

Hannah felt a shiver run through her.

'I mean, everything you went through.' She glanced at Indy, back at Hannah. 'With your dad.'

Hannah straightened her shoulders and pushed her chin out. Her family history had been big news over the last few years, of course strangers would know.

Laura spotted the body language and recoiled, stumbled over the kerb. 'I'm so sorry, I shouldn't have said anything.'

'It's fine.'

Hannah listened to the chatter from nearby diners, a clatter of cutlery, the coo of a woodpigeon in the oak tree.

'I should...' Laura pointed a thumb down the road. 'I just ... I'm sorry.'

Hannah shook her head. 'It's fine, Laura, honestly. It was good to meet you.'

Laura switched on a smile. 'OK. Bye.'

'Bye.'

Indy waved after her. 'Bye, Laura.' She turned to Hannah with a grin. 'Somebody has a crush on you.'

'Shut up.' Hannah watched Laura walk away and tried to remember, but she was pretty sure she'd never seen her before in her life.

4

DOROTHY

Leslie's Bar was the kind of old-school pub that was vanishing from Edinburgh. Carved wooden gantry, stained glass and burgundy upholstery. Dorothy sat with Danny Frame in the snug, separated by more dark wood and glass from the main bar where the wake was happening. The noise of reminiscing and condolence drifted over the divider as Dorothy sipped her Lagavulin and felt the peaty burn. Danny glugged a pint of cloudy IPA, took off his black-framed glasses and ran his thumb and finger across his eyes.

'Takotsubo,' he said, putting his glasses back on.

'Sorry?'

Danny drank, nodded to himself. 'Takotsubo cardiomyopathy, that's what they said Mum died of. It's like a heart attack except there's no obvious clinical cause. The left ventricle balloons up. That's how it gets its name, it looks like a pot used by Japanese fishermen to trap octopuses.'

He touched a hand to his chest and held Dorothy's gaze. 'Also known as broken-heart syndrome. Brought on by extreme emotional distress. I Googled it.'

'I'm sorry.' Dorothy examined Danny – young, smart, desperately lost.

She was a little surprised the wake had gone ahead. After Kathleen's body had tumbled from the coffin, Danny and Mike separated and sat getting their breaths back. Archie and Dorothy hurried over to sort the casket, lifted Kathleen in with as much decorum as they could muster, then secured the lid. What a clusterfuck. Hard for Danny to see his mum like that. The rest of the ceremony went off quietly, just the minister's religious murmur drifting through the air.

Dorothy heard a laugh from the other side of the pub. People *should* laugh at a wake, remember the good times. But Danny scowled at the wall and gulped more IPA. He waved a hand at Dorothy.

'I owe you an explanation.'

Dorothy sipped her whisky. 'You don't owe anyone anything. You just buried your mother.'

His face crumpled. He ran his tongue around his lips. 'That bastard.'

Dorothy knew it was often best to let people talk it out. That carried over to the investigator business, where people would give themselves away if you left enough silence.

Danny straightened his shoulders. 'So. My dad went missing a month ago.'

So that was why Danny hadn't mentioned him while arranging Kathleen's funeral.

'His car was found next to Seacliff Beach in East Lothian. He told Mum he was going stand-up paddleboarding. He had his wetsuit. He was spotted going into the water by some horse riders on the beach. His clothes were at the car. No sign of the board or paddle. Just vanished on a calm day.'

It was clear from his tone what Danny thought of that.

'The police think he got into difficulties. There are weird tides, he got sucked under.'

Dorothy sipped her whisky. A voice floated over the divider, telling an anecdote or joke. 'But you don't think so.'

Danny snorted and gulped his pint. 'No chance. He's experienced, a good swimmer. If he died, where's the body?'

'Washed out to sea?'

'I spoke to a coastguard guy. He said bodies usually wash up in the few days after. Think of all the people who jump off the Forth Road Bridge. They find almost all of them.'

'That's more built up. And it's in the narrow part of the firth. Seacliff is almost open sea.'

Danny stuck his bottom lip out. 'He's not fucking dead.'

Dorothy looked at him. Denial was human nature, the first part of grieving according to theory, followed by anger. Danny seemed halfway between the two. Not that the theory stood up. Dorothy had dealt with more grief than she could comprehend in the funeral business and it didn't follow a nice, easy pattern.

Danny lowered his head. 'Shit, I can't believe we did that at Mum's funeral.'

'Don't be too hard on yourself. You're under a lot of stress.'

'She would've found it pretty funny, she had a fucked-up sense of humour.'

Dorothy smoothed her skirt, rested her hands on her knees.

Danny looked at her. 'She was convinced something happened to him, he was carried out to sea and drowned. She wouldn't entertain the idea he might've faked it. I hinted at it once and she shut me down. Said he wouldn't do that.'

He puffed his cheeks and breathed out. Took a big slug of beer. 'I don't know about breaking her heart, but it definitely killed her. There's scientific evidence that grief makes you physically weak. You hear about couples where one dies not long after the other. Mourning is stressful, gives you high blood pressure, blood clots, reduces your immune system.'

Dorothy knew that from the funerals and her own grief. When Jim died she felt sick, didn't eat, drank too much, threw herself into crazy situations to cope. She always hated that phrase, 'what doesn't kill you makes you stronger'. Bullshit. What doesn't kill you can make you weak, can destroy you in a million different ways. Can make your existence miserable.

Danny finished his pint.

Dorothy understood his need for oblivion right now. 'So that's what the fight was about?'

'Uncle Mike is Dad's brother. They're pretty close. I'm sure he knows something. He acted weird when Dad went missing, like he didn't give a shit.'

Dorothy finished her whisky, felt the stickiness on the glass as she placed it on the table. She could smell the stale booze of the drip trays and a hundred years of drowned sorrows from the bar. 'Plenty of middle-aged men don't show their emotions. It's a badge of honour.'

Danny ran a hand through his hair. 'This is different.' He rubbed at his neck. 'You lot investigate stuff, right? As well as doing the funerals.'

It wasn't exactly a secret in a small city like Edinburgh. They took cases when they felt right, and sometimes when they felt wrong but needed to be done. This felt right to Dorothy.

'We do.'

Danny's eyes looked sharper suddenly. 'I want you to find my lying piece-of-shit dad. Will you help?'

Dorothy took him in. Already so much on his shoulders. One parent fresh in the grave, the other lost at sea. Or maybe not. Either way, he needed help.

Another ripple of laughter came from the other side of the bar.

'Of course,' she said, and went to buy another round.

5

JENNY

Indy drove the body van southeast towards the Royal Infirmary while Jenny stared out of the window at the ghosts. If you lived somewhere all your life, memories haunted you at every corner. They turned at Grange Cemetery, where Jenny picked up a PI case from oddball twins a year ago. They drove past The Old Bell, where Jenny remembered flirting with Craig early in their romance. If she'd known how things would turn out, she would've run a mile. But then she wouldn't have Hannah, so no. They hit the roundabout at the Cameron Toll shopping centre, where Jenny lost Hannah for a heart-bursting fifteen minutes when she was a toddler. Her cheeks flushed thinking about it now, the kind old man who found her in Waterstones reading a kids' book about the solar system.

'How's therapy going?' Indy said.

Jenny turned. Indy never seemed to do chitchat with her. Those eyes always looked into Jenny's soul, uncomfortable but weirdly reassuring. Jenny was glad she had this relationship with her daughter-in-law, although that meant she was a mother-in-law and fuck that shit.

'Happier and healthier every day.' Her voice rose at the end and she sounded manic, kind of on purpose but also not.

'I know you don't believe in it,' Indy said. 'But Hannah appreciates you trying. We all do.'

Jenny swallowed. Christ, how did a woman in her twenties who'd cremated her own parents get to be so smart?

'It's not that I don't believe in it...' Jenny didn't know how to finish the sentence.

They hit roadworks on the A7 at the entrance to Craigmillar Castle Park Cemetery. The lights changed but the traffic didn't move. Fucking Edinburgh.

Indy nodded at the cemetery entrance. 'Got one in there soon. A toddler.'

'Jesus.'

'It's tough.'

The engine idled, a lorry rumbled past the other way.

'Did Dorothy tell you about my ideas for the business?'

Jenny shook her head.

'I'm researching more eco-friendly funerals.'

'Like Archie's mum in Binning Wood?'

'That's one option. I mean, I love this work but did you ever stop to think what we're doing?'

Jenny scrunched up her face. 'I try not to.'

Indy waved her hands above the steering wheel. 'We're either pumping bodies full of embalming chemicals then throwing them in the ground to poison the earth, or we're setting fire to them, using up tons of energy and generating a shitload of carbon dioxide. We're in the middle of a climate catastrophe and our carbon footprint is terrible.'

Jenny felt guilty that she hadn't thought about it more. Hannah and Indy's generation took the climate crisis more seriously, for obvious reasons.

'What else is there?'

The traffic moved and they edged forward, almost at the lights when they changed back.

'Natural burial with no embalming, for a start. And there's a company doing human composting, you can use your remains to grow trees or vegetables.'

Jenny stuck out her bottom lip. 'I think some of our older punters might baulk at that.'

Indy nodded. 'We have to keep the old options on the table, but things need to change. There's promession, which is freeze drying and shaking to bits, but that's not well developed yet. Or you can get buried in a mushroom suit.'

Indy got her phone out and searched, showed Jenny a picture of a small Asian woman giving a TED talk, in a black outfit covered in white lines branching like lightning strikes.

'It's covered in spores that digest your body in the ground, neutralising harmful stuff like pesticides, medicines, heavy metals.'

'Heavy metals?'

'The average cremation releases four grams of mercury into the air, from fillings and other stuff. It's crazy. And now they're finding microplastics in corpses.'

'We are so fucked.'

The traffic light turned green and they were through. Jenny was suddenly aware of the car fumes around them.

'We can do better.' Indy's voice was soft and upbeat, as always. 'Environmental doomism is not the answer. It's fixable.'

'With a mushroom suit.'

'It's a start.'

They turned into the RIE site, negotiated more building work and closed lanes, then drove to the back of the main building. The mortuary had its own entrance, away from the living. Indy parked and they took the gurney out the back, telescoped the legs and wheeled it to the entrance. Indy buzzed and they were let in, met by a young woman in scrubs with Nancy on her nametag.

Nancy and Indy chatted, so maybe it was only with Jenny that Indy didn't do small talk. We're all different versions of ourselves with different people. She thought about herself as a mother, daughter, ex-wife, middle-aged woman full of anger.

'Rhona Wilding,' Nancy said, opening one of the doors on the huge wall of body fridges. So much space for dead people in a hospital. 'Born sixth of January, 1977.'

Shit, two years younger than Jenny.

Indy pulled on blue nitrile gloves from a box on the desk and unzipped the body bag down to Rhona's chest. She had black hair that needed washing, blue lips, small nose. Indy checked for jewellery, compared Rhona's face to a picture on her phone. 'Visually confirmed.'

They'd never picked up the wrong person before, but this procedure had saved them a couple of times from making that mistake. There were a lot of corpses in the world.

Jenny looked around the room. No windows, a yellow tinge to the artificial light. A desk and a computer. Could've been any office in the city, except for the fifty fridges and a huddle of gurneys cowering in the corner.

'How did she die?' she said.

Nancy snapped off her gloves, balled them and threw them in the bin like a pro. 'Stomach cancer. Ate her up from the inside.'

Jenny breathed out as she thought about that.

'Come on,' Indy said gently.

Jenny put on gloves too and took Rhona's legs, Indy behind her shoulders. Indy counted to three and they lifted her from the tray to the gurney, strapped her in. Indy signed some paperwork and they were out into daylight, wheeling Rhona to the van, sliding her inside. The whole visit took ten minutes.

Back on the road, they turned left out of Little France to avoid the roadworks, drove through Craigour and Moredun, turned north towards The Inch. Jenny didn't know this road well, her only reference was that Mount Vernon and Liberton Cemeteries were over to her right. She wondered how Mum and Archie got on at the service this morning.

'But the most promising eco-funeral tech is resomation,' Indy said, as if they'd never stopped talking about it. 'I think we should buy a Resomator S750. They're expensive, but it's an investment. Water cremation, you stick the body in a boiling water-and-alkaline solution, it dissolves in a few hours. The water can be used as fertiliser or cleaned in standard water treatment plants, and they dry out the remains so you still get ashes. It uses a fifth of the energy and produces no greenhouse gases. It's miles better for the planet.'

'Not sure about pumping human remains into the ocean, Indy, I swim in there.'

Indy smiled as they turned past King's Buildings up Esslemont Road towards home. 'It's cleaner than normal sewage. Besides, there must be millions of dead bodies in the world's oceans already, and you're happy to swim with them.'

Jenny imagined Craig's corpse doing the front crawl, racing through the water towards her. They passed Grange Cemetery again and she wondered if she would ever escape the dead.

6

DOROTHY

Dorothy put the large bowl of rice in the middle of the table. She went back to the big pot of veggie chilli on the stove and gave it a final stir. She turned and took a moment. Hannah, Indy and Jenny were fussing around the table, sorting out tortillas, guacamole and salsa, cutlery and plates. It made her heart swell. She tried to appreciate having these women in her house, but the moments always slipped away. She thought about the Buddhist idea of impermanence, how everything changes.

'In one of your dwams, Mum?' Jenny smiled at her. A running joke for decades, how Dorothy tended to fall away from what was happening, try to gain perspective. Jenny could never understand that mindfulness.

Dorothy took the chilli to the table. 'How was therapy?'

Jenny made a face and Indy laughed. 'Don't, Indy already asked.'

Indy and Hannah's flat was not far away and they ate here more often than not. Dorothy cooked to stop her house feeling empty since Jim died. Anything that kept these women in her life was worth it.

She remembered something and went to the large whiteboards on the wall. Rhona Wilding was now on the funeral board in Indy's handwriting. She moved to the PI board, got a marker and wrote *Eddie Frame* in big letters.

Schrödinger came in and slinked around Dorothy's legs. She bent and touched his back. He hadn't been the same since their dog Einstein died, who knew a cat could give a shit? Dorothy remembered Einstein's ravaged body on the funeral pyre in the back garden. That dog saved her life.

The cat walked over to the armchair by the window and Dorothy looked out. It was already dark, lights buzzing along the paths of Bruntsfield Links. The undulating grass looked like shifting dunes in the yellow light. Jim's ashes were scattered out there, grains of him in worms and flowers, or floating in the air, circling the planet looking for a home.

'I took a case today,' she said, returning to the table.

The majority of cases were walk-ins or phone calls, but sometimes the funeral work brought a mystery to their door.

'The same Frames as today's funeral fight?' Jenny said.

Archie had already got the rest of the women up to speed on this morning's debacle.

Dorothy nodded.

Indy looked at the funeral board. 'We buried Kathleen and Danny arranged it, so who's Eddie?'

'Danny's dad,' Dorothy said, spooning rice onto her plate. 'He went missing while paddleboarding in East Lothian a month ago.'

Jenny frowned. 'And his body never showed up?'

Dorothy shook her head and added chilli and guacamole to the rice.

'Very Reggie Perrin,' Jenny said.

Hannah threw Indy a look. 'Who's that?'

Jenny rolled her eyes.

Dorothy smiled. 'A television comedy in the seventies, he faked his own death, left a pile of clothes on the beach and walked into the sea.'

Indy grinned. 'The seventies were so weird.'

'Seventies television made me who I am today,' Jenny said. 'Which explains a lot.'

Indy turned to Dorothy. 'So Danny thinks he faked it?'

Dorothy forked chilli into her mouth. Not enough cumin. 'He wants us to find Eddie, if he's alive. The fight was between Danny and his Uncle Mike.'

'Fucking men,' Jenny said.

The anger in Jenny's voice made Dorothy's heart ache. She wanted her daughter to find peace but that seemed a long way off. Her instinct was to help but that closure had to come from within. All Dorothy could do was be here. It made her feel sick, if she was honest, but that was parenthood.

The house phone rang from out in the hall. The business was closed but they always picked up, it could be a grief-stricken relative, a body to pick up, someone in need.

Indy was already out of her seat, but Dorothy rose and waved her back to the table. 'I'll get it.'

She went to the hall and lifted the handset. This was connected to the line downstairs, their personal and business stuff tangled up forever.

'The Skelfs, Dorothy speaking, how can I help?'

'Yes, Mrs Skelf, I remember you.'

An old man, Asian accent. 'Call me Dorothy, please.'

'Very good. I am Udo Hayashi, do you remember me?'

Elderly Japanese gentleman, they cremated his wife a few months ago. She was Scottish, Dorothy pictured her name on the funeral board, Lily.

'Of course, Mr Hayashi, I remember.'

'Call me Udo. You helped with Lily, you were very kind.'

A lot of funeral places just did the service and sent the bill. Dorothy wasn't casting shade on that but she'd always prided the Skelfs on their aftercare, checking on the bereaved, paying visits for a few weeks after a funeral, or even longer sometimes. It didn't make any money, but she was drawn to help. So often, it was after the funeral was over that the bereaved fell apart. A funeral provided scaffolding for them to cling to. But once that structure was removed, what was left? Relatives and friends returned to their lives, but those closest to the deceased were left in an empty house.

'How are you, Udo?' Dorothy said. She could hear the chatter of the women in the kitchen.

'I'm well, thank you. But I have a problem, I'm looking for help.'

It took guts to say that out loud.

'Is it to do with Lily?' Dorothy said.

Hannah and Indy laughed in the kitchen.

'I don't know,' Udo said.

Dorothy tried to jog her memory. He was a retired academic with a granddaughter living down south, maybe?

Udo cleared his throat. 'I speak to her.'

Dorothy nodded, we all did that. 'Of course.'

'Using my wind phone.'

Schrödinger came out to see what she was up to, nestled at her feet. He was much more clingy than he used to be. 'I'm sorry, what?'

'In my garden.'

'Wind phone?'

'But I'm worried she's not happy.'

'Your wife?'

'Either that or maybe I have a mischievous yōkai.'

Dorothy took a moment. 'Yōkai?'

'Do you know Japanese folklore?'

'I'm sorry, no.'

He sighed. 'Maybe it's easiest if you come and see for yourself.'

Dorothy remembered a flat in Leith somewhere, she'd need to check the records. 'I'm happy to help if I can, but what exactly is it you want me to do?'

'Find out whether my wife's spirit is unhappy or whether I have a demon. Will you come? You're a detective, are you not?'

7

HANNAH

Professor Gabriel Galatas had a smooth Greek accent that danced around the lecture theatre. Hannah looked at the screen behind him, which had a large, glowing, orange doughnut on it, flares stretching around the outside, black in the middle. In the lowered lights of the theatre, the doughnut seemed to throb. Hannah stared at it.

'This is a very famous picture, of course,' Galatas said. 'The first direct image of a supermassive black hole, at the galactic core of Messier 87.'

He flashed a laser pointer at the brightest part of the edge. 'This is the radio emission from the heated accretion ring. It's orbiting the black hole at 350 AU, ten times larger than the orbit of Neptune around our sun.'

As always with cosmological distances, Hannah failed to get her head around the scale. That wee doughnut had a radius 350 times the distance from Earth to the sun. And the black hole itself was six and a half billion times the mass of the sun, and 38 billion kilometres across.

And that wasn't even the biggest black hole out there. Galatas had shown a league table earlier and Messier 87 was thirty-ninth biggest of the ones discovered so far. It was too much to comprehend. That's why she preferred the exoplanet research she was doing. While the distances from Earth were mind boggling, at least the planets were comparable to planets in our solar system.

But she was bored with the day-to-day grind of her work, and this trip to listen to a visiting expert was an attempt to get out of the rut. The astrophysics department had a programme of evening events from the cutting edge of the discipline. She'd wandered over here to the campus on Blackford Hill after dinner at Gran's house.

Galatas ran through more data gleaned from the Event Horizon Telescope and the Very Large Telescope. Hannah smiled at the deadpan humour of physicists. There was a new generation of telescopes being built, one of which was called the Extremely Large Telescope, due to get its first light in the next few years. All of this was exciting, but frustrating too. Everyone needed more data and the telescopes were always playing catch up. It felt like there would never be enough information. That applied as much to the nature of the universe as it did to what had happened to her dad's body.

The door at the back of the lecture theatre creaked open and Hannah saw a glimpse of light from the corridor outside, a silhouetted person entering. A couple of heads turned, Galatas paused then went back to his next slide, a familiar picture of the Milky Way. Hannah thought of Douglas Adams' line at the start of *The Hitchhiker's Guide to the Galaxy*, that Earth was located 'far out in the uncharted backwaters of the unfashionable end of the western spiral arm of the Galaxy'. Perspective.

'Fancy meeting you again.'

Hannah jumped at a voice too close, felt the heat of breath on her ear. She turned and saw Laura Abbott sitting next to her, her bag at her feet, throwing over a conspiratorial smile.

'You look like you've seen a ghost,' Laura stage-whispered. The two students in front of them turned their heads and Galatas peered into the gloom. Laura opened her eyes wide and put a finger to her lips then leaned closer. 'What have I missed?'

Galatas's next slide was the recent picture of Sagittarius A*, the black hole at the centre of the Milky Way. It was tiny compared to other supermassive black holes, but still unimaginable. The professor paced up and down in front of the screen, talking about the difficulties in detecting it, all the stuff in the way, the barrage of radio waves and signals from infinite sources that clutter telescopes' images.

'Are you OK?' Laura said.

Hannah wanted her to shut up. What was she doing here? It couldn't be a coincidence. She remembered Indy teasing her about Laura having a crush. Maybe she'd followed her. But that was nuts, they met hours ago. Hannah had been home and to Gran's house since then.

'I'm fine,' Hannah said through her teeth.

Laura leaned in until their shoulders were touching. Hannah shifted away. If Laura had been a guy, she might've said something about personal space.

Galatas put up a picture of a glowing dumbbell shape, the Milky Way at one end, Andromeda at the other, each surrounded by a cluster of smaller, satellite galaxies.

'It's cray that we're both here,' Laura said.

Hannah cringed.

'What are the chances?'

More heads turned.

'Please stop talking,' Hannah said.

Galatas was discussing the Local Group, more deadpan understatement from the physics community. This was the name for a collection of over eighty galaxies, including the Milky Way. Then zooming outwards, the Local Group was a small part of the Virgo Supercluster, which was a small part of the Laniakae Supercluster, which was a small part of the Pisces-Cetus Complex, a galactic filament a billion light years across.

Laura nudged Hannah. 'Puts our shit in perspective, yeah?'

Hannah caught some of Laura's flowery scent. There was a hint of something acrid underneath, like nervous sweat. Hannah tried to give her the benefit of the doubt, maybe this was a coincidence, maybe she had a crush, maybe she didn't have boundaries. Hannah had encountered that a few times around campus, strangers talking to her as if they knew her because she'd been in the news with all the shit between Mum and Dad.

A shadow of anxiety lurked over her. She glanced across and

Laura beamed in a way that made Hannah's teeth itch. Give her a break, she's just trying to get through life, same as anyone else. What was that Robin Williams quote on socials every now and then, 'Everyone you meet is fighting a battle you know nothing about. Be kind.' Fine, but you had to protect yourself too.

Galatas was back to his dumbbell slide, the Milky Way and Andromeda. He clicked a button and it became animated, the galaxies spinning towards each other.

'Thanks to blue shift measurements, we know Andromeda is heading towards us at a hundred and ten kilometres per second,' he said. 'The galaxies are predicted to collide in four and a half billion years.'

The swirls bounced off each other and flipped away, then came back in, spinning round and away in a coy dance. But they couldn't escape each other, eventually merged into a single glowing whirl of light.

'Mathematical modelling is unclear as to the fate of our solar system in such a collision,' Galatas said. 'Some predict we will be sucked into the supermassive black hole and torn apart. Other models suggest we're thrown out into the blackness of space. Either way, we won't be around to see it.'

He smiled and threw it open to questions from the audience. Hannah stared ahead, worried Laura would put her hand up. Someone else asked if it was true that all galaxies had supermassive black holes at their cores. Galatas waved his hands as he explained it was still an open area of research. He talked about different models and formation mechanisms, got into complex stuff over Hannah's head.

'But in essence it's because of the basic rule of gravity,' he said, 'Objects attract each other and eventually form bigger objects. And the biggest objects are also the darkest. So yes, every galaxy we know of has a black heart.'

Laura nudged Hannah and smiled too wide. 'A black heart, I like that, very Gothic.'

8

JENNY

It was more gin than tonic, burned her throat as she downed it and ordered another. She sat at the bar to feel less alone, as if she was friends with the cute barman, though she knew from working in bars as a student that was delusional. She watched Jamal pour gin into the glass, bend down for bottled tonic, underwear showing as his jeans slipped. She smiled and paid. He didn't look twice, why would he, he was a fucking baby, she was invisible to him.

She glugged gin and looked around. Bennets Bar was beautiful, plenty of old locals, a smattering of students and tourists. The room was long and thin, the bar on one side, a bank of seats and mirrors on the other, sodium glare bleeding through the windows at the front, gloomy to the rear.

She watched Jamal serve a pot-bellied beardie three pints of IPA, froth spilling on his hand. Behind him, the top level of the gantry was all whiskies, decorative small barrels and chalkboards with malt offers and cask ales. It was lit up like a fairground and Jenny felt the gin fuzzing the edges of things. She imagined it was a coconut shy, pictured herself throwing wooden balls and smashing the spirits to smithereens.

She glanced to her right, saw therapist Brandon at a table with three friends. She caught his eye briefly and looked away. So the dance begins, blah blah blah.

She wondered what Liam was doing now. Jenny had first met him when his wife hired her to find out if he was having an affair. He wasn't, the wife was, so Jenny fucked Liam. He was handsome and uncomplicated, and she loved that to begin with. He was there for her when all the shit with Craig kicked off. She dumped him for his own safety then hooked back up eventually, but things were never the same. She grew to hate his puppy-dog face, the way he accepted her bullshit even as it got worse. So she pushed him away, a self-fulfilling prophecy. Easier to be unattached, disconnected.

She watched Brandon lift a pint to his lips, his Adam's apple dancing. The act of talking through her problems was supposed to help, but she was done talking. Easier to stay silent and drink. She downed her gin and smacked her lips so loud that Jamal looked round.

'Another,' she said, waving the glass.

A flicker of a look in his eyes, who is this alky woman in my bar. She paid and smiled, and he smiled back like it was his job.

She downed her drink, slid off her stool and walked the length of the bar. She put something into her hips, Brandon watching her all the way. As she passed his table, she lifted her chin.

She walked on and turned into the gents' toilets, the smell of piss in the air as she went into the last cubicle, flipped the seat lid down and waited.

She heard him come in. Not his quickest time, but still keen. The cubicle door opened and Brandon stood there. She pulled him in, kissed him hard, pushed her tongue into his mouth and began unbuckling his belt, felt his erection pushing underneath. He shoved her jeans and underwear to her knees and pushed himself inside her. The door clattered shut as they circled in the cramped space so that she could lean against a wall. She felt his hands on her bum cheeks, gripping tight as he thrust. She was nowhere near coming, nowhere near losing herself. But that wasn't what this was about. She smelt beer on his breath, sweat, the deodorant he used, and she felt less lonely, as if she was part of something more than just her sad little life.

He grunted and came inside her then went soft immediately. He took a moment getting his breath back and she placed her hands on his back, squeezed then released him. He tucked his cock away and zipped up, looked sheepish.

'We have to stop this, Jenny.'

Every time, like a broken record. 'You can stop anytime you want.'

'It's unethical.'

'OK.'

'And unhealthy.'

'But you love it or you wouldn't be here.'

Brandon lowered his head. 'I'm ashamed.'

She shoved him playfully in the chest, but it was stronger than she intended and he looked surprised.

Her phone rang in her bag and she dug it out. Fiona, Craig's other ex-wife, Jenny's sister in betrayal. She hadn't heard from her in a while and it was late for a random chat. She answered.

'Have you seen the news?' Fiona said. 'A body washed up at Wardie Bay. Someone on Twitter says it's charred.'

'Fuck,' Jenny said, yanking her jeans up with one hand and opening the door. 'Is it him?'

She left the toilet and started running.

೫

She held her card to the machine then jumped out of the cab on Lower Granton Road. She ran down the path to the bay, heard the murmur of the sea. An ambulance and a cop car were parked on the rough grass before the beach, lights flashing. Behind her the streetlights glowed orange, out at sea was black. Wardie Bay was a rough sliver of beach stuck between Granton and Newhaven, bumping against the harbour breakwater to the left. She ran to the vehicles, which were empty. On the beach were bright spotlights, figures milling around a ring of police tape. She felt heartburn as she stumbled over to them, her head pounding. The lights seemed to throb, the rumble of the waves made her queasy.

She reached the tape and was blocked by a cop half her age.

He put his hand out. 'I'm sorry.'

'Have you IDed the body yet?'

He frowned. 'There's no public information at this time. Please clear the area.'

Why did cops speak in that weird tone like they were constipated? She went to go round him and he moved quickly to block her.

'You need to leave.'

An older woman in uniform joined them from behind the tape. Jenny craned her neck to see over there but everything was covered, white tarps already erected.

'I'm a good friend of DI Thomas Olsson,' Jenny said. 'He said I could see the body.'

The woman laughed. 'You could be best pals with the Dalai fucking Lama, you're not getting any closer.'

Jenny started to run around the young guy and was surprised when he tackled her. They fell over, sand spraying into her mouth as her hip bumped a hidden stone.

'Jesus, Callum,' the female officer said. 'Careful.'

The cop released her and she got up, wiping sand from her clothes. She thought about Brandon inside her, Liam's face when she dumped him, Craig pointing a gun at her.

'Are you OK?' the female officer said.

Jenny stared past her at the spotlit area.

The male cop looked sheepish but stood his ground.

She turned and walked to the water's edge, splashed into the wash, felt resistance against her legs as she got deeper, cold seeping into her clothes. She went up to her waist and imagined the millions of corpses in the ocean, a gigantic dead-body soup. She felt herself become part of it, welcomed into its embrace.

9

HANNAH

The early morning haar matched her foggy mind. She hadn't slept well, tossed and turned since three, worried she would wake Indy. So she pushed the covers off at first light, grabbed a coffee and jumped on a bus to Liberton Cemetery. Keeping busy was supposed to take your mind off things.

She walked in the side entrance of the graveyard, but couldn't see the usual spread of the city, all of it shrouded in damp mist. She sauntered past the graves, pretending to check them out. She looked around, no mourners or staff this early in the morning, which was good. She was here to place a surveillance camera at Kathleen Frame's grave, in case the allegedly dead husband paid his respects. It was a long shot, but private investigating was taking a load of long shots in the hope one came off.

But she was thinking about two other things. The first was this situation with Laura. Hannah had no recollection of seeing her around campus before, yet she was suddenly in her face as if they knew each other well. It felt wrong. And twice in one day was so obvious. Maybe Indy was right about the crush. But if so, what should Hannah do about it? She didn't want to encourage her, but also didn't want to burst the bubble and hurt her. After the lecture last night, Laura suggested going for a drink, which Hannah declined. When it looked like Laura would try to walk her home, Hannah made a bumbling excuse about work and headed to her office on campus. She sat there for an hour, waiting until the coast was clear. Then she'd walked home with shivers up her spine, worried that Laura would jump out from each dark passageway she passed. She felt a residual of that now, imagined she would turn a corner and bump into Laura examining a grave.

Then there was this other shit with the body on the beach. Scrolling through her phone last night she'd hit the news story that a body had washed up in Wardie Bay. She'd initially struggled with her dad's dreadful behaviour, worried that she carried his genetic legacy. But over the last year she'd got back on an even keel, thanks to Indy. She wanted to talk to Indy about this body last night, but she had used her as a sounding board too much, worried about all this bad karma affecting her.

She turned a corner in the cemetery and jumped when a fox darted out from behind a tombstone. It paused on the path, stared at her, then slinked into a large hedge running along the east wall.

'Fuck,' Hannah said through heavy breath.

She leaned on the gravestone nearest her, felt the damp granite under her fingertips, a patch of spongy moss. The inscription told her this belonged to Morris Anderson, died 2017 aged fifty. At the bottom of the stone was inscribed:

To live in the hearts of those we love is not to die.

She thought about her dad, maybe lying in the mortuary right now, maybe at the bottom of the North Sea. It was impossible to reconcile the conflicting images she had of him. He had been a good father to her growing up, despite the divorce, attentive, supportive, caring. A good man to be around, or so she thought. When she uncovered his dark side – affairs, coercion, violence, murder – it hit her like a hammer, swiped her feet from under her. For better or worse he was still very much alive in her heart. She would never be rid of him.

She walked to Kathleen's grave, newly turned soil on top, a small slate headstone with her name and dates. She did a three-sixty. A single cherry blossom tree stood ten yards away. She walked over, took the motion-sensitive camera from her pocket and switched it on. She synched it with her phone app, checked the settings, waved a hand in front of it to make sure it was working. Then she pulled out a cable tie, reached to where the trunk split into three wide limbs, wedged the camera in a gnarly crook and secured it with the tie.

She walked to the side then back again, checked the camera was on and transmitting to the cloud. She watched footage of herself, gawky and uncomfortable, in and out of shot in a gloomy grave-yard. It was like a vintage horror movie.

She left the grave and walked towards the entrance, traffic noise coming over the wall. At the gate her phone buzzed. The camera had triggered already. She watched the fox wander along the path, sniff the ground, piss on Kathleen's headstone. It looked at the tree. Hannah held her breath as it stared straight at her. Eventually it turned away. Her heart thumped in her chest, letting her know she was still alive.

10

DOROTHY

She helped herself to another pancake, drizzled maple syrup, threw brambles on top. This was a leftover from her Californian upbringing, the need for a proper breakfast. When she first came here she was amazed that Scots didn't give a shit about eating early in the day. Cereal or a piece of toast, never a communal experience. As a kid and young woman in Pismo Beach she got up early to linger and chat over breakfast. There were a million such differences, of course, and she loved having a foot in both worlds. But breakfast was serious business.

Thomas pushed his empty plate away. Being from Sweden he had his feet in another culture too. Thinner pancakes, muesli rather than cereal, generally healthier. He had a well-toned body for someone heading into his late fifties. He now had more grey sprinkled through his hair and beard than when they met, but his eyes were still bright. It seemed weird to call him her boyfriend, but there wasn't a better word. Partner seemed very serious. Companion felt like the pipe-and-slippers club. Lover? Puke. She was seventy-two and had a fifty-seven-year-old boyfriend, so be it.

She reached out and squeezed his hand, shared a smile.

'Beautiful,' he said, talking about the pancakes, but the glimmer in his eye suggested her too.

She got up and examined the whiteboards on the kitchen wall.

'What's on the schedule?' Thomas said. He had a stronger trace of his Swedish accent than she did of her American, and it was kind of a turn-on.

'No funerals, but I need to pay a couple of visits about cases.'

'The fake suicide?'

They'd talked about it, he was a cop after all. It was a running joke between them, it only took a few minutes after sex for them to start discussing her latest case. It was a bond, a simple way to keep them connected.

She nodded. 'I want to call on Mike Frame, see if he knows anything.'

'He won't tell you.'

'But I might learn something anyway.'

Thomas stood. Schrödinger walked over from the window and greeted him warmly. The cat was a good judge of character.

'You really think it's a pseudocide?'

It was a cheesy portmanteau created by journalists, but it worked. They'd talked this over last night. The three main reasons people faked their own deaths were to collect life insurance, avoid debts or because they'd committed a crime. Dorothy had already checked the financial side with Danny and everything seemed legit. Thomas ran a check and Eddie Frame wasn't in the police database. So why disappear?

'Maybe he just wanted a new life,' Dorothy said. 'I mean, who hasn't wanted to get up and leave at some point?'

Thomas kissed her. 'As long as you're not thinking of it right now.'

'My life insurance policy is terrible.'

Her smile faded as she thought of Danny's face in Leslie's Bar, a destroyed wee boy.

'Imagine just leaving,' Thomas said. 'Not thinking about your wife and son.'

Dorothy shrugged. 'It's not that simple. You're considering his actions as if he's mentally healthy. It's the same with suicide. People aren't in their right minds, they think the world is better off without them.'

Thomas touched his fingers to Dorothy's elbow. 'You always try to see all sides, I love that about you. But sometimes people are just bastards.'

'Maybe,' Dorothy said, running a hand through her hair. 'And maybe he's feeding the fish at the bottom of the North Sea. I hope I can find out.'

Thomas looked at the PI board, pointed at Udo Hayashi's name. 'What's this?'

'He called yesterday.'

'Is it a case?'

'Not sure yet. We cremated his wife a while ago, now he says her ghost is not happy.'

Thomas laughed then caught something in Dorothy's eyes and covered his mouth. 'Sorry, I didn't think you were a supernatural detective agency.'

Dorothy made a sarcastic face and picked up Schrödinger. 'I'm a rationalist, but I'm also a pragmatist.'

'Big words,' Thomas said, but he was smiling.

That was one of the things she liked about their relationship, they were on the same wavelength. That happened so seldom in life you had to hold onto it.

'There's stuff we don't understand,' she said. 'It's a big universe and it's all connected. Just because we can't grasp something yet, doesn't mean it isn't true.'

Thomas narrowed his eyes. 'You're taking the case.'

Dorothy laughed. 'I'm popping round for a chat this morning.'

Thomas looked thoughtful, a cloud passing briefly over his face. 'Do you still have time to join me later? What we talked about?'

She smiled and touched his cheek. 'Of course.'

'Did you see the news?' Jenny was in the doorway waving her phone.

Dorothy shrugged.

Jenny handed over her phone, the top news story on BBC Scotland, body washed up last night at Wardie Bay.

'It's Craig, I'm sure of it,' Jenny said.

Dorothy passed the phone to Thomas and took a deep breath. 'We don't know that yet.'

Jenny shaped her hands into claws, like she was summoning lightning from heaven. 'I was there last night but they wouldn't let me see the body.'

'Of course not,' Thomas said.

'Folk on socials are saying it was charred and burnt.'

'People say a lot online.'

Jenny grabbed her phone back and glared at Thomas. 'You need to find out if it's him.'

Dorothy glanced at Jenny. She wanted to wrap her arms around her but feared her daughter would jump away.

'I'm sure they're working as fast as they can,' Thomas said evenly. 'But I'll see what I can find out.'

He grabbed his jacket from the back of the chair, kissed Dorothy's cheek and turned to Jenny. 'Promise you'll let me handle this.'

Jenny shook her head.

'Jenny,' Dorothy said, reaching out a hand.

Jenny left the kitchen and headed downstairs, footsteps thudding like a drum.

11

JENNY

She walked to the bottom of High School Wynd, turned right onto Cowgate and bumped into a traffic warden. She swore under her breath and went through the mortuary's small car park to the side entrance, corrugated-iron door with access to the body fridges. This was where they brought the hearse when picking up bodies, out of sight of the road. Edinburgh's mortuary was bang in the centre of town, two minutes from the Royal Mile.

She pulled at the door but it was locked. She felt sweat in her armpits, heat on her neck. She went round the building. It was an ugly two-storey block, grubby grey and small, dirty windows. She pressed the buzzer, shifting her weight from one foot to the other. She pressed the buzzer again, rubbed at the palm of her hand with the thumb of the other.

There was CCTV above the entrance, the old camera pointing at her. She tried to put on a smile, wiped sweat from her forehead. She felt like she was posing for a school photo, face aching with the effort.

The buzzer sounded and she went through to reception, cheap wood, scratchy carpet, walls covered in crime-prevention posters. It was a bit late for the dead, being on the slab put crime prevention way down your list of priorities.

Graham Chapel came through from the back, snapping off blue gloves. 'Jenny, good to see you.'

He was a barrel of a man, like a jovial uncle. He always had a smile on his face. Considering he'd been chief mortuary technician here for decades, that was something. Jenny first met him when she was around seven years old, accompanying her dad to pick up a body. The mortuary was for all unexplained deaths. Most folk thought of murder, but the vast majority were just bad luck or bad decisions. Suicide, drug overdoses, homeless and helpless, untreated illnesses. Everyone who slipped through the cracks of society ended up here.

Jenny liked coming here as a kid, Graham had a jar of lollipops on the desk through the back next to the fridges, before health and safety put an end to it. And he always had a daft joke ready for her, something with a black sense of humour. But when she hit her teenage years she rebelled against her family and refused to come with Dad on his weird body-collecting missions.

But she was back to it now that Dad was dead, and found Graham the same as before. He was bigger round the waist, hair now thin and white, but he was the same man.

'To what do I owe this pleasure?' He gave her a knowing look. He knew why she was here, he just wanted her to say it.

'The body that washed up last night,' Jenny said. 'Is it Craig?'

Graham rubbed his stubbled chin. 'You know we don't know yet, Jenny. DNA takes longer than that.'

'What about a visual ID?'

'Police are tracking down next of kin now.'

Jenny thought of Craig's mum, Violet, for the first time in a long time. Jenny had been focused on Craig's impact on herself and Hannah. But of course Craig was someone's son. What must it feel like for your son to be exposed as a murderer? To have his body go missing after someone set fire to him in self-defence and watched him float into the shipping lanes. All the work that the Skelfs did drilled home the idea that everyone has a story made up of both good and bad. But she couldn't square that with the man who tried to kill her, who killed one of Hannah's classmates, who stole his other daughter, Sophia, from her mother and tried to start a new life with her.

Jenny swallowed. 'Thomas said I could ID him.'

Graham gave her a look which made her want to curl up under

the reception desk and hide. 'I don't believe Thomas said any such thing.'

She straightened her shoulders. 'He said it would be the quickest way.'

Graham took his phone out of his pocket. 'I'll call him to check, will I?'

He made no move to press any buttons, just stared at her.

'Don't do that,' Jenny said eventually. 'Please, let me look.'

'It's not pleasant.'

'I've seen worse.'

'I'm sure you have,' Graham said. 'But that's not the point.'

'Please.'

Graham shook his head, kindness in his eyes. 'We have to do things by the book, you know that. It's still an open case that you're involved in. Go home, and I promise I'll get news to Thomas as soon as I have it.'

Jenny remembered being here once with her dad, picking up a young man for burial. Rather, picking up the parts of him they found on the railway tracks after an InterCity 125 smashed into him, spraying blood and guts for over half a mile outside Dunbar. The body bag seemed like it contained a bunch of butcher's cuts or dog food. These were her childhood memories, no wonder she turned out so normal.

'Are you OK?' Graham said, stepping forward. 'You look pale.'

Jenny held the edge of the desk, leaned on it. 'Could I get a glass of water?'

Graham went to the water cooler behind reception. Jenny flipped the hatch in the desk and ran through to the examination room. She felt cool air on her face, saw the spotlit metal tables, the glow of the fridge doors along one wall. There were no corpses on any of the slabs. She opened the first fridge and slid out the tray, unzipped the body bag and saw a young girl, maybe ten years old, red hair. She thought of herself at that age, all the endless potential she had.

She felt Graham's big hands on her shoulders, dragging her out of the room and down the corridor. She staggered as he released her, brushed her hands on her jeans and looked at the floor.

'Go home, Jenny,' Graham said, and the pity in his voice made her burst into tears.

12

DOROTHY

Dorothy loved Leith's vibrancy. There was an edge here, a hint of danger that bonded the community together. Despite the tram works on Leith Walk there was still a hustle to the main drag and its arteries, a diverse and inclusive mix of newcomers and old-timers. She found a parking space on Dalmeny Street, reversed the van into it. She and Hannah got out and stretched. Hannah had been quiet on the drive over and Dorothy wondered about that, it wasn't like her.

To their right was a community arts centre, a dim-sum bar and a graphic design workshop. At the end of that corner was the ornate old kirk, recently injected with new life by the Ukrainian Catholic Church. Dorothy had done a couple of services there, loved the showmanship of incense and holy water.

To their left was a small park, the basketball court surrounded by skaters, a playpark beyond. Dorothy smelled skunk. Most of the street was late Victorian tenements, three-story blocks built to last. She found Udo's door, number forty-five. He was ground floor, had his own entrance. She rang the doorbell and shared a quiet smile with Hannah.

Two young black women in ripped jeans walked past laughing at their phones. It was a sad truth about Edinburgh that the most multi-cultural areas were also the most deprived. Dorothy saw mostly white faces in Bruntsfield but it was a different story in Niddrie or Wester Hailes, where housing was more affordable.

The door opened. Udo was short and trim, about eighty, neat white beard, bald on top but a crescent of white hair above his ears.

'Mrs Skelf.' He spoke carefully, strong accent.

'Dorothy, and this is my granddaughter, Hannah.'

He bowed to them both and smiled, a sparkle in his eyes. 'Come in.'

He led them through the flat to his kitchen at the back. They walked past family photographs, Udo, Lily, their daughter and a granddaughter, Willow, about Hannah's age. The Hayashis' daughter died in middle age, leaving Willow as their only family. And now Lily was gone too.

They walked past Japanese woodblock prints, a frog, a deer, a bat. Delicate lines evoking the animals in a few simple strokes.

In the kitchen, Udo waved at the table where a tea set was already laid out. Dorothy and Hannah sat. The kitchen was clean, worktops free of clutter and dust. Dorothy wondered if Udo had someone helping him since Lily died. The tea set was like something from a seventies sitcom, chunky orange-and-brown cups.

'Thank you for coming,' Udo said. He raised his eyebrows asking if they wanted tea. They both nodded and he poured. There was a small jug of milk, but none of them touched it.

'So how have you been?' Dorothy said.

She'd read the few notes that she made when arranging Lily's cremation. They'd been married more than fifty years, since he met Lily when he moved to Edinburgh to teach at university. He'd shared his retirement with her until two months ago. She died six weeks after being diagnosed with oesophageal cancer, too advanced for surgery or treatment. She'd apparently handled it with good grace, though Dorothy knew cancer was never pretty. It robbed you of dignity, often left bereaved relatives suffering PTSD at the shocking deterioration.

'As well as can be expected,' Udo said, sipping tea.

Dorothy drank hers too. 'Does Willow stay in touch?'

Udo glanced at Hannah. 'She's a wonderful young woman. We talk every week, yes. But she has her own life.'

Silence, just a clock ticking on the wall. Dorothy saw Hannah looking at a dresser at the side of the room in an alcove. It held a wooden box on a stone plinth. It was surrounded by small brown sculptures – a monkey, rabbit and mouse – and a stone statue of an enlightened Buddha, hands clasped in his lap.

'Lily's *butsudan*,' Udo said, smiling. 'It is not a proper shrine but it's enough.'

He got up and opened the doors of the wooden box and Dorothy recognised the urn they'd used for Lily's ashes. It was flanked by two incense burners, a small bell in front. Not too different from the Catholic church up the road. We all need our rituals and ceremonies, ways of remembering.

Hannah joined him at the shrine. He picked up the mouse sculpture, rubbed its nose then handed it over to her. 'She loved *netsuke*. So delicate and fun.'

Hannah turned it in her hands. 'It's beautiful.'

He took it back from her, replaced it and closed the shrine doors.

'You must miss her a lot,' Hannah said.

'She is still with me.' Udo stood looking out of the window. 'I speak to her.'

Hannah nodded. 'Of course.'

Dorothy thought of the number of times she'd spoken to Jim after he died, forgetting he was gone, looking for reassurance, an old pattern to fall back on. Something that wasn't loneliness. She realised she didn't do it so much these days, since Thomas, and felt a stab of guilt.

'I mean out there.' Udo pointed into the garden.

Dorothy stood and looked. At the bottom of the garden was a white phone box nestled amongst beech trees.

Dorothy looked at Udo. 'The wind phone you mentioned?'

'Come.'

He walked to the back door, unlocked it and went down three steps to the garden. Dorothy and Hannah shared a look then followed, the rumble of road works and traffic in the distance. As they reached the phone box, Dorothy heard the beech branches whispering in the wind.

Udo opened the door and Hannah stuck her head inside. Dorothy saw a small ledge with a red rotary-dial phone on it. The cable from the phone dangled down, unconnected.

'I use this to speak to Lily.'

'Nice,' Hannah said.

'I'm not crazy, I know it is unplugged.' Udo stepped into the box. 'In Japan, a man named Itaru Sasaki built a wind phone in his garden in Ōtsuchi to help him cope with his cousin's death. A year later, after the tsunami, he opened it to the public. Many people use his phone to speak to the relatives and friends they lost, it is quite famous. When Lily died, I bought this to talk to her.'

Udo looked up at the block of flats behind them.

'I told my neighbours they could use it to talk to their ancestors. I told them to tell others. My wind phone is very busy. Many people in Leith want to stay connected.'

Dorothy looked at the buildings stretching in both directions. The tenements of Sloan Street whose gardens backed onto Udo's. People in their little boxes getting on with life, separated from each other, from their pasts, their ancestors. But this phone box connected them, thanks to Udo.

'That's a beautiful idea.'

'But Lily is not happy.' Udo picked up the receiver of the phone, looked at it, placed it to his ear. He stared into the trees and Dorothy strained as if she might hear a voice.

Hannah frowned. 'Why not?'

Udo moved the receiver away from his ear as if he was getting feedback. 'She thinks I betrayed her. I let her down.'

'Why does she think that?' Dorothy said.

Udo placed the receiver into the phone cradle. The wind rustled in the trees, clouds scudded east, a hundred pairs of eyes on them.

'I don't know,' Udo said. 'She doesn't just say things. She hurts me.'

Dorothy frowned as Udo stepped out of the box, letting the door swing shut behind him.

Hannah was still peering through the glass at the phone inside. 'Hurts you?'

Udo untucked his shirt and lifted it up, revealing a stomach and chest covered in bruises, black and blue, some browning and yellowing as they healed. He stared at Dorothy then Hannah for a few seconds, then lowered his shirt and let it hang loose.

'Can you help me?'

13

HANNAH

She sat on the grass and put the bag of lunch stuff next to her. Two baguettes, avocado and olive tapenade, bottles of some healthy rhubarb soda from a deli on Tollcross. She looked around the park. She was round the corner from the big house, nearer the Meadows. The sun shone, lots of people spread over the slope. It was weird to think there were thousands of ancient plague victims buried under the grass. This whole area was a massive plague pit five hundred years ago. She imagined the grass was glass and she could see hungry zombie faces below, staring at her avocado baguette. She pictured an earthquake ripping the ground apart, letting all the corpses out so they could finally have lunch.

She smiled at a toddler who waddled close by, his dad keeping a watchful eye. The toddler looked confused by her and went to examine a piece of litter down the hill.

Hannah looked for Indy. She felt a trill in her stomach thinking about Laura, when she might pop up next. But that was ridiculous. Laura might have a crush, might be clingy, but she was harmless. And a small part of it was flattering. It doesn't do your ego any harm to know someone fancies you.

She glanced at the trees on the path. This was close to where she and Indy encountered the Beast of Bruntsfield, a rogue black panther loose in the city last year. Some ex-zoo madman breeding them in his garden. Just another case for the Skelfs.

Her phone buzzed. An alert from the spycam at Kathleen's grave. There had been a few triggers since yesterday but nothing out of the ordinary. Most had been that stupid fox. That part of the cemetery was obviously its patch. Each time she checked, Foxy was padding around the grave, weaving in and out of the stones, sniffing and lifting a leg. A few times it stared at the tree, straight into the camera. Was it just wondering what that thing was in the branches? Maybe Kathleen's spirit was trapped in the fox, trying to tell her something.

She laughed at how ridiculous that was, realised she'd been spooked by Udo earlier. He was a sweet old guy who missed his wife, and the wind phone was lovely. She'd Googled the original one and felt a rushing darkness when she thought of the thousands of people who died in the tsunami. Most of them missing forever. Or corpses discovered weeks, months, years later, unidentifiable. She thought about the person who'd washed up across town. Anxiety fluttered in her stomach, rose up her throat. Sometimes death was overwhelming, impossible to put into words. And the connections, Udo in his garden, the body in Wardie Bay, all those people off the coast of Japan somewhere, waiting to go home.

Then there were Udo's bruises. Dorothy told him to go to hospital but he refused. Perhaps because it was inexplicable. Or maybe because of shame, the shame felt by abuse victims. Another Skelf mystery to add to the list.

'Hey.'

Hannah turned and saw Indy backlit by the sun, a halo around her head.

'Hey.'

Indy shifted her weight but didn't sit down. 'Do you want to tell me something?'

Her voice sounded off, serious tone.

'Sit down,' Hannah said.

'I don't want to sit.'

'What's this about?'

'Why don't you tell me?'

'Indy, I don't know what you're talking about.'

'Really?'

'Really.'

Indy dug into her bag, pulled her phone out.

Hannah stood. 'What's going on?'

Indy scrolled and brought up a picture, showed Hannah. It was a dark selfie, framed at a jaunty angle, of Hannah and Laura side by side in the lecture theatre last night. Laura was smiling widely, leaning towards Hannah and angling her head, throwing her eyes at Hannah behind her. Hannah wasn't looking at the camera but she wasn't entirely unconnected either. She must've been absorbed in something Galatas was saying, because she hadn't realised it was being taken. But the way Laura set it up, it looked like they were there together.

'She just turned up at the thing I was at,' Hannah said, hating the sound of her own voice. 'Attached herself to me. I was trying to ignore her.'

Indy took her phone back and shook her head. 'It doesn't look like that.'

'Indy, come on.' She touched Indy's elbow, looked in her eyes. 'This is me you're talking to. You're right, maybe she has a crush, maybe she followed me.'

Indy narrowed her eyes, touched her hair. 'It's more serious than that, how the hell did she get my number? This was texted to me.'

'I don't know, honestly. Are your contact details public somewhere?'

'They shouldn't be. Did she get into your phone?'

'Nothing like that.' Hannah tried to remember. Her phone was in her bag last night, was it near Laura? 'She wasn't on my phone, she just sat next to me. I fobbed her off afterwards.'

Indy glanced back at the screen. 'What do you mean?'

'She wanted to go for a drink, I said I had work to do.'

'That's why you were late home, avoiding her?'

'I made it clear I wanted to be alone.'

Indy raised her phone and Hannah winced at the screen. 'I think you need to be more clear.'

'I didn't know about the picture,' Hannah said. 'I thought this whole crush thing was nothing, now I'm not so sure.'

'Why didn't you tell me last night?'

Hannah shrugged and it felt overexaggerated, like she was pleading for forgiveness. 'It was late, you were tired. I didn't think it mattered.'

Indy put her phone away. 'It always matters. Don't keep things from me, that's a slippery slope.'

'I'm sorry, please, it's nothing.' She pointed at the lunch bag on the ground. 'Come on, you can help me figure out what to do about her.'

Indy's face softened a little and Hannah felt the knot in her gut loosen.

Her phone vibrated and she tensed up, then remembered the gravecam. She opened the app, played the most recent footage.

She felt sick as Laura came into shot in Liberton Cemetery, walked carefully down the path, stopped at Kathleen's grave and looked at the headstone for a moment. Then she turned and stared straight at the camera hidden in the tree and smiled a big smile.

14

JENNY

'You see how it looks.'

DS Griffiths sat with her elbows on the desk, fingers templed like she was pondering a fucking riddle. She was younger than Jenny but that wasn't saying much. Fair hair in a neat pony, smart grey suit, a real achiever. Jenny took in the interview room. Not the windowless shithole you'd think from television dramas. She could see the car park out the back of St Leonard's station, cop cars and vans lined up, ready to go. The walls and carpet were sickly beige. The chair she sat in wasn't even uncomfortable. But this place wasn't a patch on Thomas's office upstairs, with views to Salisbury Crags. A guy had pushed his wife off there recently, it was in the news. On their honeymoon. She wondered how different things would've been if she'd pushed Craig off a cliff the day after their wedding.

'I don't care how it looks,' Jenny said, putting on a smile.

Griffiths had a notepad in front of her, but she didn't consult it. Jenny wondered if it was a prop.

'You turned up at Wardie Bay last night not long after a body washed ashore, and had to be physically restrained by an officer.'

'I could do him for assault,' Jenny said. 'Police brutality.'

Griffiths angled her head. 'I can send you the link for complaints but I wouldn't recommend it. From what I've heard, you needed restraining.'

Jenny shifted her weight forward, fists on the table. Griffiths tried to hide it but she flinched. It felt good to put the shits up her a little. If Jenny was on fucking edge, everyone else should be too.

Griffiths cleared her throat. 'Then you had to be restrained again, at the mortuary this morning.'

Graham wouldn't have offered that up voluntarily, Griffiths must've weaselled it out of him.

'I was just visiting an old friend.'

Griffiths chewed her lip. 'Anyone would think you know something about all this.'

Jenny straightened her shoulders. They'd been in here a while, but she'd waived the solicitor stuff, it was just an informal chat, apparently. 'We've been over this. I need to know if it's Craig.'

Griffiths glanced down at her notepad. 'You mean the man you set on fire and cast adrift in a boat on the Firth of Forth.'

'In self-defence.'

'So you say.'

'I thought this was all sorted.' Jenny was being disingenuous, Thomas had made it clear it was still an open investigation, but she wasn't about to admit that.

Griffiths sighed. 'Far from it.'

'So?'

'So what?'

Jenny leaned forward. 'I could walk out of here anytime, you're not arresting me, I'm just "helping police with their enquiries".' She did air quotes around the last part. 'The reason I'm still here is that I need to know if that is Craig McNamara's body in the fridge down the road. And if you don't tell me right now I'm leaving.'

Griffiths stared at her for a long time and Jenny felt the false bravado draining from her.

Griffiths gave a tiny nod. 'DNA came back. It's him.'

The room swam. She touched the edge of the table to keep herself steady. 'Are you sure?'

'We're sure.'

Jenny sat back and rubbed her eyes, felt tears bubble up, a hot flush along her spine and through her arms. She saw Craig with the gun pointing at her, sure she was going to die, angry that she would be killed by a no-good piece of shit on a beach in Fife in the dark. But it hadn't worked out like that. Life was a knife edge. A sliver of bad luck and it could all crumble. She was still here and Craig wasn't, that was the size of it.

'It's over.'

Griffiths frowned. 'It's far from over, you're a person of ongoing interest in this case, and I'd advise you to contact a solicitor.'

Jenny stood up. 'I don't care. He can't get me anymore.'

But that wasn't true. He was still in her nightmares, still made her feel hot with shame. And he was Hannah's dad, that would never change. They were connected forever.

Griffiths looked at her. 'And don't think being friends with my boss or Graham at the mortuary will do you any favours.'

Jenny shook her head and headed for the door.

Griffiths shouted after her. 'I'll be in touch.'

༄

'It's him.' Jenny shoved Brandon's office door open without knocking. Fizz spilled from the Prosecco bottle she gripped as she swung into the room. She grinned and swigged from the bottle, felt bubbles up her nose.

Brandon stared at her. He was sitting on one of the low chairs in the therapy corner across from an attractive young woman, brown skin, black hair, dark eyes. They were leaning close to each other and Brandon had a look on his face, guilt and anger. The girl stared at Jenny like she was a mad harpy, which was pretty accurate.

'Beat it,' Jenny said to her.

'Jenny, this isn't appropriate,' Brandon said. 'I'm in a session.'

Jenny stuck her chin out at the girl, who looked confused. 'Are you fucking him too?'

The girl's face blushed as she got up. 'Maybe I should come back another time, Dr King.'

Jenny laughed. 'He's not a doctor yet, darling.'

The woman left and Brandon stood. 'What the fuck?'

Jenny leaned towards him, waved the bottle. 'It's Craig. The body washed up last night. It's him, he's finally dead.'

Brandon still looked angry. 'That's a lot to process, but this isn't the way.'

Jenny drank more Prosecco. 'You're right.'

She thumped the bottle on the desk and grabbed the front of his shirt, kissed him hard, pressed her hips against his, forced him back until he was against the wall.

He broke free. 'Stop, this is my office.'

She grabbed his crotch and he winced. 'You know you want to.'

He moved her hand and pushed his head away from her until it clunked the wall. 'No.'

Jenny narrowed her eyes and burped. 'It's OK to fuck me in the toilets at Bennets, but not in your office?'

'Neither is OK, you know that.'

'And it's OK to fuck me when I'm messed up about my ex-husband, but not when I'm happy that he's dead?'

'None of this is OK.'

Jenny reached for the fizz on the desk and swigged. 'Then why are we doing it?'

'We're not anymore. I'm happy to help with therapy, but the other stuff.' He looked sheepish. 'We can't do that.'

Jenny laughed at his boyish face. 'Fuck's sake, Brandon, lighten up. It was just a bit of fun, a quickie against the wall every now and then, no harm done. You're a better fuck than you are a therapist, that's for sure.'

She felt the weight of the Prosecco bottle in her hand, thought about swinging it at him. 'Anyway, I don't need therapy anymore. Craig is dead and everything's fine.'

She blew him a kiss and walked out of the office, desperate to feel fresh air on her face.

15
DOROTHY

The moment before the drums kicked in always contained a frisson, potential about to be fulfilled. Dorothy sat behind her beautiful sunburst Gretsch kit, light streaming across the attic floor, dust motes arguing in the air. In her headphones, Julia Jacklin was strumming on electric guitar and singing. After the first verse, Dorothy threw out a simple three-beat fill and locked into the rhythm, quiet at first, simple but subtle, the right jigsaw piece to make the song fit together. Jacklin was an Australian singer-songwriter that Dorothy's drum student Abi brought to her attention. Abi was more than that, of course, had lived with Dorothy for months, sleeping in this studio while she sorted things with her family. She still came to lessons, though she didn't really need them anymore, she was finding her feet with her own band, The Blood Queens. This track was on a playlist Abi sent her called *Badass Bitches for Mrs S*, six hours of women musicians, alternative pop, rock and indie. It was great there were so many young women making their way in a shitty industry. Abi had all these role models, what a future.

The song swelled in the middle, Jacklin unleashing her voice, repeating that everything changes. Dorothy switched to the ride cymbal for the middle eight, some flourishes around the toms and snare, sitting inside the beat and feeling the band play in synch. Out of the middle eight the song dropped, Dorothy hunching as she tapped the hi-hats and snare lightly. Jacklin sang about her love for a city and Dorothy thought about Edinburgh. The song bottomed out on a gentle fill and crash, the shimmering ring of the cymbal, sound waves spreading into the universe.

She flicked through *Badass Bitches for Mrs S* looking for another good song to drum to. Went past Phoebe Bridgers, Sasami, Wet Leg, stopped at Illuminati Hotties, more punky than the others. She flexed her shoulders and launched into 'Pool Hopping', stick clicks in dropped verses, full-on choruses. She thought about Udo's bruised body, his shamed look, his unconnected phone. And she thought about Hannah and Jenny. In the end, did it matter if this poor washed-up person was Craig? Where does closure come from? She still had waves of grief from Jim's death years ago. The same for her dog, and the hundreds of people she'd help bury and cremate across this beautiful, complicated city. Death was the one thing that linked everyone.

The song finished and the playlist moved onto Cassandra Jenkins, a dreamy spoken-word thing with a jazzy groove, repetitive snare shuffles. Dorothy thought about Danny and Mike at the funeral, Kathleen dead not knowing, her husband vanished. It was too late for her to get closure. In Dorothy's ears, Cassandra Jenkins told her to breathe and count. She tried to follow the advice.

Ferry Road was such a long artery through the north of the city that it changed character umpteen times. Private schools, big houses and rugby pitches made way for tenements and corner shops, all mixed up together. Dorothy passed the turnoff for Warriston Crem, tried to think if they had a funeral there this week.

She found the place, a sturdy semi-detached with ivy up one wall, a short driveway with a black Audi in it. She parked in the street and got out. The traffic was endless and she tried to still herself and block out the noise.

She walked to the front door and rang the bell.

It took a while, then the door was opened by Mike's wife,

Roxanne. She wore tight yoga trousers and a loose tank top over a luminous sports bra. She was sweating, red hair in a bun. She'd aged well or had good work done. She frowned at Dorothy.

'The funeral woman. What do you want?'

'I was hoping to speak to your husband, Mrs Frame.'

'Roxanne.' She wiped sweat from her brow and drank from a water bottle. 'This about yesterday?'

'Is he in?'

Roxanne stepped forward. 'Emotions were running high, these things happen. You must've seen a fight at a funeral before.'

Dorothy had, but usually at the wake once drink was flowing.

'We don't blame Danny,' Roxanne said.

'I never said you did.'

'He's got this crazy idea that Eddie isn't dead.'

'He told me.'

Roxanne looked at Dorothy. 'Is that what this is about?'

'He wants me to look into it.'

Roxanne smiled and looked Dorothy up and down. 'No offence but you don't look like a sleuth.'

'None taken.' Dorothy threw a look back at Roxanne, eyebrows raised.

Roxanne laughed. 'What, I don't look like my sister-in-law just got buried? Life goes on. Fucking Peloton is gonna kill me, but it's worth it. We all grieve in different ways, you must know that.'

'I do.'

'And yet you believe Danny's thing. He's clearly just grieving for his parents.'

'I didn't say I believed him.' Dorothy straightened her shoulders a little. 'I'm just helping him.'

Roxanne stuck out her lip. 'But you're taking his money while you do.'

They hadn't actually agreed a fee. Most of her cases were ones she would've taken whether there was payment or not.

Roxanne smiled. 'Anyway, Mike's not in.'

Dorothy glanced at the Audi in the driveway and got a card out of her pocket. 'Can you give him this?'

Roxanne looked at it for a long time, had another swig of water then took it. 'Sure, but there's nothing in this.'

'Isn't it worth knowing what happened? This is Mike's brother we're talking about.'

Roxanne flicked the card between her fingers. 'I'll give it to him.' She gave Dorothy a deadpan look.

'Thanks.'

Dorothy walked down the drive, turned at the bottom and saw Roxanne still watching her. She went to her van and got in, saw the front door close. She waited three minutes then got out, walked to the Audi and stuck a digital tracker under the rear wheel arch. She returned to the van without looking back, then started the engine and pulled into traffic.

❧

Morningside Cemetery had a glut of notices at the entrance, warnings about headstones and dog shit, all the usual council stuff, a map of famous graves, although most were famous by association – a friend of Florence Nightingale, Robert Louis Stevenson's nursemaid.

Thomas smiled when he saw her. She felt a sliver of melancholy in her heart and smiled back. He was holding flowers, not for her.

They took the long way past the old graves and statues, a Celtic cross, a weeping angel. Morningside conjured up images of millionaires' mansions, but they were overlooked by blocky sixties flats and anonymous tenements. They walked down the central path flanked by huge oak trees, light dappling through the branches.

'How's everything going?' Thomas said. 'With the cases.'

She squeezed his hand. 'Fine. We can talk about it later. How are you?'

He just nodded and looked away.

They reached the grave, at the far end amongst newer stones, and stopped. Dorothy read the inscription, Morag Olsson, 1968–2018. She hadn't quite reached her fiftieth birthday, today would've been her fifty-fourth. A heart attack while riding her bike, dead by the time the ambulance arrived. The Skelfs had buried Thomas's wife, although Dorothy had been friends with him before that.

Below Morag's name was a short quote from a Mary Oliver poem, 'When Death Comes'. She'd helped Thomas pick it out when he told her Oliver was Morag's favourite poet. She wished she'd known Morag, felt sure they could've been friends.

She felt guilty, of course she did. She'd asked Thomas if he was sure about her coming today, but she understood as well. Her husband was dead, his wife too, but they still had to live, right? And just as her grief over Jim was a big part of her now, so Thomas's grief about Morag was the same. They just had to suck up the guilt, do they best they could.

Thomas knelt and placed the bouquet on Morag's grave. It was a colourful array – irises, delphiniums, lisianthus.

'Hi, love,' he said, standing up. He rubbed at his chin and blinked a few times. Sighed deeply. 'I miss you.'

Crows called out in the trees. Dorothy saw a squirrel dart from one trunk to another. She thought about all the years before she'd known Thomas. She would never understand what he had with Morag, just like he could never comprehend her life with Jim. So much of us is a mystery to others, ourselves too.

Thomas reached out and Dorothy took his hand, felt his body tremble with emotion as they stood there, both lost in the endless maze of grief.

16

JENNY

The sky was too bright as she staggered home across the park. The bumpy grass made her lose her footing. After leaving Brandon's office she'd drunk the rest of the Prosecco before she reached Bennets. She wasn't sure how long she spent in there, a few doubles anyway.

She got to the house and squinted at the campervan in the driveway, a load of flashy bikes leaning against the hedge. She crunched over gravel and threw the door open hard enough that it banged off the wall. She made a cartoonish face at Indy on reception and closed the door, paying too much attention to her hands.

She felt like a teenager again, sneaking drunk into the house after partying in the park or a pal's house, trying not to puke on her dad's shoes. She remembered those same fucking shoes on fire as Dad lay on a funeral pyre in the garden, feet melting inside, body shrivelling into nothing. Holy shit she missed him. She hadn't realised what she had when he was alive, never really told him what he meant to her, blocked by some ridiculous thing inside her.

She glanced towards the chapel, saw a funeral service, Mum standing by a plain bamboo coffin. A middle-aged woman in dungarees, her blonde hair in braids, stood at the lectern trying not to cry.

'Shit,' Jenny said in a stage whisper to Indy. 'Who died?'

'Roger Brown,' Indy said, taking Jenny's arm and guiding her towards the stairs.

'Roger that,' Jenny said in a stupid voice.

'Are you OK?'

Soft piano drifted from the chapel and Jenny saw her mum glance at them.

'I just want to...' Jenny said, pushing towards the chapel. She felt dizzy from all the booze as she stumbled into the room. There were thirty people sitting in rows, most in cycling gear.

Jenny caught a look from Dorothy that reminded her of all the arguments they had when she was a teenager. Some mourners looked at her in confusion as she slumped on a chair at the back of the room.

Hair Braids paused to wipe away tears. She stared at Jenny but seemed to look right through her. Jenny felt like a ghost. Hair Braids looked about the same age as Jenny but contented. How was that even possible? She stared at a piece of paper trembling in her hand.

'I want to finish by reading these words by Ram Dass.'

That seemed to mean something to the congregation of cyclists and hippies. Hair Braids cleared her throat.

'"As if in each of us there once was a fire, and for some of us there seem as if there are only ashes now. But when we dig in the ashes we find one ember and, very gently, we fan that ember. Blow on it. It gets brighter and from that ember we rebuild the fire. The only thing that's important is that ember."'

Her voice was low and sonorous and Jenny felt the words go into her.

'"That's what you and I are here to celebrate", she continued. '"That though we've lived our life totally involved in the world, we know, we know that we're of the spirit."'

Jenny struggled to breathe, wondered if she was having some kind of attack. Her breath came out in jerky jumps and she realised she was crying.

Hair Braids looked around the room and her gaze landed on Jenny, who wanted to sink through the floor.

'"The ember gets stronger, flame starts to flicker a bit. And pretty soon you realise that all we're going to do for eternity is sit around the fire.'"

Jenny pushed her chair back and staggered out of the room, scared to listen anymore. She strode past Indy to the back of the house.

She wiped at her cheeks and slammed into the doorway of the embalming room. Archie glanced up from the body on the table in front of him. He was embalming her, pink fluid pumping from the slushie machine, down the tube and into the hole in the woman's carotid. He tapped the tube, checked the dial on the machine, rubbed at the woman's hand. Jenny knew it was to get all the blood out, the fluid in. If the blood wasn't all removed it would rot inside her body.

Archie looked at her.

'You're drunk,' he said, but not unkindly.

'I am.' She tried to regain her composure. She walked into the room, closed her eyes briefly, the lids felt heavy. She opened them and touched the metal table, tried to stop herself swaying. She recognised the woman on the slab, it was the one she and Indy had picked up from the hospital yesterday.

'Rhona Wilding,' she said. 'Two years younger than me.'

Archie nodded. 'And me.'

Jenny forgot they were the same age. Archie's stocky frame, trimmed beard and bald head made him seem older. But maybe Jenny was kidding herself. She used to feel young, before all this shit. Now she felt ready for the grave.

She watched Archie as he worked, attentive to Rhona, gentle with his hands.

She leaned against the table. 'Archie, how come we've never fucked?'

Archie raised his eyebrows. 'You really are drunk.'

'It's a reasonable question.'

She wanted to shock him but he just smiled. 'I'm not sure we'd be a good fit.'

'You wouldn't forget it.'

'I'm sure I wouldn't.'

For a moment she imagined she was twenty again, tight body and endless energy. She'd last felt properly desired by Craig, how fucked up was that? When he came back into her life she felt young again, and every dumb thing she'd done since then had been a pathetic attempt to get that back.

She breathed out and shifted her weight. 'How are you doing, Archie?'

Archie came to the Skelfs twelve years ago when Dorothy spotted him hanging around at funerals and stopped to talk. She gave him a job and, when he said he felt like he was dead, took him to see a psychiatrist. Eventually he was diagnosed with Cotard's Syndrome, a rare condition where patients believe there's no point interacting with the world because they're already dead. In extreme cases they starve themselves to death. Archie was prescribed a combination of antipsychotics, mood stabilisers and behavioural therapy.

'I'm fine.'

There was a firmness in his voice. Jenny didn't blame him, who wants to talk about how dead you feel inside? She watched the embalming fluid flow into Rhona and wondered what it felt like, cold toxins rushing through your veins.

'She looks good,' Jenny said.

Archie nodded. 'I don't know why I'm bothering, I don't think anyone's coming to the funeral. She doesn't have any close family and Dorothy hasn't tracked down anyone who knew her well.'

Jenny thought about Roger Brown in the chapel, friends and family off on a celebratory bike ride, scattering his ashes somewhere scenic, telling stories about him. She imagined doing the same for Craig, raising a massive gin to that fucker's death. Then she thought about Rhona, lowered into the ground or pushed into the incinerator with no one there.

She felt the room spin and swallowed hard. She left and turned towards the workshop. Shelves stacked with caskets, a workbench and tools, the smell of sawdust. There were half-constructed coffins on the floor, a completed one on the low bench, soft lining stapled into the corners. She lifted a leg and climbed into it, using the wall to brace herself. She fixed her clothes as she lay down, felt the material against her head. The sides of the coffin were comforting, they would stop the world getting at her. She placed her arms across her chest and closed her eyes, waited for the release of sleep.

17

HANNAH

Hannah heard Indy's key in the door and tensed up. She was in bed watching an old episode of *Taskmaster* to distract herself. She closed her laptop. She hated when they argued, all that shit earlier about Laura. But she hadn't mentioned seeing Laura's face on the gravecam, and she'd wondered about that all day. Maybe it was because she'd just talked Indy down about the photo at the lecture, didn't want to start things up again. And maybe she was a little tired of leaning on Indy for everything. She kept telling herself it was nothing, she could handle it alone.

'I'm sorry.' Indy stood in the doorway with her work flats in her hand and a tired look on her face. 'About earlier.'

'Babe, I'm sorry too.'

Indy took her jacket off and sat on the bed.

'Anyway,' she said. 'There's more important stuff. Dorothy told me they confirmed it was your dad at Wardie Bay.'

Hannah shifted gears in her mind, felt guilty she hadn't given more thought to her dad. She'd had a similar grind of gears when Mum called earlier to tell her. There was a manic edge in her voice, the slur of alcohol. If anyone had a right to flip out it was Hannah, this was her dad, right? But Hannah felt she'd dealt with his toxic energy when she found out he'd murdered her friend Mel after an affair. The counselling had helped and these days she was on a much more even keel. Did his body turning up really make a difference? She'd assumed he was dead for the last year.

'I'm OK,' Hannah said, clocking the concern in Indy's eyes.

Indy rubbed her arm. 'If you need to talk, I'm here.'

Hannah leaned forward and kissed her. It started as a reassuring peck but she felt a tingle in her stomach and they kissed for a long time. Eventually they came up for air.

'How was work?' Hannah said, wrapping a strand of Indy's hair round her finger.

'Long day.' Indy gave her a worried look. 'Your mum turned up drunk at a funeral.'

Hannah sighed. 'Did she make an idiot of herself?'

Indy shook her head. 'Just sat at the back then walked out crying.'

'God, I'm worried about her. I thought going to therapy would help, but she seems worse than ever. And the alcohol, she's losing the plot. It's a fucked-up situation, I get that, but if I can deal with it, I don't know why she can't.'

'You're applying logic to the situation. It's not logical. *She's* not logical.'

'I know.'

'Do you want me to talk to her?'

Hannah ran a hand through her own hair and shook her head. 'I should do it.'

Three hard raps on the front door made them jump. Hannah raised her eyebrows. It wasn't late but it was dark outside. Plus it was a knock, not the buzzer, so it was either a neighbour or someone who bypassed the downstairs security.

Hannah jumped out of bed and threw on an old sweatshirt and joggers. Indy went to the spyhole, stepped back. She mouthed, 'It's Laura,' and Hannah felt a knot in her stomach. She waved Indy away from the door, as if Laura could sense them. There was a noise, Laura crying and sniffling.

'Hannah?' she said between sobs.

Indy gave Hannah a look and Hannah held her hands out, she didn't know what to do. The crying continued and Hannah wondered if Mrs Wilson across the way would step out of her flat and intervene. They couldn't leave her out there, but Hannah didn't want to open the door either. How did she know where they lived? The sight of Laura smiling in Liberton Cemetery came back to her.

Indy opened the door. Laura had her face in her hands as she sobbed into a tissue. She looked up then threw herself into Hannah's arms, buried her face in her shoulder. She smelled musky, like she'd been spending time with the graveyard fox. Hannah placed her hands on Laura's back. The crying got louder and Hannah wondered about snot and tears on her sweatshirt. Eventually the sobs quietened and Hannah prized herself out of the hug. There was resistance but she pushed hard, kept her hands on Laura's upper arms.

'What are you doing here?'

Laura dabbed at her nose with a tissue. 'I didn't know who else to turn to.'

Hannah looked at Indy, who had narrowed her eyes.

'I never met you before yesterday.'

'I had to come here, I had to see you.'

Hannah folded her arms to create a barrier. 'Why?'

'Mum's dead.' Laura's face crumpled.

Indy angled her head. 'What?'

'I got home today and she's dead.'

'Jesus, I'm sorry,' Hannah said, her mind churning.

'How?' Indy said.

Laura glanced at her but replied to Hannah. 'A heart attack, I think. She had a faulty mitral valve.'

'Where is she now?'

'Still at home, of course.'

'Don't you have any family?'

Laura sniffed. 'It's just me and Mum. It *was* just me and her.'

This caused another sob, a shiver through her body.

'I'm not sure what we can do to help,' Indy said.

Laura didn't look at her, kept staring at Hannah. 'I want you to do the funeral, of course.'

Hannah glanced past Laura to Indy, who was shaking her head.

18

DOROTHY

Dorothy walked into the kitchen and saw Jenny stroking Schrödinger on her lap. The cat had a sense of when people needed his company. Jenny looked like shit, still wearing yesterday's clothes, face crumpled and hungover. It made Dorothy's heart ache. Morning light splayed through the windows behind her. She had a huge mug of black coffee and a piece of toast, untouched.

'Hey,' Dorothy said.

Jenny winced and Schrödinger leapt to the ground.

Dorothy held her phone up, showing the tracker app, red dot glowing. 'I need to go on a stakeout, want to come?'

'No.'

'We can get bacon rolls and Irn Bru on the way.'

'Make it a Maccy D's and you're on.'

Dorothy scrunched her face up. 'You're such a philistine.'

❧

It was a ten-minute drive from Greenhill Gardens to Braid Hills, but the detour to McDonald's doubled that time. Dorothy had her window down to get rid of the smell of the sausage-and-egg McMuffin. It looked like a toy version of food. Jenny slurped from a large full-fat Coke and Dorothy wondered about her daughter's guts. Dorothy wasn't a food snob by any stretch, she'd grown to love Greggs, for God's sake, but this felt bad.

Jenny let out a sigh like an orgasm.

'Better?'

Jenny groaned and took another bite.

Dorothy turned up Craiglockhart Avenue, dropped gears to get up the hill, straight over the junctions and past Craiglockhart Hill. She tried to remember Edinburgh's seven hills. Castle, Calton, Arthur's Seat, Corstorphine, Craiglockhart, Blackford and Braid Hills, which for some reason was always plural. She had a flash of perspective, imagined five hundred years ago when they were all outside the city boundary except the castle. The grind of travel on horseback or foot, few paths, wolves waiting to pick you off. The idea of people thriving here for thousands of years was so alien to her as an American. Of course, that was her white privilege, the indigenous peoples of America did exactly that for thousands of years before her kind fucked it all up.

Jenny slurped more Coke and finished her breakfast as they headed along Braid Hills Approach, past the golf course. Dorothy checked her phone then pulled up near the entrance to the park. She had a good view of the house on Bramdean Rise with the black Audi parked on the road outside, Mike and Roxanne's car. The house was a big post-war build, not old money but worth a packet in this part of town. It was detached, large garden, two cars in the drive, a sporty thing and a people carrier. Dorothy thought about what sort of person had a life here.

Her window was down, the smell of honeysuckle and grass from the park. It was quiet up here, like you weren't in a city. So much of Edinburgh was like that, peaceful pockets of parkland and trees, hills and wilderness, right amongst the thousands of people. She heard the clack and ping of a golfer over on the course.

'So what's this about?' Jenny said, nodding at the Audi.

'The possible pseudocide.'

Jenny burped. 'Suicide?'

'Pseudocide, pretend suicide. Faking your own death.'

'This is your funeral fight from the other day.'

'The Frames.'

'Sounds like a band, I was into their early stuff.'

Dorothy got most of Jenny's references these days, thanks to being in proximity for the last few years. She loved that more than she could say. She remembered when Jenny was a toddler and had no secrets, then when she started lying, transparent at first, then more clever. The shock the first time Jenny talked about something happening at nursery Dorothy didn't know about. The girl she'd given birth to was beginning to have an independent life. Natural, of course, but devastating too. The rebellious teenage years when everything was secret, the student years when she moved out, getting married, having Hannah, getting divorced. All someone else's life, no longer a part of Dorothy. As it should be, but brutal all the same.

'Danny wants to find out if his dad faked his death.'

'Thus causing his mum's death.'

Working in the funeral business you got used to spouses appearing on the slab not long after each other.

Jenny pointed a thumb out of the window. 'What about the Audi?'

'Tagged it outside Eddie's brother's place. Danny thinks Mike knows something about it. I was hoping Mike might be stupid enough to lead us to his brother.'

'Unlikely.'

'People are very stupid sometimes.'

Jenny puffed her cheeks out. 'Tell me about it.'

Dorothy reached over and touched her clammy hand.

'Jen, there's a lot going on. Craig turning up in the water is a lot to work through.'

Jenny shook her head. 'I haven't been working through anything. I'm still the same self-pitying arsehole I've always been.'

'Listen to me. You're not like that.'

Jenny tried to pull her hand away but Dorothy held on.

'I mean it. Think of all the good you've done.'

Jenny scoffed. 'Like what?'

'Helping people. The funerals. Everything you did for Fiona, you got her daughter back, that's something.'

Jenny looked around, trying to avoid the truth of that.

'And look at Hannah,' Dorothy said. 'She's an amazing young woman, that's down to you.'

'That's despite me.'

Dorothy felt her face heat up. 'Jen, come on. That can't be what you really think. You're a great mum to her and a great daughter to me.'

Jenny shrugged. 'OK.'

Dorothy squeezed her hand as tight as she could, felt the knuckles crack under her grip. 'Say it like you mean it.'

Jenny pulled her hand free, flexed it in pain. 'OK, fuck, I'm amazing, don't break my hand.'

A dog walker passed the car and entered the park, let his golden Lab off the lead. It raced up the slope and Dorothy felt a twinge about Einstein. That led to Jim, another twinge, so much life behind her now in her seventies. But there was still life in front of her too.

'Hey.' Jenny raised her eyebrows and looked out of the window.

Dorothy saw the front door of the house open and there was Roxanne in sports gear, her hair down and shiny on her shoulders, big smile on her face. She was followed by another woman, thin and beautiful, short black hair, sharp features, ten years younger. Roxanne pushed the woman against the doorframe, kissed her hard, rubbed a hand against her crotch then her bum, pressed their bodies together. The other woman kissed her back and they stayed like that for a while before separating.

Roxanne headed for her car and the other woman watched her go with a spark in her eyes.

'The plot thickens,' Jenny said.

It was the first time Dorothy had seen her smile in a while.

19
HANNAH

She rubbed at her eyes, tired and heavy. She felt bloated from drinking too much coffee to stay awake. She looked down Middle Meadow Walk. She'd sat at the adjacent table with Indy two days ago when Laura approached them, now they were entangled with Laura in ways Hannah couldn't fathom.

Across the table, Indy looked calmer than Hannah felt. She was more used to dead bodies, calls at all hours, the raw pain of the initial grief. Hannah had come to realise she had no problem with the deceased, wasn't squeamish. But the emotional weight of the bereaved was hard to stomach, impossible to avoid taking it on your own shoulders. And of course, it was more complicated with Laura.

'Some night,' Indy said, sipping a green tea.

Hannah stared at the dregs of her cappuccino. A breeze fluttered her two empty sugar packets across the table. Crows in the trees cawed out a warning, feathery clouds scuffed across the sky, a waitress dropped a saucer. A thin stream of people walked up and down the lane to her right.

'I can't even...' Hannah didn't know what she wanted to say.

The first thing they'd done last night was calm Laura down, take her to the living room and get her to do a breathing exercise Hannah had learned for her anxiety. Then they called for an ambulance and police, told them to meet at Laura's place. Indy drove the three of them to the house Laura shared with her mum on Lismore Avenue, off Jock's Lodge, one of a low terraced row on the rump of Arthur's Seat.

They got there in ten minutes round Holyrood Park, the roads empty. Hannah had hoped the emergency services would be there already, but the street was quiet. So they went in, Laura anxious and crying, Hannah and Indy nervous. And there was Elizabeth Abbott crumpled in a heap on her bedroom floor. Pale skin, blank eyes, wet patch on her lounge pants where her bladder had emptied, acidic tang in the air.

They took Laura downstairs and waited, Indy putting the kettle on. No one ever talks about this time between finding a dead person and what comes next. A weird limbo, a void opening up. We all want someone else to take charge, that's why Laura came to Hannah.

The police arrived first. Two officers not much older than them, asking routine questions, filling the small kitchen with their bulky uniforms and stab vests. The female officer stayed with Laura as the male one went upstairs, returning visibly paler. Maybe it was his first dead body. When the paramedics arrived they didn't hang around, declared death, put her on a stretcher and took her away. They made Laura sign something, gave her a leaflet about what to do next and a handful of sleeping pills. Hannah made sure she took two then put her to bed. She and Indy headed home in silence, numb from the grief and weirdness.

'Morning, ladies.'

Hannah jumped, but it was just Thomas pulling up a chair. They'd decided in the early hours they needed to tell him about Laura's behaviour.

It seemed weird having coffee with Gran's boyfriend. But he'd become a close friend of the Skelfs in the last few years and was super helpful with the police angle on anything.

'Are you OK?' he said, looking from Indy to Hannah. They'd explained on the phone why they wanted to talk.

'Fine,' Hannah said.

Indy smiled. 'Tired.'

'I'll bet.'

A tall waitress took Thomas's order.

Indy raised her eyebrows at Hannah when the waitress left. Hannah cleared her throat and laid it out. It sounded crazier out loud than it felt. Laura introducing herself two days ago, turning up at the lecture, the picture sent to Indy, arriving in tears at the house. It felt like being invaded.

Hannah's cheeks flushed. 'There's one other thing.' She got her phone out and showed Thomas the picture of Laura smiling on the gravecam. 'This was yesterday, from a motion-sensitive camera I set up in Liberton Cemetery.'

Thomas gave her a look. 'I won't ask why you're spying on a grave.'

Indy leaned in and went wide-eyed as she stared at the picture. She grabbed the phone off Thomas and shook it at Hannah.

'What the fuck, Han? I thought we said no secrets?'

Hannah swallowed and felt her cheeks redden.

Indy shook her head. 'Did you know about this in the park yesterday?'

Eventually Hannah nodded.

'And you didn't tell me?' Indy stared at the picture again, then at Hannah. 'This means she was following you all yesterday, right? Otherwise how would she know the camera was there.'

'I guess so.' Hannah felt the rush of shame from Indy challenging her. Indy was right, she'd been stupid.

Thomas looked at Hannah. 'Let me go through this. The woman claimed to know you but you've never seen her.'

'I don't think so.'

'She turned up at a public event you were at the same day.'

Hannah nodded.

'She took a picture without you realising, then somehow got Indy's number and sent her the picture. She also knew about the cemetery camera, so we can assume she saw you put it there. And she knew the address of your flat, and got past the downstairs buzzer.'

Indy rubbed at her neck. Hannah knew it was a reflex when she was tired. 'And there's the dead mother.'

Thomas drummed on the table as his espresso arrived and he thanked the waitress. 'The dead mother.'

Hannah's leg twitched under the table. She thought about impulses from her brain firing through her body. The brain was a control centre in the dark, receiving and sending out messages, trying to keep its shit together.

'What do we know about her?' Indy said.

'We'll hopefully get the post-mortem done today, but the preliminary suggestion is a heart attack.'

'But it could be something else?' Indy said.

This conversation was running away from Hannah but also seemed inevitable.

Thomas nodded. 'Could be. Let's wait and see what the mortuary says.'

A young woman walked past their table, a toddler with curly red hair strolling in front of her. She kept an eye on the girl as she picked up a stick and waved it around. Mothers and daughters. Hannah thought of Mum, spiralling and drunk yesterday.

'This is something, right?' she said.

Thomas lifted his coffee and drank it in one go. 'It could be something.'

Hannah felt suddenly aware of her brain scrabbling in the dark, trying to make sense of all the information it was drowning in.

She looked at Indy and didn't like what she saw. Indy was doubting her and it hurt like hell.

❧

She knocked on her mum's bedroom door. She'd walked Indy to work, where Dorothy explained Jenny had gone back to bed. Hannah knocked again then went in.

Jenny woke with a start and blinked at her. 'Hey, Han.'

Hannah stood in the doorway wondering why she was here. 'Big night last night?' She hated the tone of her voice.

Jenny sat up, ran a hand through her hair. 'Not really.'

'Special occasion.'

'What is this?' Jenny patted the bed. 'Come sit.'

'I guess you were out celebrating Dad's body finally turning up.'

Jenny looked crushed and Hannah felt guilty, but not too much.

'It's not like that.'

This felt all wrong, their roles reversed. Hannah was the scolding mother, standing in her daughter's bedroom, catching boozy fumes in the air.

'Mum, I know that to you he's just a crazy ex-husband, and he was obviously a bastard of a man, but he was still my dad.'

'Oh, Han.' Jenny got out of bed and hugged her. She was in a T-shirt and pants, smelled of sweat and McDonald's.

Hannah let herself be held as if she was little again, a grazed knee or a falling-out with her best friend. Eventually she pulled back but still held on. Jenny tucked Hannah's hair behind her ear, held her cheek and looked in her eyes.

'If you want to talk about it, I'm here.'

Hannah could tell she meant it, but Jenny was only just hanging on. The truth was, Hannah was in a much better place about all this than her mum.

'He's always going to be part of us, isn't he? Part of our story.'

'Yes.'

'I just … Mum, I need you to have your shit together.'

Jenny dropped her arms to her side and stepped back. 'I have my shit together.'

Hannah swallowed and held her gaze. 'We both know that's not true. I'm worried about you.'

Jenny looked crushed again and Hannah felt guilty again. But not too much.

20

JENNY

The front door opened and Fiona grabbed Jenny into a hard hug. She was small and wiry but strong, and Jenny felt fingers digging into her back, smelled her tropical shampoo. Eventually Jenny eased her off. Fiona looked healthier than last time Jenny saw her, clear-eyed. She'd been through the wringer with Craig as much as Jenny had. Craig abducted her daughter Sophia and fled to the East Neuk, tried to set up some happy-families shit with another woman he duped along the way. Jenny found them and dealt with it, and Fiona made it clear every time they spoke that she was in her debt forever.

'Come.' Fiona headed through the house to the kitchen. She still stayed with her mother in Cramond, where she'd ended up when her house with Craig had to be sold. She was on her feet now and could afford her own place, but Sophia had settled at school. And there was her mum's support, something Jenny could relate to. Society might think it's failure to move back in with your parent in middle-age, but society can get fucked.

The kitchen table was covered in documents, an open laptop and a large cafetière, half full. It made a change from the morning wine Fiona resorted to back in the day. Now she was an established freelance PR trying to forget about the past, at least until Craig's body appeared.

Fiona poured coffee, slid the cup over. 'So it's really him.'

Jenny had called to let Fiona know about the DNA.

'You saw him?' Fiona said.

'No.'

'Then how can you be sure?'

'I'm not sure I would recognise him anyway. He's been in the sea for twelve months.'

'You'd know.'

Jenny thought about that. She wasn't convinced about gut instincts. She'd followed her gut her whole life and look at where it'd taken her.

'They don't get DNA wrong.'

Fiona shook her head but was smiling. 'You hear scare stories about that stuff. Half-brothers, bone-marrow transplants, blood transfusions.'

'Trust me, it's him.'

Jenny looked around the kitchen. Fiona's mum hadn't decorated in forever, it was homely in a retro way. Stained-wood cupboards, old cooker, very lived-in. Jenny liked it.

'It's over,' Fiona said.

Jenny took a deep breath. 'I mean, as much as it'll ever be.'

She couldn't say she felt free of Craig. Hannah's words rang in her head, it was fucking embarrassing having your daughter worry about you. She was drinking too much, fucking her therapist, sleeping in coffins. Maybe she needed to reset. That's one reason she was here, talk to someone else who went through it from the same perspective. She and Fiona were the same age, had both been married to him, both had his daughters, were both duped by his charming façade.

'We should start a support group,' Fiona said, a lightness in her voice that Jenny loved to hear. 'Craig Survivors.'

Jenny lifted her coffee cup. 'We kind of have. Is Sophia not around.'

'School.'

Jenny remembered being tied to Hannah's every breath when she was little. Every ache and pain, every broken heart, every after-school club and pimple and period. Until she's not yours anymore, she's just a strong, independent young woman. Mum was right, Jenny hadn't done a bad job with Hannah.

'How's she getting on?'

'Lots of new friends, happy. It took a while, after what he did. I've explained that he's never coming back but I haven't mentioned the body. Maybe when she's older. She'll ask questions eventually and I don't want to lie. How's Hannah taking it?'

'Fine, I think. She has Indy, they're very strong.'

'Still, he is her dad.'

'Was.'

Fiona stared at Jenny. 'Are the police sniffing around you because of what happened?'

Jenny ran a finger across the scuffed table. 'A little. But the forensic evidence will back up my version. I'm not worried.'

'Liar.'

Jenny smiled. 'OK, a little.'

Fiona reached over and took her hand. 'If you need anything you just have to ask.'

'Thanks.'

'I mean it. You brought Sophia back, I owe you everything.'

Jenny sipped her coffee. Magpies called outside in a tree, the grumble of a car down the street.

'I don't want to lose this,' Fiona said, waving a hand between the two of them. 'Know what I mean? We're more than friends.'

'Craig Survivors.'

'Craig Survivors.' There was melancholy in Fiona's voice and Jenny understood. They might have physically survived but there would always be scars. Jenny ran a hand over her stomach where he stabbed her, felt the hard tissue. And his ghost would live in their hearts. That was his legacy, two beautiful daughters and a ghost.

'So, what now?' Jenny said.

'Maybe we just live the rest of our lives.'

It sounded easy.

She pushed through the water until she felt the burn in her biceps and thighs. Her lips were salty, body shivering as she stopped and treaded water, looked around. Granton harbour wall dominated her right, to the left was the grubby promontory of Ocean Terminal, ships docked. She looked to shore, could see her pile of clothes on the sand. Overhead, a patchwork of white clouds nudged eastward, beams of sunshine through the gaps.

She normally swam off Porty but she was in Wardie Bay because of Craig. She thought about what Fiona said, they were survivors, but now they needed to live. Jenny felt better than she had for a while. She owed Brandon an apology. Maybe it was all over. She didn't feel it in her heart, but maybe she just had to bluff her way through, fake it till you make it.

She swam towards shore. There were other swimmers in the water and she swapped smiles when she passed them. She felt like a normal human being living her life. She headed for the sand and didn't think about Craig, not really, just wondered what she would do with the rest of her day.

21

DOROTHY

Dorothy put the phone down and rubbed the bridge of her nose. She looked around the cluttered home office, files and invoices, quotes and order forms. Rows of old documents from when Jim ran things, which she hadn't touched.

She'd been phoning round about Rhona Wilding, the woman Jenny and Indy picked up from hospital. She had no one in her life. Dorothy called the hospital but they knew nothing and were understandably busy. She called Rhona's most recent workplace, but she'd only worked part-time in odd jobs for years. No note of any family except a distant cousin in New Zealand who was paying for the cheapest funeral possible. Someone from the council was going through her possessions but hadn't uncovered anything. The council woman also knocked on neighbours' doors, but Rhona lived in a flat off the Royal Mile surrounded by Airbnb apartments. How could someone live in the middle of a city and know no one? We can drift through our years if we're not careful, our connections to others become weaker, until they dissolve.

'Dorothy?' Indy in the doorway, knuckle hovering over the door. 'There's someone at reception for you.' Her face gave her away, it was bad news. She glanced behind her. 'It's Hannah's other gran.'

Dorothy felt a weight descend on her. She'd been subconsciously expecting this, she realised. Of course Craig's mother would be here, now that his body had turned up. Her son was dead, and here she was.

Dorothy lifted herself out of the chair, felt her heavy bones and aching muscles, and walked downstairs. Violet McNamara was sitting with her hands in her lap. She was a few years older than Dorothy, white hair in a bob, small frame, neat trousers and blouse. When she saw Dorothy she put on a thin smile, a flicker in her eyes.

'Dorothy.'

'Violet.' Dorothy slid her hand down the bannister for the last few steps, didn't want to let go in case she wobbled. She raised a hand and showed Violet to one of the grieving rooms, a quiet space for the bereaved to sit and cry. Appropriate.

Violet sat on a plush sofa, Dorothy on the armchair opposite. There was a large vase of lilies on a coffee table, filling the space with a powerful scent. Two seascapes on the walls, a gauze curtain giving a diffuse light. Violet looked smaller than Dorothy remembered, but they hadn't been in the same room for over a decade. They got along fine at Jenny and Craig's wedding, a handful of occasions since, and of course when Hannah was born they were both doting grandmothers. Violet lost her husband five years ago. Dorothy sent a condolence card and felt guilty she didn't do more.

'How are you?'

Violet moved her bottom lip out and back in. 'Not great.' Her accent had a hint of Perthshire.

'I can imagine.'

Dorothy felt like she was walking on rice paper. Violet's son tried to kill her and Jenny. He did kill one of Hannah's friends. But he was still Violet's child. Dorothy imagined Jenny on the slab in the back room of the house.

Violet looked up. 'Can you?'

Dorothy felt her lungs lifting and falling, oxygen filtering through her blood into her brain. She didn't speak.

Violet's hand trembled in her lap. She rubbed at an imaginary spot on her trousers. 'I've been to the mortuary to identify him.'

'I'm sorry.'

Violet's tremor grew bigger and Dorothy wanted to reach over and steady her hand.

'What's left of him. A year at sea, burned beforehand. By Jenny.'

Dorothy angled her head. 'Wait—'

Violet's hand raised up as if out of control. 'That's not why I'm here. I'm not delusional, I know what Craig was. But I'll never understand why.'

Dorothy watched her carefully. She heard Indy on the phone at reception, the creak of something moving in the house. A hundred years old and still settling down.

Violet clenched her jaw, talked through it. 'I was a good mother.'

'I don't doubt it.'

'He was a sweet boy. Kind, considerate. He had a boisterous side. What boy doesn't? But he had a good heart.'

Dorothy stayed silent.

'What happened to my boy?' Violet's voice broke on the last word. 'That's what I keep asking. As they grow up, they become strangers to us, don't they?'

Dorothy nodded.

'That's the worst thing about parenthood,' Violet said. 'They fill your life as babies, consume you, push out any sense of self so that your entire life is theirs. Then gradually they become their own people. Their own thoughts, personalities, friends, lives, secrets. What are we left with?' Violet looked at Dorothy. 'We're hollowed out, nothing where they used to be. They go into the world, make mistakes. Take the wrong jobs, marry the wrong people.'

Dorothy remembered Jenny and Craig on their wedding day. Dorothy hadn't thought he was wrong for her. He was charming and kind, attentive and fun. They had a future together. And so it turned out, just not what anyone expected.

'All you can do is be there if they need you. But Craig never needed me. He always coped on his own, even when I knew he was hurting. Maybe I did this to him, I should've shown more love.'

'This isn't your fault.'

Violet's head snapped up and she stared at Dorothy. 'I'm his mother, of course it's my fault.'

'You said it yourself, we can't control their lives.'

Violet's trembling hand was back in the air. 'So nothing we do makes any difference? That's worse.'

'We can only love them and point them in the right direction. Hope they keep their ships afloat.'

Violet narrowed her eyes. 'Well, Craig's ship sank. And I'm the one who's drowning.'

She closed her hand into a fist and lowered it, covered it with her other hand.

Dorothy couldn't help thinking about losing Jenny. She nearly did because of Craig. And he killed Melanie, whose family would always grieve, a lifetime of loss. To be honest, Dorothy cared less that Craig had tried to strangle her, more about what he'd done to Jenny and Hannah. They would always have this legacy. She looked at Violet, tears in her eyes. It wasn't easy for anyone, life was never easy.

Violet wiped tears from her cheeks and stood up. 'I don't know why I'm here, this was a mistake.'

Dorothy stood and took Violet's hand, wet with tears, the skin as loose as her own. 'No, I'm glad you came.'

'I'm so sorry for what my son did to your family. But I'm also sorry he's dead. How can those both be true? How does any of this make sense?'

Dorothy pictured Craig with his hands around her throat. She imagined his bloated remains in the mortuary.

She put her arms around Violet and held on.

22
HANNAH

She hadn't been to King's Buildings in a while. Since she started her PhD, all her work was at the observatory campus up the road, but she had fond memories of sitting on the grass here between undergrad lectures, surrounded by boxy buildings with random vents. She walked into James Clerk Maxwell Building and up the stairs. Stood across from the lecture theatre and checked her watch. A few minutes later, students piled out of the double doors. This was the Fourier analysis class, one of the core subjects for Laura's year. Half the students headed downstairs and out of the building, the other half drifted towards the Magnet Café.

Hannah examined their faces as they passed. She followed them into the café, a long and airy room, thin carpet, cheap sofas and dining area. She approached some kids from the class and asked about Laura. Got a few shrugs and knock-backs before she reached two girls on a sofa at the far end.

'Excuse me, do you guys know Laura Abbott?' She was about to give a description when she clocked the look they shared.

'Who are you?' said the nearest girl. She was tall and gangly, striking in a goofy way. Long brown hair halfway down her back.

'My name's Hannah, I'm a PhD in the Astronomy department. Laura asked about doing some work experience but I can't get hold of her. She's not answering phone or emails. I just wondered how to find her.'

'Join the club,' Goofy said.

'What do you mean?'

She glanced at the other girl and got the go-ahead. 'We haven't heard from her in a week. Totally ghosting us.'

Hannah put on a concerned face. 'She hasn't been to classes?'

Goofy shrugged then looked guilty. She only now realised that maybe she should've been worried. 'No.'

The second girl looked at Goofy. She was short and slim, hair undercut on one side, punky pink tinge on top. 'I've messaged her loads of times.'

'Did you try calling?'

'Like a phone call?' Undercut said.

Hannah didn't like talking on the phone either. 'Anyone tried her home?'

Goofy straightened her shoulders. 'She lives, like, way out with her mum.'

There was disdain in her voice, a student living with her mum. Hannah didn't mention Laura's mum just died. And the house wasn't way out, Jock's Lodge was ten minutes from the city centre. But it was easy to live in a student bubble, think of the Southside flats, uni buildings, bars and clubs as the only part of town. Hannah was grateful the Skelf businesses had widened her horizons.

'Are you sure it's been a week?'

Undercut looked at Goofy. 'She wasn't in our thermo tutorial, was she? That was seven days ago.'

They shared another look.

'What?' Hannah said.

Goofy turned. 'It's not the first time she's ghosted us.'

'What do you mean?'

Goofy looked for support, Undercut nodded.

'She's quite ... intense about some stuff.'

'Like?'

'Boys,' Undercut said.

'It was six months ago,' Goofy said. 'She was going out with this guy Antoni. She started hounding him, turning up unexpectedly, checking his socials all day. Finally he finished it and she just disappeared. We found out later she kept hassling him. He had to get a restraining order.'

A boyfriend was unexpected, but maybe Laura was bi. Or maybe she didn't fancy Hannah after all.

'And has there been anyone else, another boy?'

'I don't think so.'

Hannah nodded and looked around. Every person in this café had a secret, stuff they didn't want anyone to know. The truth doesn't always look pretty in the light.

'Any idea where I can find this Antoni guy?' Hannah said.

She knew from their faces that they did.

Her phone buzzed and she checked it. A message from Indy: *Come and see me now.*

Hannah felt sick.

She breathed deeply before opening the door to the Skelfs' reception. Indy was on the phone, facing to the left. When she turned, the rock in Hannah's stomach hardened.

Indy finished the call and stood.

'What's up?' Hannah said.

Indy shook her head. 'Is there something else you want to tell me?'

'Like what?' Hannah thought hard, felt guilty and didn't know why.

Indy was trying to gauge her.

'Indy, please. What's this about?'

Indy took out her mobile, swiped and scrolled, then pressed. She held it out and Hannah stepped close. It was a picture of Hannah, one from her own camera roll, in a strappy, low-cut top, bright eyes and a sly smile.

Indy moved her thumb up and down, and Hannah saw it was a profile on lesbian dating app HER. She went to take the phone and Indy pulled it away and started reading.

'"Looking to connect with cute girls in Edinburgh, up for anything."'

Hannah laughed. 'Come on, you don't believe that.'

'I got a message from the app inviting me to connect with Hannah Skelf.' Indy's face was tight, furrowed brow.

'Obviously I didn't set that up. Why would I? I don't even have the app on my phone.'

Indy raised her chin. 'Show me.'

'What?'

'Show me your phone.'

Hannah pulled her phone out of her pocket and handed it over. Indy swiped a few times, stared, showed the screen. The app was on its own on a final home screen. Indy opened it and there was Hannah's profile, messages in the inbox. Indy pressed, whole flirty conversations with strangers.

'Indy, I swear, I don't know anything about that. Christ, you have to believe me.'

'Why?'

'It's Laura,' Hannah said. 'She must've got to my phone at that lecture the other day. She must've been there longer than I realised. She downloaded the app, set up an account. That would only take a couple of minutes. And now she's accessing it from her own phone or something, I don't know how it works. Jesus, this isn't me.'

Indy shook her head and breathed heavily. 'Honestly, I don't know what to believe. You said you'd never met her before two days ago, but she seemed to know so much about you. There's the picture of your two together, the gravecam thing, and now this.'

'This is what she wants, don't you see? She's trying to come between us, fuck things up. She's delusional, maybe thinks that if she does this, somehow she'll get me.'

Indy stared at the picture of Hannah on the phone for a long time.

'Please, Indy.'

Hannah thought she might vomit. Every nerve in her body sang. She stood there, waiting for a reply, for anything that might make her feel better. But it didn't come.

23

DOROTHY

She was in lotus pose, felt the mat under her thighs, hips open, knees and back complaining. She didn't do yoga as much as she used to, but she still tried to find time to meditate. Jon Hopkins' 'Singing Bowl' played over the speakers and she closed her eyes and tried to empty her mind. But Violet's face kept coming back, the emptiness in her gaze, a mother without her son. How do you get over that?

Her phone rang and she tensed, felt a twinge in her left glute. She opened her eyes, saw her drum kit across the studio floor and imagined bashing the crap out of it. She untangled her legs and straightened them, gave a low stretch, then reached for the phone behind her. It was a number she didn't recognise.

'Hello?'

'Is this Dorothy Skelf?' A young woman, business-like but harassed. Noise and shouting in the background jarred with the sonorous bell sounds floating around the studio.

'Yes.'

'This is Accident and Emergency at the RIE. Do you know a Mr Hayashi?'

She pictured his bruised torso when he lifted his shirt next to the wind phone in his garden. 'Is he OK?'

'He handed us your card, said to contact you.'

'Did something happen?'

'He just had a fall, a few cuts and bruises. But we need someone to come and get him.'

She gave Udo's name at reception and was told to sit. Most of the bolted-down plastic chairs were taken. She wondered what everyone was here for. Some were obvious, a decorator with his hand in a bloody makeshift bandage, a rugby player holding an ice pack to his teammate's head. But others were just suffering, in wheelchairs or standing, moaning or silent.

A doctor in scrubs called her name and she went through the plastic doors to the cubicles. She was shown to one on the right where Udo sat on a hard, raised bed. He had a white bandage around his head, a wisp of hair poking out. There was a cut with several butterfly stitches on his left cheek. He looked pale and tired. Some blood-soaked cotton pads and wipes were on a tray next to him. The doctor followed Dorothy in. She was tall and nervy, high ponytail and sleek features, Home Counties accent.

'Mr Hayashi had a fall,' she said, cleaning up the bloody scraps and throwing them in the clinical-waste bin. 'A couple of cuts, nothing serious, but you'll need to watch him.'

Dorothy looked at Udo, head bowed.

The doctor gave her a leaflet on concussion. 'There are no outward signs, but you have to keep a look out for twelve hours, just in case. It's all in there.'

Dorothy turned to him. 'Don't you have any family?'

'Willow is in Manchester.'

Dorothy shook her head and scanned the leaflet. Blurred vision, nausea, vomiting, memory loss, blackouts.

'Any questions?' the doctor said. 'Only we need the cubicle. You saw what it's like out there.'

Udo looked sheepish as Dorothy helped him off the bed. She held his arm and walked him slowly through reception then out of the hospital to the car park. The hearse was easy to find.

Udo laughed. 'I'm not dead yet.'

Dorothy unlocked it, helped him into the passenger seat then got in. 'Someone has the van on a pick-up.'

Udo put on his seatbelt and touched his bandage. 'You mean picking up a body?'

'That's right.' Dorothy started the engine, drove out of the car park and into traffic on Little France Drive.

Udo smiled. 'Well, I'm glad I'm only in the passenger seat.'

His hand went to the cut on his cheek, fingers running along the stitches like they were braille.

'Are you OK?' Dorothy glanced at the concussion leaflet she'd dumped between their seats.

'Fine.'

'Do you want to tell me what happened?'

'An accident. When you get to my age, it's a wonder you manage to stay safe. The world narrows as you get older.'

'You think so?'

Udo wasn't that much older than Dorothy, and the idea of her world narrowing scared her. She wasn't as physically capable as she used to be, and that made her anxious. When you're young, you're invincible. She didn't want to be reduced.

'I didn't fall,' Udo said as the hearse turned at Cameron Toll.

Dorothy stopped at a pedestrian crossing. 'What do you mean?'

'I couldn't tell them what really happened.'

Dorothy felt a trill in her stomach as she started the hearse up again.

'It was Lily.'

Dorothy swallowed.

Udo touched his cut again. 'I was cleaning her shrine but I was clumsy. I dropped her ashes.'

'Oh, Udo.' They drove past King's Buildings and headed north at the next junction.

'It shouldn't matter, it's not about her remains.'

Dorothy pointed at his bandaged head. 'But how did that happen?'

Udo looked out of the window. 'I was on my knees with a

dustpan and brush, sweeping her up. The Buddha on the altar fell on my head, cut it open.'

'You must've bumped it.'

'It fell on its own.'

'It was unstable, on the edge.'

'I know what happened, Dorothy.'

They drove in silence through the Grange.

Udo looked at his knees. 'Will you help me find out what she wants?'

Dorothy thought about her life narrowing, her universe becoming smaller. She drove into Greenhill Gardens. 'Sure.'

He placed his hands together. 'Thank you.'

Dorothy turned into her driveway and pulled up outside the house, switched the engine off. Udo looked out of the window.

'This isn't my home.'

Dorothy pointed at the leaflet. 'I need to watch you for twelve hours, so you're sleeping here tonight. It's not up for debate.'

24
JENNY

She walked past Bennets, felt the tug but didn't go in. She could still smell the salt in her hair from Wardie Bay, heard the rumble of buses heading to Tollcross, thought about Brandon, how she owed him an apology. She walked across the Links, their house lit up like a beacon ahead. They'd been looking over this park and this city for a hundred years, that counted for something. Providing help in a moment of need. But who helped the Skelfs when they needed it? Each other, was the truth.

She reached the house and stopped, stared at the sky, stars popping out. She thought of Hannah's astrophysics, the crazy distances and sizes, the extreme cold of space peppered with incandescent fiery stars, the power of black holes. She didn't have a scientific bone in her body but she could see the appeal, the wonder.

She went in the back way, past the coffin workshop, saw Archie in the embalming room and stopped. He had a tray slid out of a fridge, was fussing over a body with his back to her.

'Working late,' she said.

He turned. 'Last-minute checks, we're burying her tomorrow.'

Jenny went in and swallowed hard when she realised it was a toddler in a pretty yellow dress covered in flowers.

'Jesus.'

'Sorry,' Archie said. 'Should've warned you.'

Jenny couldn't take her eyes off the girl's face. She felt a rock in her gut when she thought of the parents. Her little hands and feet, Christ.

The vast majority of people they buried or cremated were

elderly, folk who'd had a good life and their time had come. It was sad, of course, but an inevitable part of life. But this was just monstrous. How Dorothy had put up with it for decades was beyond Jenny. She pictured Hannah as a toddler, into everything, every street corner a potential danger. She was just discovering the world, we all have to do that. But not this little girl, she'd never put the wrong thing in her mouth, pee her pants while pottytraining, put her hand up to answer a question for the first time in class.

'Mia Welbeck,' Archie said. 'SIDS.'

Cot death was insane. Even in the twenty-first century, the best doctors in the world didn't have a clue why babies and toddlers died in their sleep. It was fucking unacceptable.

Archie checked the skin of Mia's neck, wrists, seemed happy with what he saw, then pushed her back into her slot in the wall. Jenny imagined her sleeping in the cold bed inside.

'Sometimes this is hard,' Archie said with a sigh.

'Yeah.'

He looked at her and smiled. 'You seem happier than last time I saw you.'

'And more sober.'

'I didn't want to say.'

'I owe you an apology.'

Archie waved that away.

'I mean it,' Jenny said. 'I was an arse.'

Archie moved to the worktop, began tidying away his instruments. 'There's a lot going on. It's not easy. And now with Violet turning up—'

'What?'

Archie's face fell. 'Sorry, I thought you knew.'

'When?'

Archie's eyes went to the door. 'She came to see Dorothy earlier.'

Jenny headed out as Archie called after her. She strode through the house, ground floor dark, upstairs to the light of the kitchen.

Dorothy was sitting at the table with an elderly Japanese man, his head in bandages.

'Mum.'

'Jenny, this is Udo.'

The man bowed his head.

They had a pot between them, small cups of green tea steaming. Schrödinger was wrapped around Udo's legs.

'Mum, Violet was here?'

Dorothy nodded.

Jenny eyeballed Udo. 'Can we talk in private?'

Udo placed his hands on the table and pushed out of his seat. 'I should retire to bed.'

Jenny made a WTF face at her mum.

'He's staying tonight, upstairs in the studio.'

Udo tapped his bandage as he passed Jenny. 'Your mother insisted, in case of concussion.'

Jenny shook her head and watched Udo head upstairs.

She turned back. 'What did Violet want?'

Dorothy splayed her fingers. 'Please, sit.'

'I don't want to sit, what did that bitch want?'

'Jenny, please. She's grieving for her son.'

Jenny went wide-eyed. 'For her son who tried to kill me. And you, right here in this room.' Her hands waved around.

Schrödinger slunk away to the armchair. The cat was here that night too, got a boot in the ribs for his trouble. Was there anyone who hadn't been on the receiving end of Craig?

'She's not defending him,' Dorothy said. 'Please sit.'

Jenny bit her tongue to make sure she was still alive. 'She defended him plenty in the divorce.'

'She only heard his side, I suppose. But she knows what he did. She's not here to cause trouble.'

'I find that hard to believe.'

Jenny tapped at the kitchen worktop, pushed herself over to

the whiteboards and the giant map. Cases, funerals, life and death, all a big fucking mess. And the map, an impossible network of connections, people wasting their time going from here to there, all the while getting shat on from a great height.

'Why did you speak to her?' Jenny said eventually.

'Why not?'

'She's Craig's mum.'

'Exactly.'

'What does that mean?'

Dorothy clasped her hands together and breathed deliberately. That meditative shit she liked. 'Violet has just lost her son, imagine how that feels.'

'Her son was a monster.'

'To you, yes.' Dorothy stared at her and Jenny turned away from the look in her eyes. 'He was violent, manipulative, a liar, cheat, abuser, murderer. All of those things. I understand he's your monster, your villain. But Violet is a loving mother whose son's body just washed up after being missing for a year. She's not denying who he was, but she has her own relationship to him.'

Jenny shook her head and turned back to the map. She placed a finger on Wardie Bay then moved it up into the firth, tracing the route she swam earlier. Then further out, north and east, past Inchkeith towards open water. Next stop Norway. Why couldn't Craig's body just have kept going to the North Sea, round Scandinavia, along the Russian coast, Japan, Alaska, across the Pacific, keep going forever so she would never have to think about him again?

The logical part of her knew that Dorothy made sense. Craig was Hannah's dad and Violet's son, despite everything he'd done. But he'd stabbed Jenny in the stomach in this kitchen, in her childhood home. Her blood was in the floorboards. He would've killed her, several times over, if he could. It was all still too raw. Too many ghosts, just too many.

'I just…' she said.

She looked at Dorothy sitting at the table and felt over-whelmed. She left, walked downstairs and out of the front door, tears on her cheeks as she tried to keep breathing.

25
HANNAH

She was sitting on the toilet when she got the ping. Flipped from Insta to the gravecam with a flutter in her stomach, remembering Laura's smiling face. But it wasn't Laura or the fox, instead a middle-aged man sitting cross-legged in the fading light in front of Kathleen's gravestone. Hannah saw his lips move. He was talking to her. She got up a pic of Eddie Frame on her phone. She wasn't sure but it looked like him.

She wiped and flushed, walked into the hallway, saw Indy cooking in the small kitchen. Spicy aromas surrounded her as she called Dorothy, who picked up after two rings.

'Gran, I think Eddie is at the grave right now.'

'I'll come and get you.'

There was something sinister about driving a hearse at night. Who gets buried in the dark? Dorothy turned at the end of the Meadows and headed south, Hannah with the gravecam feed open on her phone.

'Any change?' Dorothy said, glancing over.

'He's just sitting there.'

They drove through Mayfield, houses getting bigger as they went south. Through a couple of junctions as Hannah felt the ad-renaline punch of trying to solve something, find an answer. They reached the cemetery and parked.

Dorothy undid her seatbelt. 'Is he still there?'

She glanced at the app. 'Shit, he's gone.'

He must still be in the graveyard, she'd looked a minute ago.

They hurried to the entrance. It was dark inside, streetlights dimmed by the high walls. Hannah ran down the hill towards the grave, turned the corner and almost tripped over the fucking fox.

'Jesus.'

The fox slunk into the hedge as Dorothy caught up with her. They reached the grave, no one around.

'Shit,' Dorothy said, hands on knees.

Hannah touched the earth in front of the stone, flattened in a circle. 'He can't be far.'

She ran back up the hill. He must've left via the churchyard, otherwise they would've seen him. She ran through the gap in the wall, pine trees and the church spire looming over her in the gloom. Up the steps, past the older graves, out into Kirkgate. She saw a figure disappearing onto Liberton Brae. She phoned Dorothy and started running.

'He's on Liberton Brae, meet me at the hearse.'

She turned the corner and saw him walking down the pavement. He stepped into the road, flagged a cab and got in. Hannah ran back to the hearse, where Dorothy was leaning on the driver's door, catching her breath.

'I saw,' she said.

Hannah smiled. 'Follow that taxi.'

They drove fast to catch up. Hannah was worried they'd lose the cab at Mayfield but she spotted it heading left and they followed.

'Think it's him?' she said.

'Hope so, otherwise we're chasing a cab for no reason.'

They went over George IV Bridge, down the Mound and into the New Town, Princes Street empty apart from a few tourists and young drinkers. Into Stockbridge, bumping over cobbles, Hannah felt it through the hearse's suspension. They turned into Glenogle Road. Cute colony terraces lined short dead-end roads to the left. The taxi pulled up at the end of a row, the guy got out, the taxi went on its way. The guy entered the second house on Teviotdale Place.

Dorothy parked, got out and strode down the road, up the path and rang the doorbell, Hannah smiling behind. The door opened straight away.

'Eddie Frame,' Dorothy said.

He looked beyond them. 'Who are you?'

'You better invite us in, unless you want to do this on the doorstep.'

He glanced behind him like he had a guilty secret, but wasn't this all a guilty secret?

He opened the door and waved them in, walked to a neat living room, original fireplace, high ceiling and cornice, wooden floorboards and rugs. All very tasteful.

'This belongs to a client,' Eddie said, sitting on a leather armchair.

He was tall and well dressed, ironed shirt tucked into slacks, polished tan brogues. Hair in a side parting, swept back. He looked younger than the picture Hannah had on her phone. Maybe just happier.

'You look well,' Dorothy said. 'For someone missing at sea.'

'Who are you?' Eddie said, resignation in his voice.

'I'm Dorothy, this is Hannah. Skelf. We arranged your wife's funeral. And your son asked us to find you.'

Eddie pulled his hands down his face and rubbed his neck. 'Jesus Christ.'

'Quite.'

Hannah looked around the room. He left his old life for this?

'What's going on, Eddie?' she said.

'I didn't mean for any of this to happen,' he said, shoulders slumped. 'I just wanted...'

'What?'

Eddie took a deep breath, looked at the door. Hannah wondered if he was thinking of running.

'I couldn't live a lie anymore,' he said eventually. 'But I didn't know how to tell Kathleen and Danny.'

Dorothy frowned. 'Tell them what?'

Eddie held his hands out. 'I'm gay.'

Hannah burst out laughing. 'Sorry, this is the twenty-first century, right?'

'Some folk aren't that open-minded.'

'People come out to their spouses every day. It's not hard.'

'You don't know.'

'Try telling my wife that.'

Eddie stared at her. 'It's easier for your generation.'

Hannah rubbed her earlobe. She wanted to have sympathy, but really. 'You thought faking your own death was easier?'

Eddie's face dropped. 'I wasn't thinking straight.'

Hannah waved a hand around the room. 'What about this? This isn't sustainable. You still have a son out there. Had you forgotten?'

'Of course not.' Eddie's eyes were wet.

Hannah thought about Danny, his mum dead, his dad sitting feeling sorry for himself. She thought about her own dad, lying in the mortuary. Fucking fathers.

Eddie looked out of the window, then around the room. He avoided catching Hannah's eye, spoke to Dorothy.

'This was all supposed to be temporary, until I figured out the best way forward. Then Kathleen died and I didn't know what to do.'

'Takotsubo cardiomyopathy,' Dorothy said.

'What?'

'That was the cause of Kathleen's death, according to Danny. Broken-heart syndrome. Her heart swelled up until it killed her.'

'You can't make me feel any more guilty than I already do.'

Hannah wanted to try. Fuck this guy in his little house who walked away from his family, his life. We all get tired and stressed, we all want to disappear, Hannah had felt that under the black cloud of depression. But this was bullshit, a coward's way out.

'The least you could do is let Danny know you're alive.'

'How can I? After what you just said. I caused his mum's death.'

'You have to.' Hannah walked to the fireplace. Fragrant candles lined the mantelpiece, tasteful nick-nacks. 'Otherwise what kind of dad are you?'

'Please don't tell Danny,' Eddie said. 'Not yet. I'll speak to him, I just have to find the right time.'

'There's no right time.'

Eddie turned to Dorothy. 'Please. Just give me a little time to sort this out.'

Hannah watched Dorothy consider it and felt angry. But something niggled at the back of her mind. Maybe Danny was better off without this piece of shit in his life.

26

DOROTHY

She let the noise of breakfast wash over her. The crackle of eggs frying in the pan, the whoosh of the kettle, the chatter at the table behind her. She loved her own space, but the older she got the more she loved having a full house. Thomas was talking to Udo, who'd risen early with no sign of concussion. Jenny was chewing on toast, checking her phone. Indy and Hannah were talking softly to each other, then Hannah got up and went to the whiteboards. Dorothy slid the eggs onto a plate and put them in the middle of the table next to bacon, mushrooms, toast. Not the healthiest, but screw it. Your later years came with a freedom that was exhilarating.

It was windy outside, trees bending and waving, leaves shimmering. The old windows of their house rattled in their cases like they were breathing, dancing with the air outside.

Hannah wrote the name *Laura Abbott* on the PI board followed by a question mark.

Dorothy had heard all about it from both Hannah and Thomas. She sat down and Schrödinger came to her. 'What about Elizabeth Abbott's funeral?'

Hannah pressed her lips together. 'I don't think we should do it.'

'Why not?'

'Are you serious? Laura's a stalker.'

Dorothy put a hand out. 'Her mum just died, Hannah.'

'It's easy for you, you're not the one she's obsessed with.'

Dorothy helped herself to bacon and eggs. 'Of course we won't do it if you don't want to. But she came to you in good faith.'

'It doesn't feel right,' Hannah said. 'For all we know she killed her.'

Thomas cleared his throat. 'We don't know anything yet, the mortuary should have an answer soon.'

Udo looked confused.

Dorothy leaned towards him. 'It's too much to get into. Are you OK?'

She'd checked in on him occasionally through the night, made sure he was still breathing. The concussion leaflet said to wake him every couple of hours but she didn't have the heart to disturb him.

'I'm well.'

Hannah tapped the whiteboard by Eddie's name. 'And what about your ghost?'

The word ghost made Udo pay attention. It was only through a stranger's eyes Dorothy saw how weird their lives were.

She glanced at Thomas. She'd discussed it with him last night in bed. Apparently faking your own death wasn't technically illegal, as long as you weren't dodging debt. The best they could say was that Eddie wasted police time because of the search.

'What about him?' Dorothy said.

'Are you going to tell Danny you found his dad alive and well in Inverleith, living his best gay life?'

Dorothy put a forkful of bacon in her mouth and chewed, swallowed. 'I'm not sure.'

Jenny snorted. 'Sounds about right.'

'What does that mean?'

'Your compassion and forgiveness seem to come and go when it suits you. All of a sudden you're siding with a guy who faked his death.'

'I'm not *siding* with anyone. It's not about sides.'

'Sometimes it is about sides, Mum.'

'Still angry about Violet, I see.'

'I'm not angry she came here. Actually, scratch that, I am. But I'm more angry you took her side.'

'Wait,' Hannah said. 'What did you say to her?'

'She lost her son, Hannah.'

'You think I don't know that?'

'Christ,' Jenny said. 'Violet doesn't want us to do Craig's funeral, does she? Because there's no fucking way.'

Dorothy tried to tap into some inner calm but it was hard to find. 'That *would* be a bad idea, but every deceased person deserves respect, girls.'

Udo and Thomas sat quietly, this was a Skelf thing. Schrödinger leapt off Dorothy's lap and sniffed at Udo's leg. He leaned down and scratched the cat's ears.

Indy stood, took the marker pen from Hannah and went to the whiteboard.

Dorothy saw the name *Jerry Lamb* on the board behind her, an old drumming student of hers, whose funeral was tomorrow. She couldn't believe her former students were dying already.

Indy tapped on Mia Welbeck's name. 'I need some help with this today. It won't be easy.'

'I'll do it if there's no one else,' Dorothy said. 'But I should see Danny. And I need to take Udo home too.'

She looked at Udo then around the room. Ghosts were everywhere. Udo's wife on the wind phone, Craig's phantom risen from the sea, Laura Abbott's mother in a mortuary fridge. Eddie Frame, ghosting his family. She thought about Udo's bruises. She didn't believe a ghost could do that.

Hannah took the pen from Indy and wrote *Antoni Krol* under *Laura Abbott*.

'I have to see a man about a boat,' she said.

Dorothy looked at Jenny, who shrugged at Indy. 'A toddler's funeral? Why not, I need cheering up.'

27

HANNAH

The wind whipped sea spray into her face as she waited at the quayside. Heavy clouds filled the sky, the three bridges looming over her like giant centipedes. She got her ticket at the office, moved down the jetty and waited to board the *Maid of the Forth*. It was a small blue-and-white ship that did tours of the firth, under the bridges then out to Inchcolm Island.

She'd already seen Antoni Krol coming into work earlier, greeting the other staff, preparing the ship. The girls in the Magnet Café had put her on to him. A young female tour guide slid a gangplank onto the quay. Hannah got on and sat near the front, waited as the boat bobbed in the wash. Eventually they left the quayside and chugged out, the tour guide giving them some spiel about the engineering achievements of the bridges. Hannah moved forward as if to go to the toilet then headed up the steep steps to the wheelhouse.

'Antoni.' She said it loud enough to be heard over the engine noise.

He glanced back. 'You can't be up here, health and safety.'

'Antoni Krol, right?'

He looked straight ahead as the prow headed into oncoming waves. 'You've got the wrong guy.'

'I don't think so.'

One of the physics girls had told Hannah more details. Antoni tried to end it but Laura hadn't accepted that. Kept turning up at his flat, hanging out with his friends, calling his parents.

'Adam King, then.'

He sighed. The console in front of him had two levers, a spread of buttons, a digital display. Two mounted screens showed the firth, one radar, the other sonar. A pair of binoculars and a cup holder, two walkie-talkies in a charger station. The windscreen wipers were squeaking on the thick glass.

'That's me.'

'Except you're Antoni Krol.'

He scoped her up and down. He was handsome, in his mid-twenties, strong jawline, heavy brow. He was well built, looked like he could handle himself. So why change his name to escape Laura?

'Who are you?'

She flipped a business card from her pocket and held it out. 'My name is Hannah Skelf, a private investigator.'

'The Skelfs?'

Hannah sighed. It wasn't very conducive to being a private investigator to have your family's notorious past in the public domain. 'Yes.'

Down the steps, the tour guide was still talking through some bridge history as they reached Queensferry Crossing and passed underneath it. Hannah felt tiny, the colossal structure overhead. Antoni pulled a lever and the boat turned, started rocking. Hannah spread her legs and touched the wall to steady herself.

Antoni spotted it. 'You should be sitting down.'

'Tell me about Laura Abbott.'

'Fuck.' Antoni spat the word out.

'I'm not working *for* her, I'm investigating her.'

Antoni pushed another lever, checked a screen. The tour guide was talking about a seal colony on an island up ahead. Antoni ran a finger over a digital console, craned his neck to look outside.

'What the hell has she done now?'

'What happened with you two?'

Antoni shook his head. 'She was nice at first. Easy going, one of the lads.'

Hannah flinched, hated that shorthand for women, as if they could only fit in by becoming something they weren't.

'How did you meet?'

'I used to work in Pilgrim, student bar on Cowgate. She and her pals started coming in. One thing led to another.'

He ran a hand over his buzzcut hair. 'It was never serious, at least I didn't think so. Laura had other ideas. She got heavy, started checking up on me, calling me night and day. I finished with her but she acted like we were still together.'

'What then?'

'It just got weirder. She hung around outside my place. I brought other women back there. She saw them but kept acting like I was her boyfriend, making plans. I couldn't get her to understand.' He lowered his head. 'I got angry, I'm not proud of that. But I didn't know what to do. Threatened her with the police, a restraining order.'

'What did she say?'

'She called my bluff. Imagine how it looks if someone like me goes into a police station and says they've got a pretty-young-woman stalker.'

'What did you do?'

Antoni waved a hand around. 'Quit my job, got this. Moved out of the flat, got a new place. Shut down my socials, changed my name. She still sniffed around, called my mum in Poland. But I told Mama not to say anything.'

The boat was closer to Fife now, Hannah could see the rows of houses clinging to Dalgety Bay.

'If you changed your life to get away, how come her friends know where you are?'

Antoni swallowed and looked out of the window.

'You have a thing with one of them, don't you?' Hannah said. 'The goofy one.'

'Eva's not goofy.'

'You had a stalker girlfriend and you decided it was a good idea to date one of her best friends.'

'They're not that close.'

'What do you think Laura will do if she finds out?'

'You can't tell her.'

'Because it would be uncomfortable for you?'

Antoni stared at her. 'You said you were investigating her. You don't owe her anything.'

Hannah thought about Laura on the gravecam, popping up at the lecture. The thing with the dating app. Her crying face in their flat.

Antoni checked the screens, moved a lever, pressed a button. The boat slowed and the tour guide told the punters to look to their right where seals were basking on a tiny rock. They seemed so vulnerable in this big, wide sea, their lives ruled by tides.

Antoni turned the boat to give the people in the back a better view.

He glanced at Hannah. 'She's got her hooks into you, hasn't she?'

'What?'

'You look like her type.'

'What do you mean?'

'She goes both ways. Likes her women mysterious, damaged. Fixable.'

Hannah wouldn't be surprised if Antoni had been shagging Eva at the same time as Laura, so maybe her behaviour was warranted. He wasn't exactly covering himself in glory.

'You never said why you're investigating her.' Antoni pressed a button, Hannah felt the boat's gears churn, a propeller thrash.

'Her mum just died,' Hannah said, and walked out of the wheelhouse.

28

JENNY

Sheets of rain swept over the hill from Craigmillar Castle, soaking the handful of people standing around the small hole in the ground. Some umbrellas were struggling in the wind, shafts wobbling in the mourners' grips.

Jenny and Indy stood to the side under a large black umbrella that Indy brought. She was always prepared, part of what made her a good funeral director. The Church of Scotland minister at the head of the grave was a young woman, the pages of her bible getting wet. Her voice carried over the rustling trees and roadworks noise from Old Dalkeith Road.

The rain felt appropriate. God should fucking weep at this, a two-year-old dead. When babies or toddlers died you got talk about joining the angels, being too perfect for this world. Anything that got you through, of course, but Jenny baulked at the teddy bears, picture books and tiny booties lying on the graves in this part of the cemetery. Craigmillar Castle Park was the newest in the city, they had plenty of room for little ones. There were graves of stillborn babies down the slope, a scan picture laminated and taped to one headstone.

Jenny imagined Hannah coming out of her womb blue in the face. A lost lifetime of love, everything Hannah brought into her life, nappies to hissy fits, acne to first boyfriend, first girlfriend, the dog of depression, anxiety, unadulterated joy and utter devotion. Jenny was never the most natural mum in the world, always cringed at mothers and daughters who were best friends, swapping clothes and make-up tips, going out to a wine bar together. But she would happily die for Hannah.

She looked at the tiny white coffin, splattered and muddy. Raindrops landed on the lid and ran down the sides. Mia's mum and dad stood in front of it and wept hard. The mum seemed more stoic, crying but holding it together. Mia's dad dropped to his knees in the mud. The grandparents were standing back, utterly lost. This was their only grandchild. She wondered if the Welbecks would try again or if this was too much.

Funerals were supposed to celebrate a life well lived, a chance to remember good times. How could they do that for a two-year-old? There was no wake, imagine sitting in a hotel function room eating shitty sandwiches and talking about what a good girl Mia was.

This was why Jenny never had any time for God. It was a simple argument, how could a benevolent god let bad things happen? Either he was a nasty asshole, in which case, fuck God, or he didn't exist.

The minister stopped talking and two men stepped forward and lowered Mia into the ground. The Welbecks watched the wet casket in the hole for a long time, rain dripping from their noses, then they walked away, followed by the grandparents and other mourners. Jenny wanted to scream and kick at the earth, grab the coffin and open it, shake Mia awake, push on her wee chest until she started breathing.

Indy touched her shoulder and the pair of them walked back to the hearse arm in arm. Indy closed the umbrella and got in the driver's seat. Jenny got in and kicked her shoes off in the footwell.

'What a shitshow.'

Indy started the engine.

'I thought we were supposed to provide closure or some shit?' Jenny said. 'There's fuck all closure in that.'

'We do what we can.' Indy drove slowly, windscreen wipers thumping. 'Maybe we should appreciate what *we* have in comparison.'

'What?'

'Hannah.'

Jenny stared at her. Indy's eyes were wet and Jenny wondered if she'd been crying.

'What do you mean?'

'I'm worried about her.'

'Why?'

Indy reached the road, pushed the hearse's nose into traffic, crawled into the stream of cars heading into town. She braked as a car stopped in front of her. Jenny's seatbelt dug into her shoulder.

Indy stared at Jenny. 'Why do you think? Her dad's remains just washed up on a beach. You don't think that's something?'

Blood rushed to Jenny's cheeks. 'Of course—'

'No, you don't think about other people at all. This is all about you, angry at Dorothy for talking to Violet, self-destructing because your ex-husband was a bad man. Join the millions of other women around the world. This is Hannah's dad we're talking about, her flesh and blood.'

'She seems fine.'

'News flash, Jenny, other people exist. It's not all about you.'

'I'm sorry if—'

'Are you?' Indy gripped the steering wheel like she was throttling it. 'Are you sorry?'

Jenny felt shame knot her stomach at the truth of it, shock at being told off.

'And there's this whole thing with Laura,' Indy said eventually. She didn't speak for a long time. 'I'm worried. I think Han might be having an affair.'

Jenny laughed then covered her mouth when she saw Indy's face.

'You're serious.'

'This Laura girl seems to know her really well. There could be something going on.'

'Indy, there's no way Hannah is having an affair. She loves you like crazy. She's obviously just thrown herself into investigating Laura to avoid thinking about Craig.'

Hannah was avoiding her own emotions while Jenny wallowed in hers.

A car horn blared, making Jenny jump. Indy stared at Jenny, still gripping the wheel. Eventually she waved at the driver behind, then slipped the hearse into gear and drove back to their home, the house of death.

29
DOROTHY

Leslie's Bar was a welcome haven from the dreich weather outside. Dorothy loved that Scots word. She shook her umbrella in the doorway and ran a hand through her hair, wiped her feet and walked to the snug. An old man sat with a half pint and a nip, walking stick resting against his table, old collie at his feet. Danny sat at the back in the darkest corner. He had an almost empty pint and two dead shot glasses. The stickiness of the table suggested he'd had more.

'Danny.'

He hardly looked up, just waved his glass. 'IPA, ta.'

She went to the small opening in the bar and ordered. Glanced back at him, hunched over, running a finger through the spill on the table. He lifted a beer mat and pushed it through the wetness, watched it soak into the cardboard.

She sat next to him with two IPAs, slid one over.

He downed what he had, clinked his new pint with hers and gulped. 'So?'

'Are you OK?'

He snorted a laugh. 'Do you know how many people have asked me that?'

'Sorry.'

Another gulp of beer. He sighed, looked at his glass, the foamy head sliding down the sides.

Dorothy angled her head. 'Don't take this the wrong way, but maybe you need to speak to someone.'

'Maria said that to me umpteen times, up until she left.'

Dorothy heard the clatter of pint glasses coming out of the

washer in the other half of the bar, gentle murmur of conversation between staff.

'My girlfriend,' Danny said, waving a finger at the pub door. 'Ex-girlfriend. Apparently, going out with a miserable guy whose mum just died and whose dad went missing isn't much fun.'

'I'm sorry.'

'I don't blame her. If I could leave me, I would.'

Dorothy sipped her IPA. 'Danny, what's your job?'

He snorted another laugh and drank. 'Primary school teacher, believe it or not. I got one day of paid compassionate leave. One day, can you fucking believe it? And that was for Mum, I got fuck all when Dad went missing. So I'm on sabbatical or something, I haven't even been in touch. I got a message saying I needed a doctor's note for sick leave, mental stress or something. But I haven't sorted it so I'm probably out of a job.'

He raised his glass sarcastically, beer spilled on his hand. He sucked at it.

'So what about Dad, did you find anything?'

Dorothy pictured Eddie pleading to her in Inverleith. That was one of the worst things, he hadn't moved to a different country or even a new city. Just landed across town. What were the chances in a city like Edinburgh that their paths would never cross? Especially if Eddie kept going to Kathleen's grave. Imagine if Danny met him there one morning, dew soaking the grass, a fox chasing blackbirds, his missing dad sitting there chatting to his dead mum.

Dorothy wondered if she was reluctant because it was easier than facing Danny's reaction. But he deserved to know the truth. She heard traffic noise outside, conversation in the other part of the bar, the scoosh of a beer pump being pulled.

'I did find out something.'

Danny's hand stopped with his pint near his lips. He stared at her and put down his glass. 'What?'

Dorothy forced herself to look at him. 'I found him.'

'His body?'

'Alive.'

Danny clenched his jaw. It looked like his pint might break in his hand. 'Where?'

'He asked me not to tell you.'

'Fuck him.'

'I won't do that. I respected your wishes and investigated. I'm also respecting his wishes.'

'If you don't tell me I'll...'

The threat sounded weak, died in his throat. His grip on his drink loosened and he looked around at the old man. He ran his tongue around his mouth.

'That wanker. Total fucking wanker.' He stared at her. 'Does he know about Mum?'

She nodded.

'And what did he have to say about that?'

'He says he never meant to hurt anyone.'

'Cunt,' Danny said under his breath. 'Why? Is he just a selfish prick?'

'I can't say.'

'What can you tell me?'

Dorothy watched the old guy drain his whisky and pat the collie on the head. He wiped his mouth with a trembling hand.

'I understand your reaction. It must be awful.'

'Really, you understand? Fucking great.'

'Look.' She should extricate herself from this but she couldn't. 'Maybe I can help, be an intermediary. I can give him a message. Is there anything you want to tell him?'

Danny took a long pull from his pint and slammed the glass on the table, making the dog jump. He shook his head.

'Tell him he's a fucking murderer and I wish he really was dead.'

30
JENNY

The anonymity of hotel lobbies was appealing. You could walk into the Radisson Blu on the Royal Mile and sit anywhere, comfy chairs or break-out spaces, and start again. Be a high-flying entrepreneur, a visiting concert pianist, a drug dealer. A woman with no baggage. You could go to the bar and pick up any loser, wallow in the emptiness.

Jenny walked past the bar into the rabbit warren of the seated area. She checked her watch, five minutes early. She'd walked over from Greenhill Gardens, the wander through the Old Town reminding her of student days, fresh-faced and excitable beauties everywhere. She looked around. A couple of arty types with a MacBook in a wee nook, a South Asian family examining their luggage, two glamorous young businesswomen in suits and killer heels. She felt like a ghost, as if these hotel guests could pass right through her and never know.

'Jenny.'

Her stomach tightened at the sight of Violet. She looked tired, smaller too. She was still neat, contained, hair in a tight cut, creaseless blouse. But her wrists were painfully thin and Jenny imagined her frail body.

'Violet.'

'I'm glad you got in touch.'

A waitress appeared at her shoulder, a rangy girl with curly hair, waistcoat and skirt, holding a tray.

'I ordered tea,' Violet said, 'I hope you don't mind.' She waved at the seats behind Jenny.

Jenny wanted to run out and up the Royal Mile, across the Old

Town to Tollcross, slip onto her stool in Bennets, forget who she was.

She eased into the seat and watched the waitress put the tray down. Violet poured the tea, her hand unsteady with the milk, a tremor as she slid a cup and saucer across the table.

'Thanks for reaching out to me.'

Jenny had called her when she got back from Mia's funeral, Indy's and Dorothy's words running around her head. Other people existed, Violet's son was dead. But, fuck me, this was hard. She kept flashing on Craig's face in the gloom of Elie beach, the butt of his pistol slamming into her cheek. She touched her face now, no scarring.

'Mum said you were in town.'

'I know it can't have been easy to call me.'

Jenny sipped her tea and burned her tongue. 'Shit.' She put her cup down and watched people dragging luggage to the check-in desk.

She nodded to the stairs. 'How's your room?'

'Too warm. I presume you didn't come here to ask about that.'

'I just … It's all too much, you know?'

Violet stared at her for a long time. 'I know.'

'Of course you do.' She didn't know what she expected here.

Violet raised her cup and sipped her tea. Jenny did the same. The lift pinged and a middle-aged couple came out, matching rainwear and glasses.

'I need to know what happened,' Violet said.

'What do you mean?'

'That night, on the beach.'

'I don't think that's a good idea.'

'I can't deal with any of this unless I know what happened.'

'It was in the news.'

'Not the details. How it felt.'

'I don't think I can talk about that.'

Violet narrowed her eyes. 'How are you sleeping? Nightmares

and cold sweats? During the day, are you having flashbacks, constantly angry, blaming others, hating yourself?'

'You sound like my therapist.' Jenny pictured Brandon with his trousers round his ankles.

Violet raised an uncertain hand to her cheek. 'Post-traumatic stress, they call it these days.'

'I know all about it. Talk about your thoughts, make peace with things.'

'My son is dead. I need to put an end to this feeling that I might die any moment.'

Jenny thought about Indy saying other people exist. 'He was living on the beachfront in Elie. I was outside the house, about to call the police when he found me. He had a gun.'

Violet straightened her back. 'What did he say?'

'He talked about how he wanted to start again with Sophia and Charlotte. She was just another woman he'd tricked. He said he'd changed, wanted to live his best life. He killed Melanie, tried to kill me and Dorothy, kidnapped Sophia. He was delusional.'

The truth was more complicated. He did say those things, but he also knew Jenny best in the world, had appealed to her sense of being lost, said things he knew she would like, that dug deep into her and stuck their claws in. And she hated that more than anything. Not that she'd ever fallen for him, but that she still felt at some level they were meant for each other, really *got* each other.

'He beat me with the gun. Walked me along the beach, made me drag a boat to the water's edge and get in. Poured petrol over me. He was going to set me on fire and cast me adrift. But I beat him, Violet. I fought him and he ended up in the boat, on fire, out at sea. I had to.'

Violet was crying and Jenny felt like her body was disintegrating.

'I know you did,' Violet said. 'God help me.'

The last words didn't sound like a throwaway oath but a real request, beseeching whoever was up there to help.

The mood was broken by two young kids having a race with their little suitcases, running past and pulling them, laughing as they rounded a faraway chair and returned.

Jenny and Violet watched them for a while.

'Apparently I missed Hannah's wedding,' Violet said eventually.

Jenny leaned back and blinked.

'That's one of the hardest things,' Violet said. 'Because of who he was, I have two ex-daughters-in-law who hate me—'

'We don't...'

Violet raised a hand. 'Please. And two granddaughters who I've missed growing up. Who don't want anything to do with me.'

'Hannah's wedding was spur of the moment.'

'Is she happy, despite all this?' Violet turned a single finger in the air to mean every fucking thing in the world.

Jenny thought about what Indy said in the hearse. 'I don't know.'

She sipped her tea, which had cooled too much.

'I remember your wedding,' Violet said. 'You and Craig were so beautiful. So happy. You had your lives ahead of you. That's the happiest I've ever been, seeing you both like that.'

Jenny felt tears coming to her eyes. She remembered the ghost of that joy, it seemed like she was someone else back then.

'I'm sorry,' she said and meant it. Sorry for everything she'd done, for everything she'd become, for bringing so much darkness into the world.

31

HANNAH

'Next we have exoplanet HD 189773 b, where it most likely rains glass.'

Doctor Liv Pedersen was in her fifties and strikingly beautiful in the way Nordic women are – growing into themselves as they age. Tall and lean, short black hair, sharp blue eyes, endless enthusiasm. She pointed at the screen where a blue-and-grey marble was swathed in ripples and swirls as it rotated. It was an artist's impression, of course, based on the best data they had.

'Approximately 64.5 light years away in the constellation of Vulpecula, it is the closest hot Jupiter to Earth, and therefore has been the subject of extensive atmospheric examination.'

Pedersen talked about its discovery by transition across its star's path, subsequent spectroscopy and analysis of its make-up. It was insane how much we could learn about planets billions of miles away using telescopes, instrumentation and complex physics. Hot Jupiters were gas-giant exoplanets the size of our own Jupiter but with orbits much closer to their stars. They were the easiest to detect because they cast proportionally bigger shadows on the light from their stars, wobbles in brightness that we could detect from Earth.

'There is strong evidence for silicate in the atmosphere,' Pedersen said. 'And with a surface temperature of 1,300 degrees Celsius and winds of 8,700 kilometres per hour, it seems likely the silicate would form grains of glass and fall as rain.'

This was the good stuff, Hannah thought, this was her refuge. All the crap going on in her life, her dad, Laura, Indy, Mum's ongoing breakdown and Gran's crazy investigations. She could forget it all for a moment and think about the immensity of space, the bizarre nature of it. It was easy in the grind of computer simulations and number crunching to forget the big-picture stuff. Maybe she would try to get a job in science communication after her PhD. Or there was the possibility of working properly for the Skelfs, either in funerals or PI. She did a little of both, had become their tech person by default, helped out with services. But she wasn't sure if she was cut out for it. Maybe thinking about planets light years away was a cop out, a way to avoid the real world.

'55 Cancri e is sometimes known as the diamond planet,' Pedersen said.

The screen showed a glowing maroon orb with large red fires throbbing on its surface.

'It was the first super-Earth to be found around a main transition star, using changes in the star's radial velocity by measuring Doppler shift.'

She showed more graphs, talked about carbon content, tidal locking, infrared mapping. 'With such high pressures and temperatures, it seems probable that most of the planet is made of diamond.'

Jesus. This universe.

Hannah looked around the lecture theatre. It was a small one, lights lowered, and she half expected Laura to appear at her side again, her personal shadow. But she was surrounded by postgrad colleagues, post-docs and members of staff, Pedersen was a big name in the field.

'And here we have TrES-2b, sometimes known as Kepler-1b.' The screen showed a black sphere, small splash of stars around it. 'TrES-2b is 750 light years away, orbits a binary-star system and is believed to be the darkest known exoplanet, reflecting less than one percent of light. That's less reflective than coal or black acrylic paint.'

She went on about its discovery as Hannah stared at the screen. She remembered something from one of Douglas Adams' books, a spaceship that was the darkest thing in the universe. One of the characters said your eyes slid off it. She stared at the big black sphere, a heart of darkness in the room. She tried to imagine a planet so black that no light ever escaped, like it didn't exist. She thought about the last talk she went to, the supermassive black hole at the centre of our galaxy. Was the universe just made up of darkness? So much out there was cold, dead space. Watch the news for two minutes and there was darkness here too, despair and bleakness, hard to handle. It was easy for your eyes to just slide off it, but you had to look. You had to try to be a source of light.

She thought about Laura, looked around, imagined her standing and saluting, here I am with my black heart. Her ex-boyfriend was a dick, her friends were arseholes and her mother just died. That was enough to force darkness into anyone's heart.

Pedersen was now talking about OT44, a rare rogue planet that didn't orbit any star, just wandered the galaxy on its own. That sounded unbearable, no sun, no source of warmth and light to get you out of bed in the morning.

❧

For the whole walk to meet Indy she expected Laura to appear round every street corner. So it was no surprise when she opened the door to the Skelf house and saw her leaning against the reception desk, Indy with a thin smile.

Laura grinned. 'Here you are, girlfriend.'

In tears two nights ago, now she looked like she was up for a night on the town. Her hair was big, bright-red lipstick, crop top and short skirt.

'We were just talking about you.'

Indy gave Hannah the eyes.

Laura walked over to Hannah, touched her elbow. 'Fancy a few drinks?' She reached for Hannah's hair and Hannah flinched and looked at Indy.

'I can't. We have to help my gran with something she's investigating.'

'Sounds juicy, what is it?'

Laura's energy was so weird it was disconcerting. Hannah felt at sea, as if her legs might give way.

'Can't say.' She tapped her nose. 'Confidential.'

'I bet you have amazing stories.'

Laura glanced at Indy and Hannah got her phone out, made a show of checking the time.

'We really have to be going.' She touched Laura's back and moved her towards the door.

Laura resisted. 'I was talking to lovely Indy about Mum's funeral. I'm so excited you guys are doing it.'

Hannah glared at Indy.

'I can't wait to give Mum a proper send-off.'

Hannah thought about the blackest planet absorbing all light, sucking in everything so that nothing could escape. She took Laura's arm and led her to the door. Laura looked shocked for an instant then smiled.

'I see you're busy, of course. But we'll catch up soon, talk about the service. Have a proper girls' night.'

Hannah had her outside and was closing the door.

'I'll call you.' Laura blew a kiss as Hannah closed the door, leaned against it and exhaled, stared at Indy, who returned her gaze with wide eyes.

32

DOROTHY

She sipped tea from the same chunky orange cup as before. Udo's kitchen was as clean and tidy as last time. Dorothy looked at Lily's shrine in the corner, there was no sign of what Udo said happened. He was preoccupied with a plate of colourful pastries, *wagashi* he called them. Dorothy got up and went to the shrine. She glanced back, saw Udo wasn't looking, and picked up the urn, felt the weight. She knew that you got varying amounts of remains after cremation. She replaced Lily carefully and lifted the Buddha. It was substantial, square base with sharp edges. She looked for traces of blood but there was nothing.

'Here,' Udo said, placing the cakes on the table.

Dorothy sat down and took a bite of a pink thing. The texture and taste were unlike anything she'd had before, sweet but with a tang underneath.

'Made with azuki bean paste,' Udo said.

Hannah was arranging surveillance cameras elsewhere in the flat. She'd already done the kitchen, Dorothy glanced at it on top of a cabinet, pointing at the shrine. She wondered if they were recording yet, footage of her mucking around with Lily's ashes.

'I've never tasted anything like it.'

She'd lived most of her adult life in Scotland, just the occasional trip back to California to see family. In some ways, she was frighteningly inexperienced.

Udo touched the stitches on his head.

'Any headaches?'

Udo shook his head and looked at the shrine, the netsuke and urn, the Buddha.

Hannah walked past the kitchen doorway and pointed down the hall.

'I know you don't believe me.' Udo waved at the corner of the room.

'That's not true.'

'It's hard for Western people to understand.'

'I consider myself spiritual.'

Udo narrowed his eyes and nodded. 'I see that. But here, most people separate the physical and spiritual. In Japan, things are different. We live alongside our ancestors, their personalities still influence us.'

It was a common criticism of dualism. As she got older, Dorothy realised other cultures had more healthy relationships with spirituality than traditional Christianity. Other cultures celebrated death and life in a way that felt more connected, from Mexico's Día de los Muertos to Haitian voodoo to Tibetan sky burials.

Hannah went past the doorway again, heading back the way she came. 'Almost done.'

Udo smiled. 'You're very lucky to have her.'

Dorothy thought about Udo's granddaughter in Manchester.

'I need to ask about your bruises.' She nodded at his torso. 'The ones you showed me the first time.'

Udo's hand went to his midriff, touched his cardigan.

'How did that happen, Udo?'

He bowed his head and mumbled something. Dorothy imagined Lily's urn flying across the room at them.

'I beg your pardon?'

'It happens at night, I wake in the morning and feel the pain.'

Dorothy considered that. 'Can I see?'

Udo stood and lifted his shirt and cardigan. The skin was mottled blue and purple, brown and yellow at the edges.

'Did you get that seen to in hospital?'

Udo lowered his shirt and tucked it in, wincing.

'I am an old man, living alone. If I show them, I might end up in a home.'

He seemed capable of looking after himself and she understood the desire for independence.

Hannah came in, swinging a half-empty backpack onto her shoulder. 'All done.'

Udo shook his head. 'I told you, I don't think cameras will show anything.'

Dorothy rubbed a finger on the table. 'A blend of spiritual and practical is the way to go, trust me.'

'In that case you should put a camera in the wind phone.'

Of course, Dorothy was stupid not to have thought of it.

All three of them went out of the back door, walked down the garden to the phone box. It was late afternoon, scraps of blue sky between high white clouds. Hannah went into the box, flicked at the unplugged phone cable, looked around. She wedged her hips against two sides to push herself up, placed a spycam in the top corner, then climbed down. She initialised it on her phone and checked the angle. She reached up and adjusted it.

'Can we do audio in here as well?' Dorothy said.

Hannah had the door open. 'In the box or on the phone?'

'The phone.'

Hannah lifted the handset and took a small device from her bag. She unscrewed the mouthpiece and pressed the device into place, screwed the mouthpiece back on. She flipped on her phone, scrolled, spoke into the mouthpiece and recoiled at the feedback, held the handset away from her head.

'I need someone to speak into it while I check the levels.'

Dorothy took the phone and stepped inside. Hannah walked up the garden and gave a thumbs up.

'Testing, testing, one, two.'

Hannah fiddled with her phone, rolling a hand to say keep talking.

Dorothy heard a pigeon in the trees, thought of the pigeons in her garden the day she burned Jim on a funeral pyre. His atoms floating into her lungs, spreading through her blood, catching in her hair.

'Hi, Jim.' She turned away from Hannah. 'I miss you so much. You never stop missing someone. We've always told the bereaved that, but I never understood properly until you died. Everything that happens, I want to talk to you about it. I have the others but it's not the same. You knew me in a way they never will. To them I'm an old woman, a mother, grandmother. But you knew the real me.'

She gripped the handset so tight it hurt her knuckles. She leaned her head against the glass, scrunched her eyes shut. She felt light-headed, smelled moss, felt a flake of old paint come off under her finger.

'Sometimes I forget what you look like. Isn't that awful? I close my eyes but I can't picture you, I have to find a photograph. That's so fucking awful. I feel like I have a hole in my heart.'

She sniffed and wiped her nose, lowered the handset and opened her eyes.

Hannah was holding her phone up and staring at her.

33

JENNY

She threw two ice cubes and a slice of lime into the glass. The fizz and clatter in the gin and tonic was Pavlovian, made her tongue sweat. She took a swig, felt the alcohol cutting through. She looked around the kitchen, saw Schrödinger in his armchair, went over to him.

'Hey, cat.' She reached out a hand.

Schrödinger swiped a claw along her forearm.

'Fuck's sake.' Jenny rubbed at the scratch. 'Just trying to be friendly.'

She stared out of the window at Bruntsfield Links and thought about her dad. Remembered playing football with him out there in a spare moment between funerals, him pretending to be crap in goal, flopping over once the ball was past him. Then the two of them sitting on the grass eating ice poles, lurid yellow and green. The feel of it in her hand, cold and sticky.

The doorbell went downstairs. She sighed. Indy was away home, Dorothy and Hannah were out. She took her gin downstairs, ice clinking in time with her footsteps. She opened the door and saw a face she hadn't laid eyes on in years, one that was similar enough to her ex-husband that her breath caught in her throat.

Craig's sister had layered blonde hair and bags under her eyes. She was taller than Jenny by a couple of inches, lean and wiry, wearing a black hoodie and jeans, trainers.

'Stella.'

Stella smacked Jenny's drink from her hand. The glass bounced off the door and landed on the rug. The lime slice was like a little floundering fish.

'You bitch,' Stella said.

Jenny went to slam the door but Stella pushed a foot into the hallway.

'You don't get to shut me out.'

'What are you doing here?'

Stella's fists were clenched and Jenny stepped back into reception. Stella walked in and pushed the door closed. Jenny caught the smell of the lilies on the desk as she backed away.

Stella jutted her neck out and widened her eyes like a cat stalking its prey. 'Why do you think I'm here? You killed my little brother.' She stepped forward and Jenny shrunk back. 'My mum just had to look at the disfigured remains of her son.'

'I'm sorry—'

'You're sorry?' Stella said in a theatrical voice. 'I don't believe that for a second, and even if you were, you don't get to fucking say that.'

'I don't—'

'How dare you go and see Mum at the hotel.'

'What?'

'You think I don't speak to my own mum? I know what's been going on in this cosy little death house. Fucking murderous coven.'

She swept the vase of lilies off the desk onto the floor. They landed on the rug and didn't smash, just leaked water and made pollen stains.

'Because that's what you Skelf women are, fucking witches.' She took another step forward and Jenny moved around the desk. She saw the phone, thought about the police.

'I didn't do anything.'

'Are you kidding?' Stella's cheeks reddened. She put hands on her thighs for a moment as if she needed respite from her own anger. 'You lit him on fire and set him adrift in the ocean.'

'He would've killed me, Stella. He tried to more than once. He beat me, stabbed me, pointed a gun. He was a fucking murderer and a psychopath.'

Stella barrelled into her midriff, pushing them both over the desk and onto the ground. Stella swung a punch and caught the side of Jenny's face, her ear ringing as she tried to loosen Stella's grip, wriggle out. She kicked her feet, her torso writhing as Stella landed another punch on her neck which made tears come. Stella gripped her hair and pulled, sunk her teeth into Jenny's upper arm, Jesus, the pain.

Jenny tried to swing round, scratched with her free arm on the rug. Her fingers touched the edge of the vase and it spun away from her. Another fist from Stella hit her on the temple and her vision blurred. She scrabbled for the vase, gripped it by the rim and swung it down hard on the back of Stella's head, making her release her grip.

Jenny scuttled back with the vase still in her hand.

Stella pushed a hand through her hair then stood.

'I'm going to make you pay. You'll be convicted of murder. I don't care that your mum is screwing a cop. If they don't do their job I'll launch a civil case. You're ruined, understand?'

They both jumped at a noise, the door from the back of the house opening. Archie came in, headphones on, humming. He stopped when he saw the two women panting and red-faced, the mess between them. Stella heaving in breaths, hands on her knees, Jenny sitting on the floor wielding the vase like a club.

He took his headphones off. 'What the hell?'

Jenny could hear tinny beats and guitar noodling.

Stella shook her head and pointed at Jenny. 'I mean it, bitch.' She turned and left, flinging the door open on the way.

Archie helped Jenny to her feet. She felt the sting of the bite-mark on her arm.

'Who the hell was that?' Archie said.

'Trouble.'

34

HANNAH

She watched Gran as they walked to the hearse. Dorothy had barely acknowledged Udo when they left. She fished the key out of her pocket and bleeped the lock. Hannah thought about what she'd heard over the audio from the wind phone. They were all still grieving for Granddad, they always would be. But they'd taken Dorothy's strength for granted. She was as lost and alone as the rest of them. Hannah thought about Laura finding her mum dead on the floor. Violet having to look at her son's remains in the mortuary. Her own father, dead on the slab.

'Do you want me to drive?' she said.

Dorothy seemed to shake out of a dream. 'Sure, thanks.'

They got in and Hannah looked over.

'Are you OK, Gran?'

Dorothy smiled. 'You heard me back there.'

'Yeah.'

'I'm sorry.'

'Don't be stupid. It must be hard.'

She put the hearse in gear and pulled out. They headed up Easter Road, drove past Edinburgh Eastern Cemetery and the football stadium.

Dorothy frowned and got her phone out of her pocket.

Hannah saw her opening an app. 'What is it?'

'The tracker I put on Mike and Roxanne's car.'

'The Frame case? But we found Eddie and you spoke to Danny. Did you tell him about his dad?'

'I said he was alive but I didn't say where. I told him I'd pass on a message.'

'Don't get involved, Gran. The case is over, you found the guy, just pass on the information and get out. If you're the go-between, they'll both end up blaming you.'

'Danny is already angry.'

'With you or his dad?'

'Both.'

'I'm not surprised.'

Dorothy looked over. Hannah felt her cheeks flush but she was angry with Eddie too. Some of us don't have dads anymore, even if they were bastards. To hide from your kid was pretty unforgive-able, and Eddie's reason was pathetic.

Dorothy tapped her phone screen. 'We're getting off the point. The car.'

'What about it?'

'The tracker says it's in Teviotdale Place.'

It took Hannah a second to put it together. 'Eddie's house? That means...'

She had to switch down gears as traffic slowed in front of them.

'It means either Mike or Roxanne knows Eddie is still alive, and where he is.'

'Maybe Eddie got in touch since we visited.'

'Why would he contact them rather than Danny?'

'Because Danny is the one he hurt most. Sounds like he's taking the easy route again.'

'Maybe they knew all along.'

'What?'

The car crept past a tattoo place and a bakery. The pavements were busy with an eclectic mix of weirdos and misfits.

'Maybe Roxanne or Mike, or both of them, were in on it the whole time.' Dorothy stared at the flashing dot on her phone. 'The fight at the funeral. Danny thought his dad was still alive and he was right. He also thought Mike knew something about it, maybe he was right about that too.'

Hannah let a car in from a side road then nudged the hearse

forward. 'I don't know, Gran. It's one thing to fake a disappearance on the spur of the moment. It's another to recruit your brother to help you leave your wife and son.'

Dorothy wrinkled her nose. 'I think we need to pay Eddie another visit.'

'Now?'

'Why not?'

Hannah turned along London Road then up to the roadwork mess of Elm Row. They were in Broughton Street when Dorothy spoke.

'Shit.'

'What?'

'The car's leaving.' She held up her phone. Hannah saw the dot shifting on the map, heading northwest.

'Do you want to follow the car or speak to Eddie?'

Dorothy chewed it over as they went round a roundabout. They were in the New Town now, wider roads, bigger houses, smarter pedestrians. Funny how we stick to our local tribes.

'I think we should see Eddie.' She waved the phone in the air. 'He has some explaining to do.'

Hannah drove down Bonnington to Canonmills, turned left. They were almost there, sometimes Edinburgh felt so small. Everywhere connected to everywhere else, all the parts in constant communication. How could Eddie have thought that he would stay secret in a city this small? Imagine if Danny had walked past him in the street, saw him in a coffee shop, bumped into him at an art gallery or a Hibs game.

She found a space on Glenogle Road at the top of Teviotdale Place and parked. The air was cold now, the creep of sunset casting gloom over the houses.

Hannah let Dorothy go first up the path. She rang the doorbell and glanced at her phone.

'The car looks like it's back at Ferry Road.'

There was no sign of life from inside the house.

Dorothy rang the bell again, waited. Hannah felt the cold, wished she'd brought a jacket. She pictured Indy back at their place. She wanted to be warm on the sofa, forking chilli into her mouth and watching some brainless crap on YouTube.

Still no answer.

Dorothy opened the letterbox. 'Eddie? It's Dorothy Skelf. I want to talk. It's about Danny.'

It made sense that he wouldn't open his door, but you can't hide forever. Hannah felt anger rise up and breathed to quell it.

'Please Eddie,' Dorothy said. 'We need to talk.'

She straightened up and looked at Hannah. They both listened. Nothing.

Dorothy tried the door handle and to Hannah's surprise it turned. Dorothy opened the door and called again.

'Eddie? We're coming in.'

She walked down the hall and Hannah followed. The house was dark, shadows everywhere, the creak of the floorboards under their feet. They walked around the ground floor, no sign. Dorothy glanced at the ceiling then went out to the hall and up the stairs. More creaking underfoot. Hannah slid her hand up the bannister, breath shallow.

Upstairs, they walked past the bathroom first, nothing, then an office, also empty. At the end of the short corridor was a bedroom, the door ajar.

'Eddie?'

Dorothy pushed at the door and it swung open. Eddie lay on the bed, sprawled across white sheets, blood pooled around his body from knife wounds in his stomach. His neck had been slashed too, a wide gash making the skin peel away like a joint of meat from the bone. His head lolled to the side and his arms were out wide, like he was a lady in a Victorian melodrama who'd just fainted. His eyes stared at the ceiling but saw nothing.

35

DOROTHY

She blinked heavily, her body aching. She hadn't slept well, for obvious reasons. She looked around Thomas's office. She was very lucky to have him, although she hadn't exactly been devoting time to their relationship recently, what with all the death surrounding them.

She was also lucky they were able to do this in his office, not in an interview room downstairs. Thomas sat to the side in a cheap plastic chair, DS Griffiths in the main seat behind the desk. She was in her thirties, neat blonde hair, no nonsense. Dorothy liked her. Thomas couldn't take Dorothy's statement because of their relationship but he was allowed to sit in, at least that's what he told her. She was glad he was here.

Outside the window, the early-morning sun was somewhere behind Salisbury Crags, the low light casting the cliff face in eerie shadows.

'OK.' Griffiths ran her fingers along the edge of Thomas's desk. She had a recording device with a flashing red light in front of her and a notebook, where she'd been scribbling as Dorothy re-counted what happened.

'Let me just run through it.' She glanced at Thomas. It must be awkward interviewing her boss's lover with him right here. But it wasn't like Dorothy was a suspect, as far as she knew.

'You and your granddaughter arrived at 2 Teviotdale Place at around nine o'clock last night. You already knew Eddie Frame was living there, despite the fact he's been missing presumed dead for over a month. You were employed by his son to find him. You did that but didn't tell Danny where he was.'

She glanced at Dorothy. It wasn't an eye-roll, exactly, but a flat look of exasperation. She tapped her notebook.

'You went to see Eddie because a tracking device you'd placed on his brother's or sister-in-law's car showed it was in the area.'

Tracking devices weren't illegal and Griffiths knew the Skelfs were PIs. But Dorothy understood her tone and why she sucked her teeth.

'When you rang the doorbell there was no answer, so you went inside and found Eddie dead in his bedroom, stabbed and his throat cut.'

Dorothy couldn't shake Eddie's face from her mind, the blank eyes, the mess. She'd seen countless dead bodies over the decades, of course, but the vast majority were calm, peaceful corpses. It didn't always go that way, they'd buried murder victims before, picked up bodies from the mortuary that were in pieces after a bus crash or an industrial accident, skulls crushed, limbs severed, guts collected in a separate bag. But there was something about the violence of this. It shouldn't matter how we die, we all end up the same. But there were good ways and bad ways, and the trauma of Eddie's death had soaked through her skin.

Griffiths cleared her throat. 'You didn't touch anything, didn't see a potential weapon, just phoned DI Olsson.'

Dorothy knew some people had a problem with the police, and she understood that. Jenny had had run-ins with them over the years, especially in her student days. And the culture in the force wasn't great, but it seemed better than it used to be. Just look at Thomas, a middle-aged black man in a position of relative power deferring to a younger female officer. She knew good cops but she also knew the kind of people who were attracted to power. It was far worse in her home country, of course, where she fully supported change. Here, the police seemed to have less power and more accountability, but maybe that was changing in the current political climate. But it always came back to Thomas for her, he was a good man with a kind heart. If men like him were in the police, it was surely a better place for it.

'Have you spoken to Mike or Roxanne yet?'

Griffiths glanced again at Thomas. 'We're currently following a number of leads.'

Dorothy had handed over her phone when she arrived at the station, so they had the tracker information.

Griffiths flicked back and forth in her notebook. The edge of the sun appeared behind her out the window, striated filaments of cloud spreading above Salisbury Crags like fingers over the city.

'What about Danny?' Griffiths said.

'What about him?'

Griffiths angled her head and side-eyed Dorothy. She leaned back in her chair. 'He hired you to find his lying, deserting father. He blamed his dad for his mum's death, right?'

'Yes, but—'

'He had a fist fight at her funeral with his uncle Mike because he thought Mike knew something about Eddie. How did Danny react when you told him you'd found his dad?'

Dorothy pictured Danny in Leslie's, drunk and out of focus, gripping his pint like it was a lifeboat adrift in an endless ocean. The hatred in his eyes.

'He was very upset.'

Griffiths leaned forward, placed her elbows on the desk. 'Very upset.'

Dorothy looked at Thomas, a look that Griffiths clocked. Thomas kept his face deadpan.

'Did he say anything about wanting to harm Eddie?'

Dorothy ran her tongue along her teeth. 'He wouldn't do that.'

'That's not what I asked. When you told Danny his father was alive and well having faked his own death, what did he say?'

Dorothy wasn't about to lie, the truth was out there waiting. They would interview Danny, Mike and Roxanne, they would get to the bottom of this. Or if they didn't, she would.

'He said Eddie was a murderer and he wished he was dead.'

36

HANNAH

She pushed granola around the bowl with her spoon. She hadn't eaten since yesterday afternoon but had no appetite. She kept thinking about Eddie on his bed, drowning in blood, eyes blank.

She walked around the small kitchenette, tapped the spoon on the worktop, stirred her food around, thinking. She went to the window, looked over the back garden. Like a lot of the old tenements, they were packed close together and she could see four floors of life, a hundred different mornings, breakfasts, arguments, getting ready for school or work or still sleeping, maybe up all night with insomnia or a cranky baby, maybe fucking the night away and sleeping it off.

She hadn't slept much, tossed and turned, checked her phone for information about Eddie, checked again for anything on Laura, these lives swirling around her brain. She tried to read a book, a Nnedi Okorafor novella she would've normally devoured, but she realised after a while she'd been reading the same page over and over. So she got up with the sun and here she was.

'Hey.'

Indy came through the doorway in loose shorts and a sweatshirt, and put the kettle on. Hannah looked at her bare legs, lithe and dark, watched her feet on the floorboards.

'Couldn't sleep?'

'Kept thinking about Eddie.'

Indy came over and touched her shoulder. Hannah put her bowl down and hugged her, smelled her hair, squeezed her and thought how lucky she was. Despite their arguments over Laura,

Hannah knew Indy was there for her, always. She let go eventually and cricked her neck.

'I don't know,' Hannah said. '*You* see dead bodies every day at work.'

Indy gave her a look. 'That's different and you know it. I deal with people at rest, you saw an act of violence. I would be traumatised.'

Hannah stuck out her lip. 'I sometimes wonder if I'm cut out for this. Imagine if I was just a physics student, how easy that would be. Researching and writing up results. But instead I'm running around with Mum and Gran doing daft detecting, helping you all with funerals. Surrounding myself with death.'

The kettle had boiled and Indy made a pot of tea.

'Then quit,' she said, matter-of-fact. 'You have to look after yourself, that's most important.'

'But it's family. Mum, Gran and you. The whole thing with Dad, all this stuff with Laura and now Eddie...'

Indy shook her head. 'You've never been very good at self-care, Han. Think what you were like about Melanie and your dad. Helping people can't come at the expense of your own health, I learned that quickly working in this business. Funeral directors are emotional support for the bereaved, but it's their grief. You can't take that on every time.'

Hannah pouted and scratched her neck, unconvinced.

Indy poured the tea. 'You're in shock about Eddie, but it's not your grief. You care too much, that's your problem.'

'Says the most caring woman I know. Look, you made me a cup of tea at the same time as giving me a pep talk.'

She was trying to keep things light, but she knew they were both aware of the thing with Laura bubbling under the surface.

Indy kissed her on the cheek and she took a sip of tea. She remembered her counselling sessions when Dad was first exposed. The therapy she went through as a teenager with anxiety, depression and anger.

Indy was fussing with some burcha out of the fridge when Hannah's phone rang. She was always surprised when people actually called on the phone, it seemed such an antiquated concept. The screen said Thomas.

'Hi, are you with Dorothy?'

'No, she finished a few minutes ago.' His Swedish accent gave a cute lilt to the vowels.

'Want me to come and give my statement?'

'That's not why I'm calling.' He cleared his throat. 'We have the post-mortem result for Laura Abbott's mother.'

Hannah stomach tightened and she half expected to see Laura standing out in the back garden. She put the phone on speaker.

'Elizabeth Abbott died of a massive cardiac arrest,' Thomas said. 'Natural causes. But there's something else. Time of death is estimated as seven to nine days ago.'

Indy went wide-eyed. 'Over a week?'

'Correct.'

Hannah counted back. It was five days since Laura had approached them outside Söderberg. Her mum was already dead, lying on the floor of their flat. What the hell?

'Wow,' Indy said. 'So when we first met her...'

'There's another thing,' Thomas said down the line. 'In light of this news, we sent officers to bring her in. It's not technically a crime, not to report a death immediately, but it raises questions. The officers couldn't find her. She's not at her address or answering her phone.'

Hannah thought about hustling Laura out the door of the funeral home yesterday. Pictured her smiling on the gravecam, sitting in the physics lecture, at Söderberg. She was pretty sure Laura would turn up in her life again soon.

37

JENNY

'Thanks for coming,' Jenny said.

She touched Archie's knee then went back to rubbing the back of her hand. They were in the reception of St Leonard's station, waiting to make a complaint. This was probably all pointless. She thought of the police as her enemy but last night she was threatened and assaulted, what else could she do?

'No problem.' Archie threw her a smile.

His face suited it. His neat beard and shaved head made him look like an affable cartoon character, and he played on that, used it to stay under the radar. He was a quiet man but was always there in a crisis. He'd been there for Dorothy over the years and also for Jenny when she needed someone to talk to. She was guilty of taking him for granted. She looked at him, comfortable in his skin. She wished she'd known him when he first appeared at the Skelf house, unstable with Cotard's, adrift in the world, in love with the idea he was dead. In Jenny's mind that version of him was more edgy, more exciting. His medication and counselling levelled him out into a gentle soul, better for him, of course, but she preferred a fucked-up bad boy.

How stupid she was. Where had bad boys got her? Beaten and abused, stabbed, divorced, alone, desperate. Maybe it was time to go for someone nice.

Griffiths appeared from the back and walked towards them.

'Two Skelfs in one day,' she said, pointing her pen at Jenny.

'What?'

Griffiths flicked her ponytail. 'I had a wee chat with your mum earlier.'

'What about?'

'Are you for real?' She clocked Jenny's blank face. 'The murdered body she found.'

Jenny's stomach clenched. 'What?'

'Eddie Frame,' Griffiths said. 'Dorothy and your daughter found him last night, stabbed to death. Didn't they tell you?'

Jenny had gone to Bennets last night after Stella left, hammered the gin and whisky, then staggered to another bar. She didn't remember getting home. Dorothy was out the door first thing this morning. She felt like a teenager again, passing through the same space as her family, not interacting. She wondered about being a ghost, thought of Archie's condition, imagined she was dead.

'Was Dorothy OK?' Archie said.

Griffiths stared at him. 'Who are you?'

He stood. 'Archie Kidd, I work at the Skelfs.'

'Another deadhead.'

'Excuse me?' Archie had a worried frown.

'Anyway,' Griffiths said to Jenny. 'You wanted to make a complaint?'

Jenny took a while to answer. 'I didn't know it would be to you.'

'It sounds like it's connected to your case with Craig McNamara.'

'There is no *case*.'

Griffiths held an arm out to lead Jenny towards a room through the back. 'I'll be the judge of that.'

Jenny started walking and Archie followed.

Griffiths held out a palm. 'Just her. Unless you were a witness?'

Archie looked at Jenny and back at Griffiths. 'I came in at the end.'

Griffiths pointed at a chair. 'Sit.'

She walked away. Jenny followed to the same interview room as before, scratchy carpet, beaten table, view of the car park.

Griffiths sat and waved to Jenny to do the same. 'So what's this about?'

'Craig's sister came to see me last night, threatened me, swearing and shouting, then she assaulted me.'

Griffiths nodded. 'In what way?'

She made a show of looking Jenny up and down. Jenny touched her cheek where a punch had landed, but she knew there was no bruise.

'She punched me, kicked me, rugby tackled me to the ground. Then she bit me.'

That made Griffiths perk up. 'Really?'

Jenny pushed up her sweatshirt sleeve to show bite marks on her bicep. They'd faded since last night, weren't too impressive. It felt like when you were ill and got an appointment for the doctor just as the symptoms wore off.

Griffiths peered at her arm and nodded. 'OK.'

Jenny pushed her sleeve down and felt stupid. 'She threatened me too.'

'Saying what?'

'She would make me pay for what I'd done.'

Jenny wished she could've done this with Thomas, but that was privileged bullshit. Get your cop friend to take a statement, make it all go away.

'Interesting.' Griffiths made a play of flicking through her notebook. 'Because I had a visit from Stella McNamara last night complaining that you assaulted her with a heavy object.'

'What?'

'She showed me a convincingly bruised shoulder.'

Jenny shook her head. 'I only hit her to get her off me. She was punching and biting, for fuck's sake. I know when I'm being assaulted.'

Griffiths pointed her pen at the door. 'But without any witnesses, it's just your word against hers. Sounds like a cat fight.'

'A cat fight? Do they give you misogyny lessons in police training? I expected better from a woman.'

Griffiths shrugged. 'Two middle-aged women with a difference of opinion. I see worse from every hen party staggering down Lothian Road on a Saturday night.'

Jenny leaned forward. 'This is serious. I know what her family are like. Her brother tried to kill me, more than once. Maybe there's something in their genes.'

'You don't really believe that.'

'You didn't see Stella last night. She was wild.'

This was not how Jenny imagined it would go. But she should've known the police were not a source of justice. She read a news report recently about a hundred officers being investigated over sexual misconduct. She wondered how many of them even got a slap on the wrist.

Griffiths shut her notebook. 'OK, I'll speak to her.' She didn't sound convinced by her own words.

'What if she comes after me again?'

Griffiths snorted a laugh. 'You want us to assign you a body-guard? You know there are real crimes happening out there, yeah?'

Jenny swallowed hard, her fists tight underneath the table. 'I was *really* assaulted.'

'Just steer clear of the McNamaras. It should be a no-brainer, you're responsible for her brother's death.'

Jenny wanted to rise up, flip the table, pin Griffiths to the wall and scream in her face until she got it. Instead she just stood, teeth clenched, and headed for the door.

38

HANNAH

She pressed return to start the data-processing algorithm. This was the seventy-fifth data set out of a hundred and forty-six, and she was bored. It was microlensing data from a red dwarf fifty light years away, and she'd found nothing in the previous samples. She was showing her face at work because she hadn't done any in the last few days. A PhD was like that, you could disappear for a while and no one cared.

Really she was trying to block out all the other stuff going on. Life was normal here in this grey computing lab. She was on the first floor of a building at the back of the observatory site, a couple of rows of terminals linked to some heavy-duty processors next door. There was a view over Blackford Hill to the Braid Hills, like being in the countryside. She saw the chalky Liberton Tower amongst brown fields to her left, orange gorse and grass to the right.

She checked her monitor, still processing. She flicked through astronomy and cosmology websites on a browser, stopped at a story about a new exoplanet discovered orbiting a triple-star system. This was 1,300 light years away. It orbited all three stars in the system, reminding her of a novel she'd read, *The Three-Body Problem*. A species lived on a similar planet, their civilisations constantly wiped out by extremes of heat or cold, which were unpredictable because of the complexity of the planet's orbit. In the end, they decide to come to earth, nice and stable, to wipe everyone out and take over. It reminded her of Douglas Adams' *Hitchhikers* thing about a planet called Krikkit which had completely black skies. One day, a spaceship crash-landed on their planet. When they realised the universe was teeming with life, they set out to destroy it all. This was the stuff that got her mind racing, not terabytes of dry data, interminable lines of code, staring at graphs until your eyes went blurry.

'Excuse me, are you Hannah?'

She jumped at the voice behind her, northern English accent. She turned and saw a young woman her own age, beautiful with long black hair cut in a hard fringe, some east Asian heritage, strong face and small body.

'Depends who's asking.' Hannah meant it as a joke but it came out wrong. Since Laura, she was wary of randoms saying hello.

The woman gave something between a shrug and a nod of deference. 'Willow Hayashi, I think you know my *jiji*, Udo?'

'Udo, of course.' She pictured his bruised ribs, the cut on his face, bandaged head. The little shrine to his wife's ashes, all the Japanese trinkets around. 'You said "jiji"?'

'Grandpa.' Willow wore an orange patchwork jacket with high-waisted, three-quarter-length trousers and chunky trainers. She looked like an art student or a hipster model.

'He mentioned a granddaughter.'

Willow did a piss-take curtsy. 'That's me.'

'From Manchester.'

'Just off the train.' Willow threw a thumb behind her. 'I went to the Skelf funeral home to see Dorothy but she wasn't there, just a cute girl on reception.'

'That's my wife.'

Willow beamed. 'Wow, good catch.'

'Indy sent you here?'

'No. But I Googled the Skelfs, found your research page, took a punt.'

Christ, it was too easy to find people these days. Hannah had thought sitting here in an anonymous lab doing boring work would hide her, apparently not.

'So you've been helping Jiji?' Willow said.

'Kind of.'

'Cameras and audio devices all over his house seems a bit intrusive for a nice old man.'

'He wanted help.'

'Yeah, with Baba.'

'You mean your grandmother?'

Willow raised her hand to her ear, pinkie and thumb out. 'The old wind phone.'

Hannah smiled. 'I have to say, I do like that thing.'

'Me too. Makes a lot of sense for folk missing loved ones.'

'Even though it's not connected.'

'Not to 5G, but it is *connected*.'

Hannah shifted her weight, glanced at her terminal screen. Twenty percent done on the calculations. 'You think?'

Willow shrugged. 'For Jiji's generation in Japan the spirit world is right here.' She waved a hand in front of her face.

'So you think Lily is really haunting Udo?'

'Maybe.'

'And hurting him?'

'What?'

Hannah wondered what Udo had told her. 'He claims her ashes jumped out and hit him on the head.'

'An accident, he's an old man, unsteady.'

Hannah touched her own midriff. 'And there's the bruised ribs.'

'What?'

'You need to speak to Udo. This is more than him trying to get in touch with his wife. It's domestic abuse.'

'By Baba's ghost?' Willow leaned against a desk. Every movement she made was balanced and aware, and Hannah wondered if she was a dancer. 'Jiji never mentioned that.'

Hannah looked at her. Silky hair, odd clothes, languid manner, maybe lesbian or bi if Hannah was picking up right. Hannah remembered Dorothy saying Willow was all the family Udo had left. She thought how close she was to Mum and Gran.

'Go see Udo, he needs his family.'

'What are you expecting to find on these cameras?'

Hannah held her hands out. She thought of everything she'd seen over the last few years, plenty stranger things than a dead wife abusing her husband.

'We are genuinely trying to help.'

'Sounds like you're ripping off a confused old man.'

'I'd be very surprised if Gran is charging him anything. She has a weirdly Zen attitude, thinks the cosmos will pay us back somehow.'

Willow narrowed her eyes as if wondering whether Hannah was serious. Eventually she smiled and pushed herself off the desk.

'Sounds like our families are made for each other,' she said, pulling a bag of cookies out of her pocket. 'Fancy getting high?'

39

DOROTHY

Jazz didn't sing to her but she'd developed an appreciation as she got older. Sure, there was a lot of big-dick energy, a certain pissing-contest quality, showing off at the expense of the song. But sometimes, when the guys relaxed, it could be beautiful.

She sat behind the kit shuffling along to 'Dear Lord' by John Coltrane from his 1965 album somewhere between his old-school quartet and more avant-garde stuff. The track was sandwiched between two long pieces of frantic experimentation and was a moment of calm, a spiritual ballad. She felt the interplay between double bass and piano, the gentle expression of the drums, the way they all talked to each other as well as Coltrane's sax. It ebbed and flowed in a way Dorothy loved, something you only got with people in a room. That was one of the reasons she loved music, the inexplicable, emotional power, playing with other people was a sublime experience.

'Dear Lord' was the track that the Bruntsfield Bluedogs wanted at Jerry Lamb's funeral later. Dorothy tussled with the piano riffs in the middle eight and thought about Eddie. His body would be in the mortuary now alongside Craig. She thought about Violet, her boy lost. She thought about Hannah's stalker, her mum suddenly gone. And Udo haunted by his wife. It was a kaleidoscope of life and death, a spinning wheel of grief and loss, disorienting and unsettling.

Coltrane came back in for more ad-libbing over the chords and Dorothy thought about the title of the song. She didn't believe in God, or that things happened for a reason. She knew life and death were arbitrary, but felt in her bones that she was connected to the world and everything in it – Eddie and Danny, Craig and Jenny and Hannah and Violet, Laura and her mum, Udo and his wife, the jazz quartet playing in her ears, Schrödinger strolling across the studio towards the window, the people outside, trees, grass and sky.

The song ended in a lovely coda, a roll around the toms, some light cymbals. She took the headphones off and sat in silence for a long moment, trying not to think about the next thing. Just this, being here.

There was a knock on the door.

She closed her eyes for a couple of moments then opened them again.

'Yes?'

Archie stepped into the studio. 'Sorry, I didn't want to disturb you when you're drumming.'

She waved him in. 'What's up?'

'I wanted to check you were OK.'

She gave him a querying look.

'I heard about last night. You found that guy. Must've been horrible.'

She still had the drumsticks in her hand, imagined doing ba-dum tsh on the snare and cymbal. 'I'm fine. Or I will be. Who told you?'

Archie looked sheepish. 'They mentioned it at the police station. I was there with Jenny this morning.'

'Why?'

He told her briefly about Stella, him walking in on them downstairs. She felt anger rise up, tried to quell it. This was happening in her home now.

'Is Jenny all right?'

'She's OK.'

Archie glanced out the window. He clearly had something else to say.

Dorothy waited.

'Well, she's a bit all over the place. Since Craig washed up. She's drinking a lot and ... I found her sleeping in a coffin the other night.'

Jenny had gone through a phase of that as a drunken teenager, saw it as ironic or rebellious or something. Dorothy didn't like that it was back.

'You and her, you're not...?'

Archie shook his head too much. 'Nothing like that. I'm just trying to be a friend. She needs it.'

Dorothy remembered first meeting Archie at a stranger's funeral. Hiring him, taking him to the doctor. Much later, he'd helped her do some very dark things, stuff she wanted to forget. And they'd buried his mother not long ago. So much history accumulated together, like silt on a riverbank.

'She's lucky to have you. We're all lucky to have you.'

Archie held his hands awkwardly at his side. 'It works both ways, you know that.'

Dorothy knew he meant it. 'Just be careful with Jenny, she can be...'

He nodded as if he knew exactly what she meant.

She rang the doorbell and waited. Looked around the driveway, now with two black Audis in it. She wasn't even sure which one she put the tracker on. The traffic was constant over the hedge, the city always moving.

Mike opened the door. The last time she saw him, he was rolling around with Danny. He looked smaller than she remembered, blue eyes red around the rims, skin pale. He wore a large grey hoodie and joggers, which made him look softer than he had in a suit.

'Mrs Skelf,' he said. 'Roxanne gave me your card.'

Dorothy left dead air between them. She wasn't even sure why she was here. Thomas would tell her off but she needed to resolve this. Eddie's dead stare was too much for her.

Mike started crying, a sniffle at first then lots of swallowing, trying to stop the floodgates, frantically wiping his tears.

'I'm sorry, I haven't slept,' he said. 'The police took me to the station last night, told me about Eddie. Kept me there for hours.'

'I'm sorry for your loss.'

'I already lost him once. I thought he was dead. That's what made Danny's thing so frustrating, I wanted him to accept Eddie was gone. But Danny was right all along. And now Eddie really is dead. You know how that feels, to lose your brother twice?'

Dorothy rubbed the back of her neck and glanced at the Audis in the driveway. She thought about the tracking info she'd given the police. It couldn't be a coincidence that one of these cars was in the street next to Eddie's place last night. Edinburgh was a small place but not that small. She thought of Roxanne sneaking around behind Mike's back. How she'd been when Dorothy met her.

'How was it with the police?' she said.

'Horrible,' Mike said, wiping his nose. 'They think I had something to do with it.'

'How's your wife taking it?'

Mike narrowed his eyes. 'As well as expected.'

Dorothy looked past him down the hallway. 'Is she in?'

'She took a sleeping pill.'

Dorothy pictured Roxanne kissing that woman up at Braid Hills.

'How are you?' Mike said.

Dorothy was taken aback. 'What do you mean?'

'You found him, right?'

Eddie's blood-soaked body came into her mind. Maybe all of this was a big mistake, and she should retire from snooping in other people's business. Just play with the cat and practise drums and meditate and go for long hikes. But she would atrophy, this was a way of staying alive.

'It was...' She didn't know what to say.

'It's Danny I'm most worried about.'

'Of course.'

'He's lost his mum and dad. And...'

'And what?'

Mike looked at the hedges and trees, then back at Dorothy. 'You saw how he was at the funeral. So angry. And he was right about Eddie.'

Dorothy had known this was coming. 'You think Danny did this?'

Mike rubbed at the palm of his hand. 'You spoke to him. Did he seem like someone who could?'

40

JENNY

She was bored, had lost the adrenaline from the police thing earlier. She sat at the reception desk and whirled round in her seat, opened and shut drawers, flicked through her phone. She was alone in the big house except for the corpses through the back. Maybe she should go back there and snoop around. She sighed and felt like an idiot. She remembered something from a famous footballer's interview years ago, God knows why it stuck in her mind, but he said he didn't like being alone because that's when the dark thoughts came. Quite.

Dorothy, Indy and Hannah were at some jazz funeral at Warriston Crem, and Archie was at a hospice picking up a body. So she was minding reception, waiting for death to come through the door.

She remembered Stella last night, full of righteous anger. Fuck, don't we all have a reason to be angry? Technically, Jenny *had* set fire to her brother and cast him adrift. It was self-defence, but still. If Stella, Craig or Violet did something similar to Hannah, for example, Jenny would lose her mind. She didn't know what Stella's intentions were and wondered if she needed a lawyer. She didn't know if she could cope with all that. She just wanted to hibernate, wake to find all this had gone away.

She closed her eyes, tried to calm her breathing. Mum had meditated for decades and Hannah used breathing techniques to deal with anxiety. Jenny wanted some of that calm but deep inside she didn't believe it was possible. How could she, with all this shit swirling around? She listened to her breath, the pulse in her ears, the creak of the old house, a clank from a heating pipe, the buzz of the wi-fi box under the desk. Pictured Craig's body, flames dancing into the night, stars overhead, the barbecue smell of him roasting alive, his arms waving.

The door opened and Jenny flinched.

It was a tall, thin young man, dishevelled and wired, glasses and a mess of black hair.

'Is Dorothy around?' He rubbed his jaw like he'd been punched. Jenny recognised the mix of hungover and still drunk.

'She's at a funeral, can I help?'

'Depends, who are you?'

'Who are you?'

'Danny Frame.'

'Shit.'

The kid from the pseudocide thing. Jenny had checked in with Dorothy and Hannah after hearing about Eddie at the police station. Danny was better-looking than she imagined, despite his state, or maybe because of it. She liked a fuck-up.

Danny laughed. 'Yeah, "shit" seems like the correct response to my life. I presume you know the latest?'

'I heard.'

Danny pouted, pulled his earlobe, counted on his fingers. 'So my dad disappeared, then my mum died, then I got into a fight at her funeral, then it turns out my dad was still alive all along, and now he's been murdered for real.'

He ran out of fingers and looked around. 'I'm just back from the station, where they gave me absolute shit.'

'That's funny, I had the same experience earlier.'

'They think I killed him.'

Jenny kept her voice light. 'Did you?'

Danny stared at her, trying to work out her tone. 'No.'

Jenny came round from behind the desk. Danny had a lithe and reckless energy up close.

'In that case, fancy the pub?'

He looked at her as if she was crazy, and she liked it. She walked out the front door and he followed her.

❧

When they clinked glasses, a dribble of his IPA spilled into her double gin and tonic, and she watched the fluids mixing.

'Cheers.'

They were at a table in Bennets on their fifth round, and Jenny enjoyed the buzz. They were laughing at their fucked-up situations, their impossible lives. Danny was mid-twenties, young enough to be her son but she didn't think about that too hard. The way he talked to her, it was nice to be noticed. She knew how pathetic that was, seeking attention from a cute young guy, but fuck it. She liked this frisson of danger.

Danny shook his head but he was smiling. 'This is crazy.'

'What?'

He waved a hand around. 'Being in the pub. My dad was murdered. I just buried my mum.'

Jenny raised her glass. 'Welcome to the fucked-up club.'

She'd told him about Craig, because why not? How she was happily married for a decade, how it turned sour when he had an affair. How he'd come back into her life in the worst way, chaos and hatred, violence and murder. And now she was free of him, but also not really. Violet was here to remind her that she had killed someone's son. Stella was here to put a fist in her face for it. And she deserved it. She wanted Stella to walk through the door right now and give her a bollocking. She would soak up all the vitriol and hatred, use it to power through the rest of her life.

'My dad is really dead,' Danny said under his breath.

Jenny gave him a look. 'So who do you think did it? If it wasn't you.'

It was insane to flirt, but she loved it.

'Why did he fake his death and run away?' Danny said. 'It must have something to do with that.'

'Money or sex.'

'What?' Danny frowned and drank.

Jenny held two fingers in the air. 'Money and sex are the only reasons for murder. Either he owed someone a ton of money or he was fucking the wrong person.'

Danny pressed his lips together and looked cute doing it, then his expression soured. 'Two months ago, I was a normal guy. A decent job, two parents who I thought loved each other.' He looked around for answers, his eyes red and wet. 'Now I've got no one.'

Jenny imagined Dorothy and Hannah dead on tables in the embalming room. She placed a hand on Danny's, squeezed. She kept her hand there and he looked at her and smiled, and she felt something pass through her like a ghost. She imagined fucking Danny in the toilets like she'd done with Brandon. It would be easy to seduce him, fuck the pain away for a moment, for both of them. But something in her gut stopped her, and she was glad of that.

She downed what was left of her gin and went to get more drinks.

41

HANNAH

Live jazz at a cremation was a new one for Hannah. She was sitting next to Indy, both of them in funeral suits, near the front of Lorimer Chapel, the bigger of the two options at Warriston Crematorium. They sat over to the side, as unobtrusive as possible. Across the other side of the coffin, crammed into the corner, were the Bruntsfield Bluedogs, the jazz quartet that Jerry Lamb had been a member of until his quick and painful death from colon cancer. The sax, double bass and piano players were all middle-aged men in suits that were a little tight. Dorothy was behind the kit watching the other guys for the changes, feeling her way through the songs. She'd taught Jerry to play back in the eighties.

They finished a mid-tempo swing number to a smattering of applause from the congregation, unsure if they should be clapping in a crem. The saxophone player filled the echoing space with a slow build of notes, then the rest tumbled into step, finding their feet as riffs bounced off the whitewashed ceiling and walls.

Hannah felt Indy's hand in hers, slowly rotating Hannah's wedding ring. She wondered if it was a sign, if everything was OK between them. Willow had said Indy was cute and she wasn't wrong. Hannah's heart swelled, something she was used to at funerals. The proximity to death always made you appreciate the good things in your life. In an alternate universe, on a different timeline, Hannah could be the person in the casket, or Indy, or Dorothy.

Hannah felt the buzz of the weed cookies she'd eaten with Willow earlier. It had taken a while to kick in, edibles were always a slow release, but it had built to a solid high, and she felt her body's wavelengths vibrating in synch with the universe. She thought about drugs that expanded your mind. She didn't have huge experience, tended to avoid illegal stuff because you had no idea what it was cut with. Your average pill could be half parace-tamol or bleach or worse. She'd had a bad MDMA trip once, was pretty sure it was ketamine. Didn't play well with anxiety and de-pression, that's for sure.

But she wasn't against opening your mind to new stuff. She felt the spaced-out fuzz from the weed, like the jazz was passing through her, changing her, becoming her. She imagined the sound waves hitting her ear drum, sending impulses to her brain, which somehow decoded them. She'd read about people without hearing managing to rewire their brains to understand vibrating signals sent from a watch device, so they could hear again. The brain was crazy. It sits in the dark room of your skull waiting for inputs to create a picture of the world, a sense of self.

Christ, she was still high.

She looked at the faces of the bereaved and wanted to give them each a hug, tell them Jerry was OK, his energy had just been con-verted from one form to another. It would happen to all of us.

She stopped at one mourner's face at the back of the hall and her breath caught in her throat. Laura. Of course she would be here, it made perfect sense. The police couldn't find her but here she was.

Hannah stared at a crucifix on the back wall for a moment, took a deep breath, then rose and walked down the aisle, getting a few glances from the pews. Laura smiled at her. Hannah sat down, sonorous saxophone notes swirling around her.

'Are you really here?' She waved fingers in the air, imagined them moving through the music.

Laura giggled. 'Are you high? Was it the cookies you ate with that Asian girl?'

Hannah felt her face move into a frown. It took a moment to put her thoughts into words. 'You were there?'

Laura turned and looked at her. Hannah didn't know how to unpack her features.

'I'm always looking out for you, someone has to, right? I mean, you're stoned at a jazz funeral.'

'I'm fine.'

'Your so-called wife isn't taking care of you, is she?'

Laura stared at Indy. Hannah followed her look, saw Indy's eyes full of concern at the two of them talking.

'You don't know anything about me and Indy.'

'I know you deserve better.'

Hannah felt anger rise. 'Why can't you just leave me alone?'

'You need help.'

Hannah laughed loud enough to be heard over the music. The pianist fluffed his notes, a few mourners stared. Hannah heard a tut.

'*I'm* not the one who needs help. You lived in your house with your dead mother's body for days without telling anyone. The police are looking for you.'

Laura grabbed her wrist and squeezed. She tried to pull away but Laura held tight. She stared at Laura's fingers on her skin.

'Don't fucking mention my mother,' Laura said. 'You have no idea what you're talking about.'

'You came to me. You wanted the Skelfs to bury her.'

'That's before I knew you would go running to the police.'

'Nobody went running to anyone. It's a standard post-mortem, they do them on all suspicious deaths.'

Laura's nails dug in hard. 'My mother's death wasn't suspicious.'

'Tell it to the police.' Hannah yanked her arm, but Laura held on and leaned in.

'I'm beginning to think you don't deserve me.' She spat the words out.

The music came to a close, echoes of rhythms and melodies passing through them for a final time before disappearing.

'I don't deserve any of this.' Hannah felt tears coming to her eyes.

Laura let go and stood.

'See you soon,' she said, heading for the door.

42

JENNY

She felt something wet and rough on her face, grunted as bile churned in her stomach. She rolled over to escape but it followed, pressing against her cheek. She opened her gummy eyes. A big bulldog was licking her face and wagging its tail, fetid breath all over her. She pushed it away and sat up, and it sniffed her crotch. She shoved it but it kept nudging at her groin. She looked up. She was on the slope of Bruntsfield Links, light fading in the sky, a gunmetal lid of cloud, dampness in the air.

'Tyson, come.'

This was a young man striding towards her with a dog lead draped around his shoulders. He grabbed Tyson's collar and hauled him off, glancing at her. She wondered what she looked like, a dishevelled drunken old woman asleep in the park. Her head pounded.

'He's just being friendly,' the guy said.

'Tell him to be friendly somewhere else, for fuck's sake.'

The guy walked away and Jenny remembered sitting with Danny in Bennets, their faces almost touching.

She looked around. It was home time for workers and students, a stream of people walking across the Meadows and the paths behind her, cars with their brake lights on in a slow-moving snake towards Tollcross.

She got up, brushed her bum, walked down the slope and across the road to Chalmers Street. At the uni building she rattled the doors, closed. She saw Brandon through the glass, coming downstairs and heading towards the door. When he spotted her he paused, looked around for an escape. She banged on the door, raised her eyebrows. Eventually he came over, unlocked the doors and squeezed outside, locking them behind him.

'I can't see you, Jenny.'

'I need to talk.'

'I'm heading home.'

'Maybe I could come with you.'

He looked her in the eye. 'I don't think that's appropriate.'

'We've done plenty of inappropriate things.'

'And now it stops, I've had enough.'

'If you don't let me have a session, I'll grass on you. I'll tell your boss you've been fucking a client.'

Brandon scratched his chin. 'For a start, I don't believe you would do that. Deep down you're a good person. But even if you did, I don't give a shit. Go ahead, I want nothing to do with you.'

She grabbed his arm. 'Brandon, please, I'm sorry.'

He shook his head and removed her hand. 'You're drunk. Leave me alone.'

'Fuck you, you used me. I was vulnerable and you took advantage.'

Brandon thought before he spoke. 'That's true and I'm sorry. But this is obviously unhealthy, I can't do it anymore.'

He walked away and Jenny thought about going after him. She watched until he was out of sight. The streetlights were on, a faint buzz overhead and an orange tint to the smirr hanging in the air. She felt like a woman in an Edward Hopper painting.

She turned and walked home across the grass, imagined Craig springing out of the darkness, or Stella, knife glinting in the gloom, ready to gut her like a fish.

When she reached the house, she went in the back way, past the embalming room, and stopped at the doorway of the workshop, the smell of wood shavings. A spot lamp was on at the back and she saw Archie at the desk. She walked over and saw he had a chisel in one hand, a small piece of wood in the other.

'Hey,' she said.

He kept his hands still. 'Hi.'

The energy he gave off was peaceful and calm, and Jenny felt it wrap around her like a big blanket.

She pulled up a chair. 'What's that?'

The way he was hunched over in the lamplight was like a Renaissance painting, sawdust flakes floating in the air, light reflecting off his shaved head.

'Netsuke,' he said. 'Dorothy told me about them, the old Japanese guy has some in his house. I thought I'd give it a go.'

He held up what he was working on. It was a sleeping fox, tail curled around to meet its face, paws in between, its body a curved line. Elegant, beautiful.

'I didn't know you could do that.'

'Neither did I. It's not great, but it's a start.'

'It's beautiful.'

Archie shook his head and rubbed a thumb over the fox, cleaning away dust from some of the crevices.

'How did you learn?'

Archie shrugged. 'I've been pottering around for years carving stuff. We have plenty of wood and tools.'

'I could never make something like that.'

'Sure you could, it just takes time and patience.'

Jenny laughed. 'Jesus, Archie, we are completely different people.'

Archie ran a tongue around his teeth, peered at the netsuke as he turned it, then looked at Jenny. 'I don't think so. We're both good people at heart, trying to do the right thing. But we've had a lot to deal with. A few years ago I was a complete mess, but I was lucky, had help, got myself together.'

'I'm a mess.' Jenny felt the words stick in her throat.

'I know.'

'Fuck, you didn't have to say that so quickly.'

'But you'll be OK. Things feel tough right now, but you've got good people around you, people who love you.'

Jenny burst into tears, her body shaking as she sobbed and struggled for breath, drowning in the shit of the world and feeling eternally sorry for herself. She felt Archie's arms around her in a hug and she leaned into it, tears and snot streaming from her as she burrowed her face into his neck and tried to forget who she was.

43

DOROTHY

She stared at the ceiling, John Coltrane running through her head. It was always the same when she rehearsed a song over and over, it took time to leave her mind. Another thing about music that was mysterious. She thought of that Frank Zappa line, how writing about music was like dancing about architecture. How can vibrations in the air make people laugh, cry, dance, lose their minds? It was spiritual, a way to connect with others.

Thomas shifted next to her in bed and she reached out and touched her fingers to his spine, making sure he was real. He was quiet so much of the time and she wondered about that, about his grief. She remembered him standing at Morag's grave, his breath shuddering through his body like her ghost had just passed through him.

He turned at her touch and took her hand, smiled, kissed it. 'Can't sleep?'

Dorothy pressed her lips together. 'There's a lot going on.'

He propped himself up on a pillow. 'I can't even imagine what it was like finding Eddie like that. Want to talk about it?'

Dorothy felt guilty that she hadn't been thinking about Eddie. She seriously considered the question. Did she want to talk about him? She'd been around death her whole life, but not like that. She very occasionally had to deal with dismembered corpses but always the result of some kind of accident, never at a murder scene. They'd buried murder victims before, of course, but the body came via the mortuary, and she never saw the violence, just the aftermath.

'I don't think so.'

Thomas nodded. 'Well, I'm here if you change your mind. Always.'

'I know.' She stroked his arm, felt the muscle beneath. Looked at his neck, thought of Eddie's slashed throat.

Thomas glanced away. 'I'm sorry about Griffiths this morning. She's young and ambitious, thinks confrontation is the way.'

Dorothy thought about all the stuff in the news about bad cops, violent cops, sexual assault by officers. It must be a painful weight on good police officers. She thought Thomas was good, but what did she know? We all present different faces to different people. Walt Whitman's thing about containing multitudes. She wondered which parts of herself she hid from Thomas. Which parts he hid from her.

'She was fine. Aren't most officers like that?'

Thomas held her gaze for a moment. 'A lot of them.'

'You don't seem very typical of the police force.'

'Maybe not.'

'And yet you rose up through the ranks.'

'Despite the system, rather than because of it.'

She brought his hand up to her face and kissed it, brushed his knuckles against her cheek. 'There's a whole side of you I don't know, Thomas.'

He narrowed his eyes and smiled. 'Not really, I'm an open book.'

Dorothy shook her head. 'I don't think any of us are open books.'

He leaned in and kissed her. 'So what secrets are you keeping?'

She thought about it. She wondered how she got here, in her seventies and in bed with a beautiful, gentle man. She thought of Jerry Lamb earlier today, a good man gone early. People younger than her died all the time, why did she deserve to keep going when others couldn't? She pictured Hannah talking to Laura at Jerry's funeral. The police were looking for her and there she was, in broad daylight at Warriston Crem. She thought of what Archie said, about finding Jenny sleeping in a coffin.

'I'm worried about Jenny,' she said eventually.

'What about her?'

'This whole thing with Craig's body turning up. I thought it would be the closure she needs. But it's like she's gone the other way. Craig's family have reminded her that he wasn't just a monster, there were other sides to him. And she can't handle that.'

She thought about Whitman's multitudes again. All the aspects of Craig that couldn't be reconciled. All the feelings inside Jenny that she couldn't come to terms with. It pained Dorothy to see her daughter so lost and not be able to show her the way.

'She'll come round eventually,' Thomas said, stroking her hand. 'She has to.'

'I'm not sure she does.'

Dorothy's phone vibrated on the bedside table. The time said 3:15am, the call was from Udo.

'Hello.'

'Dorothy.' He sounded out of breath. 'I didn't know who else to call.'

'What is it?'

'Willow. I heard a noise, came through and she's lying here bleeding, I don't know what happened.'

'Is she conscious?'

'I can't wake her. I'm so scared.'

Dorothy was already out of bed, looking for clothes. 'I'll call an ambulance.'

❧

Udo stood next to the hospital bed, hands gripping the bedsheets as if they were the only thing keeping him upright. The room contained four beds. The lights were low.

Dorothy looked at Willow, bandaged head, eyes closed. She'd spoken to a doctor on the way in. A blow to the head, sharp object, a fair amount of blood loss, probably concussion. They'd done various scans, no bleeding on the brain.

'How are you?' Dorothy said.

Udo shook his head. 'I can't lose her.'

'She'll be OK. The young are strong.'

Udo closed his eyes like he was praying. Dorothy listened to the buzz of machines and lights, murmured voices outside the door, someone being pushed in a wheelchair. Hospitals never stopped, giant organisms always working.

Udo opened his eyes. 'I don't understand.'

'Maybe it would help to talk it through.'

Udo still gripped the sheets near Willow's arm.

'I thought I heard a noise. It's a little confused. It takes me a while to wake, at my age. To remember. I didn't know if I dreamed it. But I got up to check. She was lying in front of the shrine in the kitchen, bleeding on the rug. The Buddha on the floor next to her.'

His hand went to his head.

'Why would Lily do this? She loved Willow so much, especially after Ren and Akari left us.'

Dorothy tried to keep her voice level. 'You think Lily did this?'

Udo stared at Willow for a long time. She had bags under her eyes like she needed the rest.

'The same statue. Same shrine.'

Dorothy realised he was crying, tears falling on his knuckles. She placed a hand on his back. He flinched but didn't move away.

'I didn't know Lily, but I'm sure she had nothing to do with this. Why would she?'

'Maybe she knows something. Maybe she's angry.'

'Why would she be angry?'

Dorothy's phone buzzed in her pocket and she stepped away. Hannah. Dorothy had left her a message asking her to check the cameras, especially the kitchen one.

'Hannah.' Dorothy walked to the doorway, saw nurses swapping banter around a desk, mugs of strong tea, a plate of cupcakes.

'Nothing.' Hannah sounded confused.

'You mean there's no footage of what happened to Willow?'

'I mean nothing at all. No signals from any of the cameras in the house. There haven't been for several hours.'

44

JENNY

When she was a young woman, alcohol made her sleep like a fucking baby. Nowadays the headaches and heartburn, cotton mouth and missing memories made her wake early in an anxious sweat. She sat in the armchair at the window watching the sunrise over the Links, strong black coffee and a piece of toast. Schrödinger was surprisingly friendly, maybe sensing she didn't need his macho feline bullshit right now.

Gradually the kitchen got busier. First Mum in three-quarter Japanese pyjamas, looking a lot more rested than Jenny felt. Then Indy and Hannah turning up for breakfast. Jenny's hangover made her feel distant, like she was watching her family through a haze, and she kept closing her eyes, trying to remember yesterday. Morning trip to the police station, noised up by that cop, drunk with Danny in Bennets, then hassling Brandon before crying on Archie's shoulder. Jesus. She'd always thought she was a strong, independent woman. But here she was running between men, running away from Craig, from her dad's death.

Dorothy was standing next to the whiteboards clutching a mug of herbal tea. Jenny moved to the kitchen table where Indy and Hannah were eating pancakes and fruit. She looked at the PI whiteboard, busy with names, lines, phrases and locations. Dorothy rubbed *Jeremy Lamb* from the funeral board, another body committed to the ether. Then she went to the PI whiteboard, tapped the marker at Udo's name, turned to Hannah.

'Did you get an update from hospital?'

Hospital? Jenny had missed this.

'Willow's awake but she can't remember anything,' Hannah said, her mouth full of pancake.

'So what do we think?'

Hannah shrugged. 'Udo said I could go round this morning, check the cameras. Then I thought I would look in on Willow, unless you want to?'

'I have plenty of other stuff to do.'

Indy nudged Hannah. 'I could come with you.'

Her voice had a conciliatory tone, and Jenny wondered what else she'd missed. She felt like an interloper, an alien beamed in from a different reality. She wanted to curl into a ball.

Dorothy moved to another part of the board. 'What about your friend?'

She underlined *Laura Abbott*. At least Jenny knew about this one, Hannah's stalker who didn't report her mum's death for a week. She knew nothing about decomposition, but wouldn't that start to smell? How could you ignore your mum's dead body for days?

'The police still don't know where she is,' Indy said.

Dorothy nodded. 'It's a pity Han couldn't keep her at Jeremy's funeral.'

This made Jenny sit up. 'Your stalker was at a random's funeral?'

'She's not *my stalker*,' Hannah said. 'But yes, she was at the funeral yesterday.'

'How can the police not find her?'

'It's hard to find people if they don't want to be found.'

Christ, they knew that the hard way with Craig, missing for a year after escaping on the way to court.

'Are you safe?' Jenny said. 'She sounds crazy.'

Dorothy sucked her teeth. 'Her mother just died, Jen.'

Jenny felt like a kid again, the tone of her mum's voice.

Schrödinger strode over to Dorothy, who picked him up, stroked between his ears. She had a way with animals, with the fucking world, at ease with herself. Jenny would never have that.

Dorothy turned to the section of the whiteboard that was covered in the Frame family network. They'd already wiped Kathleen from the funeral board, but the rest of them were surrounding Eddie's name.

'What about these guys? she said.

Jenny wondered what Eddie's body looked like and felt a twinge of guilt that it was her mother and daughter who found him.

'It's a police matter now, isn't it?' Hannah said.

Dorothy nodded in a thoroughly unconvincing way. Jenny had seen that plenty of times before, her inability to let something go.

'I went to see Mike,' Dorothy said.

'And?'

'He seemed genuinely upset.'

'I feel worst for Danny,' Hannah said. 'Imagine thinking your dad is dead, then your mum dies, then your dad turns up, then someone kills him.'

'Maybe Danny did it,' Dorothy said.

'You don't believe that.'

'He was pretty angry with Eddie last time I saw him.'

Jenny swallowed and was surprised to hear her own voice. 'He came to see you.'

Dorothy turned. 'When?'

'I guess when you were visiting Mike.'

'Had the police spoken to him?'

'Yes.'

'How did he seem?' Hannah said.

She remembered sitting laughing with him in the pub. 'OK.'

'What did you talk about?'

Jenny waved a hand at the whiteboard. 'The whole fucked-up situation.'

'Do you think he could've done it?' Hannah said.

'He seems like a nice kid. Lost and angry, but who wouldn't be? I don't think he's a murderer, if that's what you're asking. And I should know, I married one.'

She regretted it as soon as it left her mouth. It was a cheap shot, Craig was still Hannah's dad, for fuck's sake. Hannah flinched and Jenny wanted to walk round the table and hug her. But she'd inflicted the damage, she didn't get to be the comfort. What a bitch.

'Sorry. I'm just a bit...'

'Hungover?' Hannah said.

'That's not a crime. I've got a lot of shit on my plate.'

'And we don't? Mum, sort your shit out. I know alcohol is your crutch or whatever, but you're spiralling. Have you even been going to therapy?'

She pictured pleading with Brandon last night and shook her head. 'I'm trying.'

'Try harder.'

Hannah pushed back her chair and stood. She left and Indy followed after a moment. Jenny glanced at Dorothy, saw pity in her eyes and wanted to jump out of the window.

'You're worried about Stella,' Dorothy said.

'She attacked me. She might do worse.'

Dorothy pressed her lips together. 'I'm going to meet Violet again, see what we can sort out.'

Jenny spread her hands out over the old table. 'How is this still haunting us, Mum? I thought it was over. I wanted Craig's body to wash up so I could be sure. But now things seem worse than before. Him turning up has just cut everything open again. Violet and Stella, I can't feel sorry for them, I just can't.'

'No one is ever really gone from our lives,' Dorothy said. 'Look at Udo and his wife. Laura and her mum. Danny and his family. They all carry those people with them. We'll always have Craig, we'll always be dealing with the ripples of what he did. But that doesn't mean we can't try to feel empathy for his family. What must it be like to have your son or brother do those things? You have to try to imagine what it's like to be other people.'

Jenny rubbed her face, felt the sheen of greasy hangover sweat. 'I've never been very good at that.'

Her voice was so low she wondered if Dorothy heard.

Silence for a moment.

'I know, love. But if you don't try, you're going to destroy yourself.'

45

HANNAH

She lifted the key from under the plant pot at the front door then looked at Indy and glanced around, hoping they hadn't been seen. They went into Udo's flat, through the corridor to the kitchen. Udo had refused to leave Willow's side at hospital, so had told her about the spare key. It was good Indy had come along, it felt like all the business of finding Eddie like that had put their arguments about Laura into perspective.

Hannah paused in the kitchen and lifted a finger. Indy stopped with a puzzled look. Hannah imagined hundreds of past tenants scurrying around them, growing old and dying, turning to dust.

'What is it?' Indy said.

'Listening for ghosts.'

'Do you think Udo is haunted?'

Indy was born in Edinburgh but her parents came from Kolkata, and her Hindu heritage informed her life. She had a closer link to her ancestors and spirits than Hannah did. Hannah's scientific brain struggled with that. But then, science and spirituality had so much in common – the sense of wonder, for one thing. Maybe they weren't so different.

Hannah walked to the shrine in the corner. 'This is where it happened. Do you feel the force?'

'It helps you to make fun of it, doesn't it?'

'I didn't mean anything.'

'You struggle with stuff you can't explain.'

'It was just a joke.'

'Sure.'

She checked the camera, saw it was manually switched off. She powered it up and it seemed to work fine. The way it was pointed, it would've been possible for someone to come in, slink along the side wall and switch it off without being seen.

Hannah put the camera back and Indy waved, checking they were being picked up. Hannah examined the shrine. Lily's ashes sat in the middle, beautiful sculptures all around, incense and candles. The Buddha was on the ground on its side. She wondered about forensics but picked it up anyway. Checked for blood but it looked clean. Did it really happen the way Udo said? No witnesses except Willow, who couldn't remember, and no footage.

She went round the flat with Indy checking the rest of the cameras. All in working order but switched off around the same time as the kitchen one. No footage of an attacker, incorporeal or otherwise. She left them all switched on.

They went out to the garden. It was colder than the last few days, leaves turning, the bird calls clearer in the air. It was starting to feel autumnal. Hannah liked this time of year but knew that Mum and Gran didn't. Indy preferred spring, rebirth and rejuvenation. Hannah liked the clarity and sharpness of autumn. We all have different responses to the world, maybe the spirit world too.

They walked to the white box at the bottom of the garden.

'The famous wind phone,' Indy said.

She strolled around it with her hand trailing across the crenulations between wood and glass. Hannah watched her.

'Can I use it?' Indy said.

Hannah nodded.

Indy opened the door and paused outside. 'Are the camera and audio off?'

Hannah stepped inside and checked, both switched off.

Indy waited for Hannah to leave, kissed her as she passed, then went inside and closed the door. She looked at Hannah through the glass then picked up the receiver. She stood like that for a while then eventually said a few words. Waited, as if for a reply, then spoke some more. She glanced at Hannah then turned to face the other direction.

Hannah thought about last year when Indy's grandparents turned up from Kolkata and insisted she was wrong to have buried her parents. They had to disinter Pratik and Giva and have a second ceremony to cremate their remains. Indy had handled it all so well but it can't have been easy. Two dead parents at her age, no wonder she wanted to speak to them on the phone.

Eventually Indy put the receiver down, stood for a long moment with her back to Hannah, then pushed the door open.

She fanned her face. 'Oof, that's quite something. Have you had a go?'

Hannah remembered Dorothy speaking to Jim down the line. 'I haven't.'

'Maybe you should, it's good therapy.'

'We can talk to the dead anytime, that's what you say to the bereaved, they'll always have their loved ones in their hearts.'

Indy pointed at the phone. 'But this, it's to do with the physical thing. Makes it seem more real. You're just alone in the box, your parents on the line, like...'

She glanced around the garden, sparrows in the hedge, a cat padding along the wall towards them.

Hannah opened her arms and gave Indy a big hug. Eventually Indy broke free and waved fingers at her cheeks again.

'Boy,' she said. 'It sneaks up on you.'

Hannah rubbed her arm then went to the wind phone. 'I just need to switch the stuff back on.'

She went into the box, switched the camera and audio device on then glanced outside. Indy was looking at the tenement windows. Hannah took out a pin-sized spy camera, checked it was working, and placed it in a corner of the box, pointing at the phone. A hidden back-up only she knew about.

46

DOROTHY

'Thanks for coming.' Dorothy looked across the table outside Söderberg at Violet McNamara. She seemed to be shrinking, smaller than Dorothy remembered from a few days ago, as if her frame couldn't handle the weight of all this.

Dorothy looked around. The tables were half full, the breakfast rush over. There was a sharpness in the air. A squirrel darted up a tree behind their table. She wished she was as agile, as determined. Students were heading to classes, youthful vitality shining from them. She envied their energy but wouldn't wish herself back to that age, nervous and uncertain, unaware of her power.

Violet held her hands over her coffee cup, warming them. There was a tremor in her fingers and Dorothy wondered if it was medical or stress. When they last spoke Dorothy felt sympathy, Violet had lost her son. But Stella attacking Jenny brought a different energy. Dorothy extended empathy as far as she could, but threats to her family were a different matter.

'So Stella's in town,' she said.

Violet tensed up. 'How do you know that?'

'Are you serious?'

It was clear from Violet's face she didn't know what'd happened.

'She came to see Jenny.' Dorothy placed her hands on the table, her green tea between them. 'She assaulted her and it might've been worse if they weren't interrupted.'

'That doesn't sound right.' Violet's hands shook as she fiddled with her teaspoon.

Dorothy kept her voice as level as possible. 'She said Jenny would pay for what she'd done to Craig.'

Violet looked down at her cup. 'She loved her brother very much, of course she's upset. But that doesn't sound like her.'

Violet's eyes were red and wet. Dorothy imagined her in her hotel room, her son's ghost standing over her, the weight of what he'd done pressing down on her frail body until she was on the floor. Then she pictured Stella attacking Jenny and her heart hardened.

'Jenny reported it to the police.' Dorothy leaned in and took Violet's hand. 'Stella is dangerous. If she keeps this up, the police will arrest her.'

Violet pulled her hand away. 'I don't think so.'

'I understand where you're coming from. To lose your boy, I can't imagine. And to know what he's done.'

Violet lowered her head and produced a tissue from her cardigan sleeve, wiped her nose.

'I'm sorry to upset you, but this needs to be said. My daughter could die.'

'Like my son?'

'He tried to kill her, do we have to go over this again?'

Violet's body seemed to vibrate like a plucked string. 'Stella is not Craig. They're different people.'

Dorothy had only ever had Jenny, no siblings. The birth was traumatic, haemorrhaging blood in the maternity room. Healthcare in those days was perfunctory, they gave her a brief inspection and sent her packing. She never managed to conceive again.

'You need to speak to Stella before she does something she regrets.'

'This just doesn't sound like my Stella. She's been so supportive. We only have each other. You know what that's like.'

Dorothy did. Jenny and Hannah kept her together when Jim died.

Violet coughed. 'But our children can hide themselves from us, you know that.'

Dorothy remembered when Jenny first started to lie convincingly as a teenager. She could no longer be sure what her daughter was thinking, the cord was severed. The curse of every parent.

Violet tried to pick up her teaspoon, clattered it against the cup.

'Stella is the only thing keeping me alive right now.'

'I know it feels like that, but—'

Violet banged the table, making both their cups jump. 'You don't get to lecture me like you know everything. Part of me shut down when my husband died, another part died when Craig went missing.'

She was crying now, tears on her cheeks, fingers clenched into claws.

'There's not much of me left. If I lose Stella I couldn't bear it. I wouldn't have anything.'

Dorothy expected her to storm off but she just sat there, hands clasped together, tears falling onto the table, staring at Dorothy until eventually she had to look away, it was too much.

47

JENNY

She knew Edinburgh's graveyards too well. From the age of fifteen until her forties she barely set foot in one but as a kid she got dragged to funerals at cemeteries and crematoriums all over the city. Childcare was expensive and it was a family business, so she went where Mum or Dad went.

She looked around Liberton Cemetery, memories coming back. Playing with her Barbies in a hearse, waiting for Dad to come back from an open grave. Sitting in the room at the back of the church with a colouring book of Noah and the flood, organ music and muffled sobs coming through the heavy curtain from the nave. Death was imprinted on her at an early age. But those memories weren't all bad, she got to spend time with her dad and she would give anything for that again.

She read some gravestones, lives well lived, cut too short, barely started, whatever. The pampas grass up the hill, the wall across the middle of the cemetery as if there was a better class of corpse on the other side. The expanse of grey stones matched the sky, leaden and sullen. Down the hill was wet grass, the view of Arthur's Seat and the dreich city.

'Hi.'

She turned and saw Danny looking sheepish. The dampness in the air suited him, like a soft filter. He was taller than she remembered, more solid. She recalled a gangly lad, but he seemed more like a man today.

'Hey.' Jenny raised her hands, taking in the cemetery. 'Why meet here?'

He toyed with the end of his scarf and pointed down the slope. 'Mum's over there.'

He walked and she joined him. She remembered running through this graveyard with her mum when she was little, hide and seek amongst the trees and stones, dirt under her fingernails.

'How are you?' she said.

'OK,' he said too quickly. 'I'm still alive, I guess, that's something.'

They passed a spread of newer gravestones, flowers and nick-nacks alongside, a soggy teddy bear, a golf ball, rusty knitting needles.

Danny touched Jenny's arm and she stopped walking, looked at him.

'Why did you call me?' he said.

Jenny twitched her nose. Why did she? 'I just wanted to check on you. We were both pretty wasted in Bennets.'

Danny narrowed his eyes. 'I don't really remember what we talked about.'

'Just life and death.'

They walked on round a corner. Jenny glimpsed a fox, tail disappearing into a hedge. They went on a few more steps then Danny stopped, turned to his mum's stone. Jenny read the dates. Kathleen was three years older than Jenny when she died. Maybe they were into the same bands and clubs, movies and books. Maybe they bumped into each other on a dancefloor thirty years ago, or sat next to each other in a restaurant.

Jenny had Googled 'takotsubo cardiomyopathy', read a list of thirteen possible triggers, an asterisk indicating it wasn't exhaustive. Everything from a car accident or asthma to public speaking could cause it, not just losing a loved one. So broken-heart syndrome seemed a misnomer.

Danny hunkered down. 'Hi, Mum.'

Jenny looked at the cherry-blossom tree nearby, leaves turning. She felt awkward listening in.

'This is Jenny,' Danny said. 'She's pretending to be worried about me, but really she's trying to find out whether I killed Dad or not.'

Blood rushed to Jenny's face. 'Danny, that's not—'

He held his hand up to stop her.

'She thinks she has some insight into who I am. She thinks she can feel my pain, see the empty heart where you should be. But there's just nothing, a black hole. Because of him.'

'Danny.'

He was still crouching and facing the gravestone.

'I miss you so much. When Dad went missing, we had each other. Then you left and I had nothing. And then that wanker turned up, such bullshit. Now I'm back to where I was.'

He stood up. Jenny expected tears from the waver in his voice, but his face was blank.

'I don't think you killed him,' she said. 'Dorothy gets these niggles she can't shake off. She has to find out the truth, it's a whole thing with her. But I genuinely did want to see how you're doing.'

She raised her hand and touched his sleeve.

He stared at her for a long time and she wondered what he would do. Walk away, hit her, throw her onto the grass and fuck her.

Eventually he took her hand, his palm cold and clammy.

'You really don't think I killed him?'

48

HANNAH

Hannah sat at a terminal in the computing lab, data processing in the background, a couple of browser tabs open. One was a discussion forum on Von Neumann machines, the other an academic paper on Dyson spheres. Occasionally she tried to discuss this stuff with Indy, but her eyes always glazed over.

Von Neumann probes were hypothetical self-replicating spaceships. The idea was that once a civilisation got advanced enough, they could design ships to head out into the universe, replicating themselves as they went. If that was the case, why wasn't the universe overrun with spaceships, robots and other tech? It was nearly fourteen billion years old, plenty of time for a species to become that advanced aeons ago and send their mechanical progeny into the void. So where were they?

Dyson spheres were another hypothetical idea about advanced species. As a civilisation develops and grows, it needs power. Eventually, it makes sense that a very advanced species would try to harness the energy of a sun, and a Dyson sphere was an imagined megastructure that surrounded a star and used all its energy. There would be specific signals sent out which were in principle detectable by our telescopes, but there was a lot of argument about the fine detail. Astronomers occasionally spotted something weird in the sky and the idea of Dyson spheres was floated again, but usually it turned out to be something natural – huge dust clouds, exploding planets, pulsars.

Working on exoplanets and astrobiology could be so frustrating. Both fields were in their infancy, scientists just about realising how much they didn't know, and the technology of telescopes and data processing lagged behind. They might find answers in twenty years, or a hundred, or never.

Her phone rang. A few other postgrads sat at nearby computers, eating snacks and scrolling. She grabbed her phone, saw it was Indy.

'Hey.' A note of caution in Indy's voice even in that one word.

'What's up?'

'Laura's here.'

Hannah realised from Indy's tone that Laura could hear her.

'She needs to hand herself in to the police.'

'She just came from there.'

'They let her go?'

'Yeah.' Indy lowered her voice. 'According to her, they said she's done nothing wrong.'

'Ignoring her mum's dead body in their home for days is fine?'

Indy cleared her throat. 'Anyway, she wants the Skelfs to do Elizabeth's funeral, she's here to arrange it. I thought you should know.'

Hannah glanced round the room, listened to the buzz of computer fans. She pinched her nose. 'I'll be there as quick as I can.'

❧

Reception was empty when Hannah came in, sweaty from hurrying up the road. She heard voices from the drawing room and went through. It was gloomy despite big windows, thanks to oak panelling, maroon wallpaper and dark-wood furniture. Hannah had wanted to brighten up the place, but maybe this was suitable for a funeral parlour. There were even painted portraits of the Skelf men going back to original carpenter-turned-funeral-director Old John. He gazed down at Laura on the sofa, Indy in an adjacent armchair. They both looked at Hannah, Indy with wide eyes, Laura grinning.

'Han!' She leapt up and hugged Hannah. 'Come sit next to me.'

She sat and patted the leather next to her. Hannah took a seat. 'Indy is being *so* lovely, but I'm glad you're here.'

'I don't arrange funerals, Laura.' Hannah threw Indy a glance.

'But you'll make an exception for little old me, of course.' Laura looked at them both. 'You guys are such a cute couple, how did you meet?'

Hannah saw Indy shake her head, a tiny movement as if her head was in a clamp.

She waited a long time before answering. 'Indy came here to arrange her parents' funeral.'

Laura's hand went to her mouth in melodramatic fashion. She lunged over and grabbed Indy's hand. 'You never said, we have so much in common. Funeral besties, and orphans too!' She turned back to Hannah. 'And the thing with your dad! We're such a perfect gang.'

Hannah reminded herself that Laura was grieving, remembered Dorothy's mantra that everyone copes differently. She recalled a tabloid story from a while ago decrying teenagers for taking funeral selfies with the deceased. She hated the paper's sneering contempt. Who has the right to judge how we deal with the massive hole in our hearts? Hannah had seen people crying with laughter at funerals, fighting, vomiting, fainting, numb, delirious. It just made us human.

She breathed deep. 'Laura, tell us what happened.'

Laura let go of Indy's hand and grabbed Hannah's. 'How do you mean?'

'At home.' Hannah didn't flinch from eye contact.

Laura squeezed her hand too hard, then a flicker behind her eyes and she looked away. 'Mum died, that's all.'

'You didn't report it.'

'I did *eventually*.' Laura sounded exasperated. 'When I came to your place.'

'She'd been dead for a week,' Indy said.

Laura whipped round and narrowed her eyes. 'I thought you

were nice.' She straightened her back. 'It just took me a moment to get myself together, that's all.' She looked at Hannah and squeezed her hand again. 'You understand. That's why I want *you* to arrange her funeral. You get me like no one else.'

'Like I said before, funerals are Indy's job.'

'But this is special,' Laura said, voice lowered. 'We're special. You understand.'

Hannah gently slipped her hand out from Laura's like it was a bomb ready to blow. She wondered how to play this. Laura was fragile, had attached herself to Hannah emotionally. If she destroyed that link, who knew what would happen? On the other hand, this clearly wasn't healthy.

'I know this is hard, but Indy is the best person to handle it.'

Laura's mouth tightened and a vein in her neck started to throb.

'Fuck's sake, I just want to bury my fucking dead mother, is that too much to ask?'

Everyone froze, then Laura broke the spell with a laugh, too loud and high.

'So, let's get the details sorted, shall we? I want a white oak coffin, red silk lining and lots of carnations. Mum loved carnations. We want to send her off in style, don't we?'

Hannah caught a look from Indy that she understood. This was a woman on the edge and they had to talk her down. But for the life of her, Hannah couldn't imagine what to say next.

49

DOROTHY

She watched Roxanne get out of the car and walk to the house on Bramdean Rise, spring in her step. The younger woman opened the door and they fell inside groping each other. Subtle stuff. When the door closed, Dorothy got out of the van and stretched her back, stiff from the drive. She presumed Roxanne and her lover would be a while, so she walked through the nearby gate onto Braid Hills, through the trees to the expanse of scrubby grass and gorse. She strode up the hill towards the trig point. There were radio masts to the left, like ancient alien artefacts left behind. The coconut smell of the gorse filled the sharp air. The gloom of earlier had lifted and when she reached the top she turned and faced the city. Remembered the seven hills, the green mounds to the west, the castle as the beating heart of the place, Arthur's Seat and Salisbury Crags endlessly dramatic, slumbering giants. So much of her life had been lived in the shadows of these hills, in the arteries and veins flowing between neighbourhoods.

Behind her was the backroad to Mortonhall Crem, Liberton Cemetery not far beyond. She liked that so many of her reference points were death-related. She thought about what she'd seen earlier on the Liberton gravecam, Jenny and Danny in animated discussion at Kathleen's grave. No audio, but something intimate in their body language.

Then she'd got a ping from Mike and Roxanne's car and jumped in the van to follow. She didn't know why, wasn't sure what she'd find. Roxanne and Mike shared their two cars, giving them wriggle room about being near Eddie's place. Surely the police would sort that. Then again, despite her attachment to Thomas, she'd learned not to rely on authorities to get things done. It was a cliché because it was true – if you wanted something done, do it yourself. That was a good ethos for life, be active, not passive. One of the issues she had with conventional Buddhism was passivity – let all things go. Sometimes you had to fight for what you believed.

She took a few big breaths, opened her eyes wide and stared at the view. High rolls of cloud scudded overhead, ravens circled, dogs off their leads sniffed the bushes below her.

She headed back down the hill and waited in the van, put on a *New York Times* podcast. It was a little pretentious and self-important, but there were worse crimes, and she liked their voices.

An hour later, the door of the house opened and Roxanne came out. She was in tight leggings and sports top like she'd just been to the gym, except her hair was down over her shoulders. She kissed her girlfriend in the doorway – they really didn't give a shit about being seen together – then made for the car. The woman went inside and Dorothy stepped from the van.

'Roxanne.'

She looked up then around her as if guilty. Her shoulders slumped.

'Dorothy, right? How the hell are you here?'

Dorothy pointed at the Audi. 'There's a tracking device on the car.'

'That's illegal.'

'It's not, as it happens.'

'Well, it's fucking dodgy.'

'It's a grey area. Can we talk?'

'No.' She unlocked the car but didn't get in.

'I want to help. This whole thing with Eddie.'

'Why are you involved?'

'I found him, I feel responsible.'

Roxanne nodded. 'Maybe you should.'

'So, can we?'

Roxanne glanced back at the house and sighed. 'Not here.'

'It's a little late to be cautious.'

Roxanne flicked her hair back. 'She has nothing to do with this.' She waved a hand as if to encompass everything, Kathleen's death, Eddie's murder, her husband's tears, the sweeping Edinburgh city-scape.

'Let's walk,' she said, and led Dorothy back onto Braid Hills, this time the lower track, closer to the golf course. Dorothy heard the ping of a golf club and imagined a ball sailing over the gorse to smack her on the head. She saw gulls and crows, two rabbits disappearing into bushes.

'I spoke to Mike, did he tell you?' she said.

Roxanne frowned. 'No, communication between us isn't what it could be.'

'Does he know about her?' Dorothy threw a thumb behind her.

'He doesn't *know* know, but I presume he suspects.'

'That must be difficult.'

Roxanne pressed her lips together. 'Her name's Adelle. I shouldn't tell you that, but I have to tell someone. We met at the gym. I fucking love her to bits. I was all set to leave Mike then his brother went missing, then Kathleen, now ... It's a mess.'

'It's never a good time.'

Roxanne ran a hand through her hair and laughed. 'True, but I think some times are fucking worse than others.'

She turned up the slope and they got a better view of Blackford Hill. 'For what it's worth, I don't think he'll mind about Adelle. I'm pretty sure he's fucking someone else too.'

'What makes you say that?'

Roxanne shrugged. 'We come and go as we please. I don't ask questions, given my situation.' She waved at Adelle's house beyond the trees. She was walking fast and Dorothy had to skip to keep up.

'What about Eddie?' Dorothy said.

'What about him?'

'Where were you the night he was killed?'

Roxanne stopped walking and took Dorothy in. 'Who the fuck are you, Miss Marple?'

Dorothy got her breath back. 'Your car was near his place that evening.'

A look came over Roxanne's face. 'The tracker, you sly fuck. That's surely not admissible in court.'

'I don't know, but it's a fact that the car was there.'

Two ravens lifted into the air squawking and flapping.

'I wasn't,' Roxanne said.

'Where were you?'

Roxanne looked towards Adelle's house. 'She's my alibi, which is complicated.'

'Surely she'd help you out.'

Roxanne rubbed at her cheek, then her chin. 'She has a husband.'

'That's convenient.'

Roxanne scowled at her.

'So what about the car?' Dorothy said.

'Take it up with Mike, he drives it too.'

'Haven't you and Mike even talked about what happened to Eddie? You could be living with a killer.'

Roxanne gave a stony stare. 'Mike isn't a killer. He's a lot of things, but he wouldn't do that.'

'Are you sure?'

The question floated away in the breeze unanswered. The ravens settled their squabble and landed. Beyond them was Edinburgh, full of secrets and lies.

50
JENNY

She sipped her gin and tonic and watched the sky darken outside Bennets. Not long until the clocks went back and they would be plunged into miserable gloom for months. She hated folk who cheerily posted on social media that they loved autumn, turning leaves, sharpness in the air. Fuck that. Give her sunshine and a beer garden all year round. She took the lack of daylight personally, felt the dark weight pressing down on her. She breathed and glanced at *The Scotsman* on the bar. It was weird to see a physical newspaper these days, like a rare bird. She hadn't bought a newspaper in years. She looked around the bar and thought about Danny and Brandon. She needed to get her shit together. Craig was dead, that's what she had to remember. He was gone and she had her family to keep her strong.

The doors swished open and there was Stella, backlit by the streetlights outside. Jenny gripped her heavy gin tumbler in her fist, ready. Stella walked towards her. She resembled Craig more than Jenny noticed last time, the same jaw, similar eyes. She held her hands up as if Jenny had a gun trained on her.

'I come in peace.'

'Fuck off.'

Stella tilted her head. 'Fair enough.' She nodded at Jenny's glass. 'But I owe you a drink, I knocked one out of your hand last time.'

'When you fucking attacked me.'

'Double G & T, I'm guessing.'

Jenny gave a nod but didn't release her grip.

Stella got two doubles, slid one over. She took a big drink and wiped her mouth.

'I owe you an apology.' She looked at the big mirrors covered in brewery logos.

'Go on then.'

'What?'

'Apologise. It's my pet hate when people say they'll apologise then don't actually do it.'

Stella smiled and Jenny saw a ghost of Craig's smile in the rise of her lips. She felt it run through her heart like a dagger.

'I'm sorry for hitting you. Truly.'

Jenny narrowed her eyes as Stella drank. 'This is because of the police, right?' She finished her drink but didn't pick up the one Stella bought her yet.

'I don't know what you mean.'

'You're worried they'll charge you. Or I'll sue you.'

'I just made a mistake.'

'Bullshit.' Jenny picked up the drink and wondered about poison. Had Stella done an Agatha Christie thing, slipped deadly powder into her glass?

Stella settled on the barstool next to Jenny. 'People are allowed to change their minds, right? I was out of order.'

Jenny took a drink and looked at her glass. 'I don't fucking trust you. But thanks, I guess.'

Stella smiled. 'I'm not the only one who's fucked up over this.'

Jenny laughed. 'Is this the bit in the movie where the bad guy tells the good guy they're actually not so different? Such a cliché.'

'Am I the bad guy here?'

Jenny shrugged.

Stella arched her back but she was still smiling. 'Fuck you. In my narrative I'm the hero and you're the bad guy.'

Jenny stared at the lime in her drink, bubbles clinging to it. 'That sounds like a terrible movie.'

'Yeah, my whole life feels like a terrible movie at the moment.'

'Tell me about it.'

Stella angled her glass to mimic Jenny. 'You see, we're really not that different.'

'Jesus.'

'In another life we could've been friends.'

'Let's not go crazy.'

A couple got up from their table and left, the traffic noise through the opened door was shocking. This place sheltered them from the outside world, all the dead bodies and murder and violence and hate and loneliness and depression and emptiness. Jenny closed her eyes and felt the weight of her eyelids. She imagined Stella bringing a gin bottle down on her head, the release of it. She opened her eyes. Stella looked at her, one woman to another.

'So what now?' Jenny said. 'You said you were going to set the police on me, drag me through the courts.'

Stella downed the last of her drink. 'I spoke to Mum, she made me see things differently. She doesn't need any of this, her son's body just washed up.' She looked as if she was holding back tears. 'I guess I don't need it either. Maybe it's time we buried Craig.'

She looked at Jenny and Jenny held her gaze. She couldn't believe Stella was for real. She wanted to bury Craig more than anything, to have all this behind her, but her subconscious refused to let her off the hook. If something felt too easy, it's because it was. But she downed her drink anyway and went to get another round, see what would happen next.

51

HANNAH

Anxiety gnawed at Hannah's brain, a tremor in her gut. She lay in bed and listened to Indy breathing, slow and deep. Hannah had been jolted awake by some drunk shouting in the street. Now the rattle of their old windows and rustle of leaves kept her company. She was jumpy about Laura, every noise from outside made her imagine Laura standing in the Meadows with binoculars, keeping a watchful eye on her. Ever since she approached their table at Söderberg six days ago, she'd thrown Hannah into old patterns of worry and stress. She still couldn't get her head around the fact Laura's mum was already dead while Laura stood chatting to them. It was crazy that that wasn't illegal. Laura clearly needed a psychiatric evaluation, but who could arrange it? The only family she had was gone.

Hannah rubbed her eyes and eased out of bed. Pulled on a sweatshirt, walked to the kitchenette and put the kettle on, threw a lemon-and-ginger teabag in a mug. She closed her eyes and imagined herself on an empty beach, waves lapping at her toes. She saw Laura emerge from the water and walk towards her with a smile. Then another figure, her dad.

The kettle clicked off and the noise ebbed away. She poured water into the mug and picked up her phone. Scrolled through her socials, eyes glazed. Swiped them away and saw a notification for the cameras at Udo's house. She opened the app, found the most recent footage, within the last half-hour. She opened a file, saw the grainy image of Udo's hallway. He emerged from his bedroom, walking slowly. It looked like his eyes were closed. His hand ran along the wall then he went out of sight. The footage ended and she clicked on the next camera. It picked him up shuffling along, hand still trailing along the wall under the woodblock prints. Eyes definitely closed. He turned into the kitchen, paused, then was lost.

She went to the next file, kitchencam. It picked him up in the doorway walking towards Lily's shrine. He stood in front of it for a while and Hannah would've thought the picture was frozen except for the time ticking over in the bottom corner. He opened his mouth and Hannah turned up the volume on her phone. He was making a high-pitched keening sound. It raised in pitch and volume, became more breathy, then dropped to something like a growl. His hands wavered in front of him as if he were staring at them, but his eyes were still closed. His hands trembled, vibrations that swept up his arms and torso, his legs were shaking and knees bent.

He stepped forward, still growling like a wild animal, and reached for the Buddha statue with both hands. He held it up in front of him, shifting it between hands. Then he brought it down onto the left side of his ribcage, hard, faster than she thought he'd be able to. He flinched and his head bowed. The noise stopped as he caught his breath. His eyes stayed closed. He straightened up, raised the statue and swung it down again on the same spot, digging into his lower ribs and the soft tissue beneath. He buckled under the hit. He began whispering and Hannah turned the volume up but couldn't make out his words. He raised the Buddha again and she cried out.

'Stop.'

But the timestamp said fifteen minutes ago, this had already happened. She wanted to stop the footage and call him but she had to see how this played out.

He hit himself three more times, the last one making him double over in pain. He dropped the statue, only just missing his bare feet, then straightened up. He was still whispering under his breath as he turned and walked out the back door. The footage ended.

She went to the last file, the spycam she'd hidden in the wind phone. It triggered as Udo opened the phone-box door and came inside. He still had his eyes closed. He picked up the handset and leaned against the door. Hannah turned the volume up full on her phone. He whacked the handset against his forehead once, twice, three times, each hit making Hannah flinch.

'Stop it,' she said. 'What are you doing?'

His head was bleeding, a small trickle at his temple. He breathed from the exertion then put the handset to his mouth and ear. He stood like that for a long time, tilted his head as if listening to someone talk. He nodded in agreement, pressed his lips together, placed his hand against the glass of the box.

'I know,' he said softly. 'Lily, I know. I miss you too. I'm so sorry for what I did. I wish I could make it up to you. Lily, please forgive me.'

52

JENNY

Another early-morning funeral with a hangover. She was forty-seven years old, so it was more than a sore head and dry mouth – bottomless darkness and overwhelming angst swamped her soul. She pressed her back into the pew, closed her eyes and felt her tongue sweat.

'You OK?' Archie said next to her.

The softness of his voice was a comfort blanket. She wanted to hug him and go to sleep, but was scared she would never wake up.

'Just tired.'

She looked at him. He had a kind smile but pity behind his eyes too, and she felt a swell of self-loathing.

'Maybe a little hungover.' She looked at her hands in her lap. She was in her funeral suit, too warm in the crematorium, she wished they would turn the heating down. Organ music burbled from the speakers.

'Regretting last night,' she said.

Archie gave her a look. 'We're a little old for regrets, don't you think?'

Normally she might've argued she wasn't old, but this morning she felt a hundred.

'Do or do not, there is no regret,' Archie said in a Yoda voice.

She got the *Star Wars* reference.

'It's like guilty pleasures,' Archie said, leaning in. 'There's no such thing. Either do something because you enjoy it or don't. Feeling guilty doesn't come into it.'

She imagined kissing him right here, feeling his scratchy beard on her cheek.

'I was drinking with Stella.'

'The woman I saw battering you?'

'Excuse me, I gave as good as I got.'

Archie looked sceptical. 'OK, Slugger.'

She punched him on the arm and he pretended to be hurt.

The organ music faded and an old female celebrant shuffled to the dais. 'We're gathered here today to pay our last respects to Rhona Wilding.'

She went on in a monotone and Jenny looked around the room. She'd never seen Seafield Crem so empty. Apart from the celebrant, there were only her and Archie on one side of the central aisle, Dorothy, Hannah and Indy on the other. Dorothy had insisted they all come and shut the business for an hour, because she hadn't been able to unearth any of Rhona's relatives.

Jenny remembered picking up Rhona's body from the hospital with Indy six days ago. Before Craig washed up at Wardie. Before she'd fought then made up with Stella.

The celebrant gave some scant details of Rhona's life that Dorothy had gleaned. It didn't amount to much. Happy child, went into insurance, lots of different jobs, never married. Liked horse riding and swimming as a kid, but didn't pursue either as an adult. Did she have lovers that no one knew about? Secret kinks? A life devoted to charity work or hallucinogens or sky diving or snakes? It was unacceptable that this woman, two years younger than Jenny, didn't have a single person she knew at her funeral. That weighed on Jenny like a ton of bricks. How easy to slip through the cracks. Or not even that, just drift along until one day a bad cramp takes you to the doctor, the next thing you know stomach cancer is eating you up and you're in a wooden box in a room with half a dozen strangers, about to go up in smoke.

Jenny wiped at her forehead, felt the alcohol sweat on the back of her hand.

They stood and said a final prayer. Jenny imagined herself in the coffin, who would be out here for her? She glanced at

Dorothy, Hannah and Indy, heads bowed. Then she pictured Craig, his disfigured corpse in a nice oak casket, expensive lace lining, a pillow for his charred and flaking head.

She thought about Stella last night, so conciliatory. Why the sudden turnaround? Jenny had accepted it, the drunken path of least resistance. But in the cold, hungover light of the crematorium, doubts crept in. It was too easy, but her foggy brain couldn't work out why.

Rhona's coffin descended into the plinth to more organ music, into the furnace in the bowels of the building, to light up at hundreds of degrees Celsius, atomise into constituent parts, throw her particles into the sky for everyone to breathe in.

Dorothy and Hannah were in conversation, animated and serious, voices low. They had secret business that Jenny wasn't part of. They were so similar to each other, and both a lot more comfortable in their skins than Jenny. She was so tired of being the fuck-up. Indy watched Hannah intently. Jenny knew it was disgusting but she was envious of their love. They were so supportive of each other and Jenny wished she had that in her life.

She glanced at Archie, who gave her a thin smile. She stared at the empty plinth and pictured Rhona burning below, toes curling, hair aflame, body fat sizzling and spitting. She imagined the same for herself and it didn't feel too bad.

53

HANNAH

'I can't believe we're doing this.'

Hannah watched Indy slow the van as they came to the big Restalrig roundabout, turning off for Lochend. Like any old city, Edinburgh's roads weren't fit for purpose, constant digging and resurfacing, tram works in Leith, too much traffic. The trick was to avoid main arteries and drive along smaller capillaries, so this was the quickest way to the mortuary from Seafield. As they drove past the tenements and semis of Marionville round the back of Meadowbank Stadium, it felt a million miles away from the castle and tourists, just lives quietly lived out of the spotlight.

'We're funeral directors,' Indy said.

'You know what I mean.'

They were on their way to pick up Laura's mum from the mortuary, take her to the house for prep.

'This is a mistake.' Hannah still had the order of service from Rhona Wilding's funeral in her hand, concertinaed like a fan.

'Dorothy was right,' Indy said. 'Laura needs our help. I know she's full on, but—'

'Full on?' Hannah squeezed the paper in her hand. 'She lived with her mum's corpse for days. She's stalked me every day since. She's trying to drive us apart.'

Indy drove round Abbeyhill, the spine of Salisbury Crags glowing in the morning sunshine to their left.

'I'll handle all the funeral stuff, you don't need to get involved.'

'I'm in the van, amn't I?'

'You know the rules, two people for a body pick-up. She's grieving for her mum, Han.'

They drove past the parliament and the white, canvassed dome of the Dynamic Earth building onto Holyrood Road, over the junction with Cowgate, into the mortuary car park. Hannah was always struck by how ugly the building was, dark bricks and dirty concrete. Indy pulled up alongside the corrugated-iron door and Hannah gripped her order of service so tight her knuckles hurt. Laura stood at the entrance, smile on her face, waving like she'd spotted them across a dancefloor.

'What the hell is she doing here?' Hannah said.

Indy's eyes were wide, smile painted on. 'She shouldn't be.'

'I told you this was a stupid idea.'

They got out and Laura skipped over and hugged them, air-kissing their cheeks. Hannah noticed perfume and make-up, like she'd dressed up for this.

'Shall we?' Laura indicated the door.

Indy held her hands out. 'It's not usual for the next of kin to be here, Laura. This is a simple transferral to our funeral home. I'm not even sure how you knew about it.'

'I called Graham at the mortuary, explained the situation, he was lovely.'

Hannah knew Graham Chapel was level-headed and hugely experienced, he wouldn't have gone along with this. But Laura was very persuasive.

Laura headed to the entrance, buzzed and was let in. 'Come on.'

'Jesus,' Hannah whispered to Indy as they followed.

In reception, Hannah looked around at the crime-prevention posters, crumpled at the edges.

Graham appeared from through the back, smiled at Indy and Hannah then frowned at Laura.

'Laura Abbott, I presume?'

'Nice to meet you face to face.'

'I told you on the phone—'

'We're here to pick up Mum.' Laura's smile was steel. 'Please take us to her.'

'I don't advise this.'

'Is it illegal?'

Graham stared at her for a long time. 'No.'

'Come on then, we haven't got all day.'

Graham led them to the room full of body fridges and pulled one open. Elizabeth was in a white body bag. He nodded at Indy and handed over some paperwork. Indy pulled on nitrile gloves and unzipped the top of the bag.

'Elizabeth Abbott,' she said, checking the paperwork. 'Visually confirming.'

Hannah looked at Elizabeth's face, pale, blue-lipped, her skin tight from moisture loss. She knew that her body would have signs of decomposition, but her face didn't seem too bad. She pictured her on the floor of her bedroom, Laura ignoring she was dead as she popped to the kitchen and put the kettle on. She looked at Laura now, like a statue.

Indy went to close the bag.

'Wait.' Laura stepped forward and stood over her mum, blinked too often. She leaned down and kissed her on the lips, stayed there for a long moment, then straightened up. She ran a finger along her mum's hairline then stepped back.

Indy closed up as Graham brought a gurney over. She and Hannah lifted Elizabeth onto the gurney on the count of three. Hannah gripped her cold ankles through her gloves, felt a chill run through her.

Graham closed the fridge and opened the large delivery door at the back of the room. Indy wheeled the body out to the van. Hannah followed and they lifted her inside. It was not dignified, struggling with a corpse, Hannah crouching in the back of the van as they slid her across.

They finished and Graham wheeled the gurney back into the mortuary. Laura was still in there, staring at Hannah and Indy. Hannah jumped down, closed the van.

'Are you all right?' Indy called over.

Laura looked at the fridge Elizabeth had been stored in, then raised a finger to touch her lips as if checking they were there.

Graham came over to Hannah and Indy at the van.

'Are you sure you know what you're doing?'

'I asked the same thing,' Hannah said.

'This is not good for her.'

Indy raised her voice. 'Laura, you OK?'

Laura snapped out of her trance and grinned at Hannah. She felt a shiver, like a memory of touching Elizabeth's ankles.

Laura bounced over to them as if she hadn't just kissed her dead mum.

'I'm fine.' She flicked her hair then squeezed Hannah's arm. It was meant to be friendly but it was too firm, like she didn't want to let go.

'I have you, don't I?' she said to Hannah, angling her head.

Hannah forced a smile and placed her hand on Laura's, but she couldn't seem to loosen her grip.

54

DOROTHY

Sunlight flickering through the tree branches made shadows dance across the metal table. The smell of coffee and pastries mingled with the undercurrent of decay from the bin further down Middle Meadow Walk. A million different forms of life moved up and down the road past their table outside Söderberg, unaware how happy they should be to still be alive.

'How's death?' Thomas said.

She came back to the here and now, sipped her coffee.

'Not great. We had a funeral this morning for someone who had no one to say goodbye.'

'At all?'

'I tried to contact friends, colleagues, neighbours. No one came.'

Thomas sighed. 'That hurts.'

Dorothy put on a sly smile. 'Promise me you'll come to my funeral.'

He took her hand. 'I always presumed we'd die together in an exotic jet-ski accident in the Caribbean.'

She laughed. 'The paperwork to get our bodies home would be a nightmare.'

But she wondered anyway. He was much younger than her, she would probably die first. Would he be there? What was in this whole thing for him? It seemed too good to be true. Or maybe she was just doubting her own worth.

'You know, in the Netherlands, they have something called the lonely funeral project. If someone dies and there's no one to claim the body or attend the funeral, they get a local poet to research the person and write a poem about them. Then read it at the ceremony.'

'That's beautiful.'

'Isn't it?'

Thomas drank his coffee, watching her over the cup. 'You're going to do that here, aren't you?'

She laughed. 'As if I don't have enough other shit to be getting on with.'

Thomas put his cup down. 'Speaking of which, how are the cases going?'

She didn't really know where to start. She looked at her watch. 'In a few minutes I'm off to visit our Japanese friend.'

'Being abused by his ghost.'

Dorothy leaned across the table. 'It turns out he was doing it to himself in his sleep.'

Thomas's eyes widened. 'Why?'

'Guilt. Grief. Loss.'

'What about his granddaughter? She was hurt too.'

'That's what I'm going to find out.'

She finished her coffee and raised her chin. 'What about Eddie? Where's the investigation?'

Thomas shook his head. 'Griffiths has interviewed them all. Still gathering evidence. She favours Danny for it, I think.'

Dorothy shook her head. 'She's wrong.'

'Why?'

She thought about her conversations with Mike and Stella. She'd promised Thomas she would leave the police to it. She should tell him she'd been to see them, but what was there to say about it? She had no more evidence to share, she just didn't think Danny was a killer.

'Just a hunch.'

Thomas narrowed his eyes. He knew her well enough to know she was keeping something from him. He'd asked her the other night what secrets she kept. Too many to mention was the truth.

She checked her watch again, leaned across the table and kissed him.

'I have to go.'

❧

She rang the doorbell, thought about the first time she came here. A nice cup of tea with an old Japanese man haunted by his dead wife. She looked at Hannah, who'd been subdued in the van on the way over. The door was opened by Willow in blue silk pyjamas with flowers on them. Her head was bandaged but her eyes were bright. Her gaze went to Hannah.

'Hey.'

Hannah pointed to the bandage. 'How's the head?'

'Sore.'

'I'm surprised you're not still in hospital,' Dorothy said. She thought about what Thomas said, the implication of what they'd seen Udo do.

Willow tapped her skull. 'So much pressure on beds, if you're not going to die immediately they throw you out with a packet of paracetamol.'

'Is Udo in? We need to speak to him.'

'He's resting.'

Hannah shuffled her feet. 'Please, Willow, it's important.'

Willow examined her long enough for Hannah to look uncomfortable. 'The cameras?'

Hannah nodded.

Willow sucked her teeth and looked at the sky. 'I suppose you'd better come in.'

She left the door open and walked tentatively down the hall into the kitchen, where she started skinning up at the table. She waved a hand for them to sit. Dorothy glanced at the shrine, Buddha and the urn in their places, netsuke keeping guard. She thought about the footage Hannah had shown her.

Willow finished rolling the joint and sparked up, taking a big inhale.

'I'm not sure that's the best idea with concussion,' Dorothy said.

'It helps.'

Willow offered the joint to Hannah and Dorothy was surprised to see her take a toke and hand it back. Willow held it out to Dorothy.

'I'm OK.'

Willow shrugged and toked. 'So.'

'I really think we should speak to Udo,' Dorothy said.

Willow waved a hand towards the back of the flat. 'I don't want to wake him.'

'Did he have a bad night?'

Willow sighed. 'Out with it.'

Hannah put her elbows on the table. 'He's doing it to himself, Willow.'

She took another hit of the joint, tapped ash into a saucer on the table. Raised her face to blow smoke into the air. 'I know.'

Dorothy watched Willow and felt things shift into place.

'That means he attacked you too,' Hannah said.

'It was an accident.' Willow examined the glowing end of the joint. 'He didn't know what he was doing.'

Hannah looked at Dorothy but she didn't speak. Leave space and someone will fill it.

'I heard him up two nights ago,' Willow said. 'The day I arrived. I found him in the kitchen, hitting himself.'

'But he *does* know he's doing it,' Hannah said. 'He switched the cameras off beforehand.'

Willow looked from Hannah to Dorothy.

'No,' Dorothy said. 'You did that, didn't you, Willow?'

Willow took another hit from the joint and offered it to Hannah, who shook her head.

Dorothy nodded. 'Because he's done this before, right?'

Willow pointed the joint at Dorothy. 'You get it. When Mum

died. He hurt himself at night for weeks. Baba was so worried about him. He does it in his sleep, has no memory of it.'

'It doesn't sound safe here,' Hannah said.

Willow shrugged. 'He's got no one else, he needs me to look after him.'

'Willow.'

She jumped at Udo's voice from the doorway.

He had a hangdog expression, shoulders hunched, tears in his eyes. There was a cut on his forehead, and Dorothy remembered the blows to his ribs and stomach. She imagined the damage under his loose jumper.

Willow put the joint in the saucer and went to his side. 'Jiji—'

'Is this true?' He leaned against the doorframe, hands shaking. 'Did I hurt you?'

'It was an accident, Jiji.'

'It can't be true.'

His legs buckled and Willow caught him, led him to the table. He shuffled along panting and favouring his right side, obviously in pain. He sat at the table, spread his hands out, shaking his head.

Eventually he looked at Dorothy. 'Can I see?'

Dorothy nodded at Hannah who handed her phone over.

Udo held it in trembling hands, peered at the screen. As he sat there, his grip tightened on the edge of the phone. Willow sat down and all three women watched him for a long time. Eventually Dorothy heard the audio from the wind phone, guilt, forgiveness, sadness.

After it finished, Udo stayed staring at the phone. He passed it back to Hannah, then looked at Willow.

'I'm so sorry.'

Willow shook her head. 'You have nothing to be sorry for.'

'I hurt you.'

'You didn't know.'

'I'm so ashamed.'

'No, Jiji.' Willow leapt out of her seat and crouched by his side, held his hand.

His eyes were full of tears and the tremble in his hands spread over his body. Willow gripped his hands as if she could stop it. She made shushing noises as Udo's head sank.

Dorothy shifted in her seat. 'Udo, what does Lily need to forgive you for?'

Willow narrowed her gaze. 'Just leave him.'

Udo shook his head. 'It's hard to talk about.'

'Jiji...'

He gave Willow's hands a squeeze then rested his fists in his lap.

'I was not faithful, there was another. A long time ago, before you were born, Willow. When your mother was little. I was selfish, Lily and I were both so tired with a small child, worn down. I was weak and stupid. Lily knew. She never said, and it ended after a while, but I'm sure she knew.'

'Jiji, you're punishing yourself. That was a very long time ago. It doesn't matter now.'

'It does. I deserve to be punished.'

'You don't deserve to kill yourself,' Dorothy said. 'I'm not saying what you did was right, but you have to think about what you have now. Willow is here, she's your family. And you've endangered her too.'

Willow took hold of Udo's hands again, held tight. 'I need you, Jiji. I need you to stop this.'

She wrapped him in a hug. Dorothy could see him shaking. She looked at Hannah, wondered what she was thinking. Dorothy had been unfaithful too, many years ago. Jenny and Hannah both knew about it. It had been a source of conflict with Jenny over the years, but they'd reached a kind of understanding, maybe even forgiveness. Dorothy still felt shame, but she had eventually forgiven herself. She hoped Udo could do the same.

55

JENNY

Jenny sat at reception and prayed the phone didn't ring. She couldn't handle the grief of a stranger right now. The scent of lilies was strong, dim light leaching through the stained glass on the stair landing. An old heating pipe clunked somewhere in the wall behind her. This house must've seen some things. A funeral home for a hundred years had stories to tell. The Skelfs had looked after the place well over the generations, it must be worth a packet. She wondered if they would ever sell. Would Dorothy expect her to take over the business if she retired? Jenny shuddered at the thought, but struggled to think of an alternative. Then she imagined burying her mum and her stomach went tight.

The front door opened and Thomas came in. He always moved with grace, something assured about his walk. Dorothy had done well with him. Daughters were supposed to resent their mother's new boyfriends, but he was a good man.

'Dorothy's not around,' Jenny said. 'She's with that haunted Japanese guy.'

She glanced upstairs, imagined her dad's ghost floating towards her.

Thomas ran a finger along the desk. 'I didn't come to see Dorothy, I came for you. I have bad news.'

Jenny felt sick, anxiety clutching her throat.

'About Craig.' Thomas glanced at his feet.

'What about him?' Jenny stood and clutched the edge of the desk.

'I got a call from Graham at the mortuary earlier. I'm afraid Stella has taken him.'

Jenny's legs wobbled. 'What do you mean, taken him?'

'We closed the police enquiry into his death once Graham performed the post-mortem. It's then down to the next of kin to arrange a funeral. It's not against the law for her to remove the body and deal with it herself. Graham advised against it, of course, but she had all the paperwork.'

Jenny gritted her teeth and clung to the desk to stop her from hitting the floor.

❧

She was sweating by the time she reached the mortuary despite the chill in the air, a ceiling of low cloud pressing down on the Old Town. She leaned against the wall and pressed the button, pressed it again, tried to catch her breath, pressed a third time.

Graham came to the door. He saw her through the glass and paused, shook his head and removed his gloves. He buzzed the door and Jenny swung it open too hard, clattering it off the wall.

'What the fuck, Graham?'

'I'm sorry, Jenny.' He held his hands out as if hoping a good excuse would land in them from nowhere. 'I tried to stop her.'

'How fucking hard is it to stop someone removing a dead body from a mortuary?'

'She knew her rights, she's next of kin.'

Jenny thought about Stella in the pub last night. That's what all that shit was about. She knew she was going to do this and wanted to see Jenny first, rub it in her face.

'I'm sure she's just going to arrange a funeral for him.'

'Then why not let a funeral director pick him up? Has this ever happened before?'

'It's very rare, but it does happen. Sometimes people want to bury a body on their own land, or organise a natural burial. They need permission but it's allowed.'

'Even if the corpse is a fucking psycho?'

'He's dead, Jenny. Craig is dead.'

Jenny leaned against the wall and breathed. She felt like she was drowning. She remembered a week ago, swimming in the sea, punching that guy who tried to help her. She felt panic rise in her chest.

'I want to see.'

'See what?'

'I want to check he's gone.'

'Jenny.' Graham gave her a look. Maybe that would've worked when she was younger, before all this shit, but not now.

'Just fucking show me.'

Graham sighed and walked to the room at the back. Jenny followed. He went to the wall of fridges, opened a door and pulled the empty tray out.

Jenny checked the name on the door – Craig McNamara. She looked inside the fridge as if he might be crouching at the back, ready to pounce. She stared at the wall of metal doors, the names of the deceased on each one, then opened a door and hauled the tray out. Wendy Irvine, an old woman with wispy hair when Jenny unzipped the bag.

'Jenny,' Graham shouted. 'Stop.'

She hauled another one out, Trevor Spencer, barrel-chested old man with a birthmark on his face.

'Jenny.'

She opened a third, pulled the tray out, then felt Graham's pinning her arms.

'Stop it.'

She tried to break free, looked at the body trays sticking out into the room, the dead lying there. Not Craig, he was long gone as always.

She wrenched herself free and ran out of the building, across Cowgate, dodging a taxi. She went up Blackfriars Street, trainers slapping on the cobbles, then turned left on the Royal Mile into the Radisson. Only two minutes from the mortuary, Violet and Stella were so close to Craig all this time.

'Hi,' she said to Mariana behind the desk. She was young, Hispanic, beautiful, had her shit together.

Jenny breathed heavily. 'I'm here to see Stella McNamara. Can you call up?'

Mariana gave her a look but checked the screen, pressed some keys. 'I'm afraid Ms McNamara checked out.'

'What?'

'This morning.'

Jenny looked around reception as if Stella was hiding somewhere, Craig's body stuffed in a suitcase or backpack, ready to go.

'What about Violet McNamara.'

Mariana looked at the couple waiting to check in behind Jenny with an apologetic air. She found Violet in the system and called upstairs, waited. Eventually she put the phone down.

'There's no answer.'

'What room is she?'

'I can't give you that information.'

'Fuck off.'

Mariana set her face hard. 'Please leave.'

Jenny looked at the elderly couple behind her. She shook her head and went out the door, stood at the hotel entrance, watched tourists up and down the Royal Mile, buses and taxis across the Bridges, the city full of life. Somewhere out there was Craig, always just out of reach.

56

DOROTHY

She closed the door of the loft studio and leaned against it. This was her sanctuary at the top of the house, away from the death below. The sun was already down outside the big windows, the Links steadfast in the gloaming. She hated the early sunsets in Scotland, had never got used to them in all this time.

She walked over and sat behind the drum kit, lifted the sticks and felt their familiar weight, the grain of the wood. She did a few light fills on the snare and toms, rolled her shoulders. She thought about Udo and Willow in Leith. Despite what they'd seen on the cameras, he was haunted all right. By memories of Lily, his own bad behaviour, the guilt of living an imperfect life. The trick was not to let that rule your future. You had to keep moving forward, that was the only way to respect those who had gone. Keep living your imperfect life.

She plugged headphones into her phone and scrolled through, stopped at *Ignorance* by The Weather Station. They were a Canadian band fronted by Tamara Lindeman, a revelation to Dorothy, a mix of indie, jazz, country and a bunch of other things. She pressed play on 'Robber', joined in on gentle hi-hats and rim-shots. The band had two drummers, giving them real drive. The song had a dance-shuffle edge, Lindeman singing about the robber of the title. Dorothy had read her discussing the song, about anxiety over climate change. How we've gone along with being robbed of our environment by capitalism, consumerism, business. It made Dorothy heartsick to think about it. She hoped Hannah's generation were smart enough to sort the mess her generation had left behind. That guilt again, always lurking.

She threw herself into the song as it built, plaintive vocals giving way to an unhinged sax solo, drummers building and feeding off each other. She felt like she was in the room with them, the fluidity of her movement as she went round the kit and splashed out on the crash then back into the tight groove that grew in a crescendo of keyboards and drums before halting abruptly.

She pressed pause on her phone, put the headphones round her neck. She was sweating, living her imperfect life the best way she could. It was never good enough but the trick was to keep trying.

She saw a notification on her phone from the gravecam in Liberton Cemetery. She put her sticks down and opened the app. Mike Frame was kneeling in front of Kathleen's grave like he was praying. Or asking forgiveness, maybe.

She got up and left the studio.

She parked on Liberton Brae and got out. Streetlights on, traffic heading out of town. She walked to the graveyard and headed down the hill to Kathleen's grave. She turned left towards the northern edge of the cemetery, near the high wall. The slope meant she didn't have a view of the grave yet. She moved from the gravel path to the damp grass, less noise.

She darted between oak trees. There were no lights down here, just overspill from Wolrige Road behind the wall. She was wearing a black polo neck and coat, dark trousers. Like a robber. She heard someone crying. She inched forward and almost jumped out of her skin as a fox ambled out from behind a grave and froze, tail to the floor. It stared at her with glassy eyes then sauntered down the slope and was gone. Dorothy tried to get her breathing back to normal. She unclenched her fists and stepped forward.

She was behind the cherry tree where Hannah had placed the gravecam. She could see its dark shape wedged between branches.

Beyond the tree was Kathleen's grave in a row of dimly lit stones, like ghosts.

Mike was still there on his knees, crouched over, fingers splayed in the grass like he might start digging her up any minute. His shoulders shook and Dorothy heard more sobbing, followed by sniffs.

She heard a noise to her left and turned. The stupid fox walked towards Mike and he stared at it. The tree Dorothy was behind was in his eyeline as he looked at the animal. She was sure the slightest movement from her would draw his attention. The fox walked past Mike without acknowledging him then disappeared in the darkness.

Mike watched it go and Dorothy watched Mike. She was conscious of her breathing, the leaves on the tree rustling, the rumble of traffic over the wall. All connected in an endless dance.

'I'm so sorry,' Mike said.

Dorothy thought of Udo's confession in the wind phone, two men admitting what they'd done when they thought no one was listening but a dead woman.

'We were so close,' Mike said. 'I swear I was about to tell him. If I'd just told him before he fucking vanished, we'd all still be here. It wouldn't be easy, but he would've got over it and we could've moved on. We could've been together. Now...'

Dorothy heard a flap of wings above her. Mike heard it too and looked into the branches over her head. She held her breath. Another flapping sound as the magpie settled in its nest. Mike stared at the leaves of the trees for a long time then turned back to Kathleen's grave. Dorothy let her breath out, closed her eyes and waited.

57

JENNY

She sat on a stool at the window table in The Mitre and stared across the road. The pub was busy, mostly tourists but a few office types, ties loosened, pencil skirts askew, tongues full of gossip. The television in the corner played Champions League that no one was watching, the drone of the mindless commentary like white noise in her mind.

She tensed up every time the taxi rank outside the Radisson filled up, restricting her view of the hotel entrance. She sat upright, stretched her neck, tried to see between vehicles. Then they picked up a fare and were off, and she could see the archway of the hotel lit up like a Christmas tree. She narrowed her eyes every time someone came in or out but never spotted Stella or Violet. She worried that she'd missed them while nipping to the bar, but she couldn't do this sober.

She remembered being in a pub further down the Royal Mile with Craig, back when they were young and in love. The World's End was infamous, two young women killed in the 1970s were last seen drinking there, then found the next morning in East Lothian, beaten, gagged, tied up, raped and strangled. The cunt who did it hadn't even tried to hide their bodies. He was only caught decades later and died in prison.

Back when Jenny and Craig were in the place, the murderer hadn't been found, and they'd joked darkly about it. But the pub had lasted longer than her marriage, longer than Craig. And he'd ended up murdering someone in similar circumstances, a young woman strangled to death. Jenny felt sick, how she'd let that man put his dick in her for years, hands all over her. Raised Hannah together until his cheating was found out. The fucking entitlement of some men was beyond belief.

And now he was dead, his rotten body out there in the city and she didn't feel any better about it. She needed to speak to Stella and she wasn't even sure why. He had to be put in the ground or burned to ashes. She needed this to be over, but she knew it never would be.

She saw a woman in the hotel entrance and stood up, almost kicking her stool over. But the woman turned under a spotlight, not Stella. On the television, someone scored and the crowd roared and she flinched. She sat back down, took a hit of gin and stared at the hotel. Waited.

In no time at all she'd finished her drink. She headed to the bar, glancing out the window. She ordered the same again, got her card out, looked back across. An older woman stood inside the entrance, sorting the zip of her jacket. Jenny heard the chink of ice in the glass. Another goal on the football. The woman stepped into the street – Violet. Jenny bolted out of the door and almost got hit by a taxi on the cobbles. Then she was there in front of Violet, who seemed unsurprised to see her.

'What the fuck?' Jenny had been waiting for hours, but this was the best she could come up with.

Violet put her hands to her chest. 'I don't know where they are.'

'They?'

'Stella and Craig.'

'Craig is dead, Violet.'

Violet's hands went to her neck as if clawing at something that was preventing her from breathing. She listed like a ship in a storm and steadied herself against the hotel brickwork. A passing couple eyeballed Jenny as if she'd done something wrong.

Violet started sobbing, her small body shaking. The sobs turned into a guttural, feral wail. Jenny was amazed at the power of it.

'You think I don't know that?' Violet screamed.

Jenny felt shame creep over her but batted it away. Fuck this family all the way to hell. 'What is Stella doing?'

'I was going to arrange the funeral but Stella said she would take care of it. Then she went and did this.'

'Where is she?'

'I honestly don't know.'

Jenny puckered her mouth like she'd been sucking a lemon. 'Try to think, she's your daughter. Where would she take him?'

Violet wiped at her tears.

Jenny's phone rang, a number she didn't recognise. She stared at Violet.

'Hello?'

'I guess you've figured out I took Craig,' Stella said.

Jenny looked up and down the road as if she might materialise. 'What the fuck are you doing?'

Violet held out a hand. 'Let me speak to her.'

Jenny waved her away. 'Stella, you can't just take a body.'

Laughter down the line. 'I did my research, I filled in the forms.'

'But what's the plan? You going to have him stuffed and put on the mantlepiece?'

Violet went wide eyed and Jenny felt a twinge. Maybe she shouldn't have said that so loud.

'I'm going to say goodbye my own way,' Stella said.

'Your mum wants to talk to you.'

'Tell her I'm sorry.'

'Tell her yourself.'

'She's not part of this,' Stella said sharply.

'Craig's her son, for fuck's sake.'

Violet reached out for the phone but Jenny didn't want to hand over control. As if she had any fucking control, as if she ever did.

'If you want to say goodbye to Craig for good,' Stella said, 'meet me at Wardie Bay. Now.'

Jenny swallowed. 'What about Violet?'

'This is between me and you, and it ends tonight. Come alone.'

The line went dead.

Violet stared at the phone as if it might burst into flames. 'What did she say?'

Jenny looked at the busy street then back at Violet. She hailed a taxi.

'I have to go.'

58

HANNAH

She lay on the sofa and clicked through the *New Scientist* on her laptop. The usual catastrophic climate-change headlines, with the odd nugget of positivity thrown in here and there, we might not get totally destroyed. Hannah gravitated towards the space articles. One about the possibility of an ancient black hole at the edge of our solar system. Another about the frequency of marsquakes related to the planet's seasons.

Then she stopped at one headline: 'A Strange Barrier Is Keeping Cosmic Rays out of the Milky Way's Centre'. Cosmic rays were background radiation scattered over the universe, but new data showed it was remarkably low in the middle of our galaxy. Hannah thought back to Professor Galatas's lecture a week ago when he mentioned Sagittarius A*, the supermassive black hole at the core of the Milky Way. It was blocking light from entering its heart. The article talked about possible magnetic winds, strong magnetic fields, but it was speculation. She remembered Laura at that lecture acting as if they were already best friends. She imagined herself as Sagittarius A* blocking Laura's advances, the radiation she was giving off.

Hannah closed the laptop and went to the window. She thought about Laura with her mum at the mortuary, Udo and Willow in Leith, Danny and his dead parents, her own dad washing up. Death was life as a family of funeral directors.

She checked the time, Indy was late. She texted, kept it light. Went through the food cupboards for a snack. Nothing appealed. Checked her phone. She went to the toilet, wiped, back to the room, nothing. She stared out of the window for a few minutes. Picked up her phone and called. Five rings then voice-mail.

'Hey, babes, just checking in. You going to be home soon?'

She could hear the worry in her own voice. She looked around the room, felt her teeth itch at how unsettled she was. Then she grabbed her phone and keys, threw a jacket on and left the flat.

Walking round the Meadows at night wasn't too bad, well-lit paths, lots of students, other women on their own or in pairs. At Bruntsfield Links she remembered walking the dog with Indy when they came across the Beast of Bruntsfield, an escaped black jaguar. It seemed like something from a fever dream now. As she got further along her stomach dropped as she remembered chasing her bleeding father across the grass, stalking him like a big cat.

All these moments made her who she was. But there were mil-lions of mundane moments too. Picnics and walks, drinks in the sun, breakfast looking out at the dreich weather, snuggling in bed on a Saturday morning. She wanted that to be who she was, not all these crazy experiences.

She crossed Whitehouse Loan and saw the house in the dis-tance. She could only see the upper floors over the garden wall, but no lights on gave her the jitters.

She kept to the path across the grass, saw a dog walker in the distance and thought about Einstein again, how he gave his life for Dorothy.

She got to the house and walked into the drive, crunch of gravel underfoot. No lights on the ground floor either. Where was every-one?

She tried the front door, locked. She got her keys, opened up while calling Indy again. Voicemail. She stood in reception in the dark and listened. Nothing for a long time.

Then she heard a noise from her right, the business end of the building. She walked down the corridor to the doorway of the embalming room. The door was ajar, a sliver of light spilling out.

There were no windows in that room, its light couldn't be seen from outside. She pushed the door open.

There were two bodies on the embalming tables to her right. She stepped into the room. As she got closer she saw the first one was Elizabeth Abbott lying naked on top of her body bag. She was ashen-faced and discoloured on her side and back by a row of internal bruises. When a body is left untreated, blood sinks to the bottom and bruises under the skin. Hannah smelled the stink of decomposition despite the air con.

As she got closer she looked at the second body and froze.

It was Indy, she recognised the smooth brown skin, her clothes, the shape of her. She appeared to be sleeping or unconscious.

'Hi, Hannah.'

She swung round at Laura's voice, saw her smiling behind the door. She wore blue nitrile gloves and held a syringe by her side as if it was nothing.

'I'm glad you're here.'

Hannah took two steps towards Indy. 'If you've hurt her—'

'She's fine.' Laura stepped out of the shadows.

Hannah put her hands out. 'What is this, Laura?'

Laura straightened her shoulders and cricked her neck. 'I wanted to see Mum, that's all.'

'You saw her earlier.'

'I don't want her to leave me, you understand. You must feel the same about your dad.'

Hannah felt sick. 'This has nothing to do with me. You lost your mum. It's hard. But this...' She waved a hand at Elizabeth's corpse.

Laura nodded at Indy. 'She wouldn't let me see Mum so I had to do something.'

Hannah stepped towards Indy, almost at her table.

'And you just happened to be carrying Rohypnol or something?'

'I don't want Mum to leave me.'

Hannah reached Indy's table, put out a hand and felt her arm. Warm, thank Christ. 'Laura, this is premeditated, you'll go to jail.'

'I'll never leave her.'

'You won't have any choice.'

Laura stepped towards her with the syringe.

'You can't behave like this,' Hannah said.

She glanced at Indy's face, remembered kissing her this morning. She looked back and Laura was another step closer. Hannah put out a hand to Laura and moved her other hand to Indy's wrist, pressed two fingers, felt for a pulse.

'She's fine,' Laura said.

'She's not fine, she's unconscious. This is assault and kidnapping.'

Hannah pressed harder, thought she felt something but maybe it was her own pulse.

She glanced at Indy again and when she looked up Laura was on her, gripping her throat as she sunk the syringe into her arm, a sting then a flow of cool smoke through her body. Hannah waved at Laura but already felt weak and dizzy as the room shifted its gravity. She let go of Indy's arm and her hand flopped to her side. She leaned on the table, cold metal against her skin, then suddenly she was on the floor, eyes so heavy she couldn't keep them open.

59

DOROTHY

The uniformed cop pulled the car over on Ferry Road and Dorothy looked out of the window. The house seemed more sinister in the dark somehow.

'I'll do the talking,' Thomas said as they got out of the car. There were two officers with them, big lads Thomas had chosen in case Mike got out of hand. Dorothy wasn't officially allowed to be here, but she'd twisted Thomas's arm. They went up the drive and Dorothy rang the bell. The uniforms lingered behind.

The hallway light came on and the door opened. Roxanne stood in sweatpants and a strappy sports vest. She eyeballed Dorothy then scoped out Thomas and the two cops.

'What is this?'

'Mrs Frame,' Thomas said. 'I'm DI Olsson, can we come in?'

She looked at him for a long time. 'What's that accent, Danish?'

'Can we?'

'Do you have a warrant?'

'Do we need one?'

'I think so.'

Dorothy put her hands together like a prayer. 'Roxanne, this is not about you. It's Mike.'

Roxanne gave her a look. Dorothy remembered their talk on the Braids, how she said Mike wasn't a killer.

'Is it what I think it is?' Roxanne's voice faltered.

'We have some new information,' Dorothy said. 'We need to speak to him.'

Roxanne rubbed her chin then turned without speaking and walked inside. Thomas went first, Dorothy after, the two big guys at the back. The house was a mix of old fixtures and new style, uncomfortable together. They walked through the hall and a large kitchen, down a few steps to a modern extension, open plan, big window looking over the garden, trees at the bottom. A desk faced the window, and Mike sat at it staring out.

'Mike,' Roxanne said.

He didn't acknowledge that he'd heard. This was the first time since the funeral Dorothy had seen them together and they still seemed like an odd couple. Sometimes we get together with people who aren't right for us, but it's easier to stay.

'Mike.' Roxanne was more firm, but he still didn't move.

Dorothy sensed Thomas and the officers on alert.

'Mr Frame,' Thomas said. 'We need to talk to you.'

Mike raised his hand to his forehead but didn't turn. 'Sometimes I see a fox out there. He looks so happy. Free.'

'What the fuck have you done?' Roxanne said. The sharpness in her voice made Dorothy wince.

Mike turned to face them. His eyes were wet with tears.

'Mike,' Roxanne said, pleading this time. She didn't want it to be true.

Mike's shoulders slumped and all the air went out of him. 'I was in love with her.'

Roxanne stepped towards him. 'Who?'

Mike didn't look at her, instead stared at Dorothy. 'You know. How do you know?'

'I heard you talking at her grave.' She didn't mention the gravecam.

Mike nodded.

Roxanne looked at Dorothy. 'Grave?' She looked back and forth between them for a moment. 'Kathleen? That's who you were fucking?'

Mike shook his head. 'It wasn't like that. We were in love.'

Roxanne put her hands to her face. 'It was you, you killed Eddie.'

Mike looked behind him as if he might see the fox in the garden. 'I didn't go there to do that. Things got out of control.'

Dorothy couldn't help herself. 'Out of control? I saw the crime scene.'

Mike's eyes were glassy as he turned to her. 'He first got in touch with me after Kathleen's funeral. I was shocked, I really did think he was dead when Danny accused me at her grave. I couldn't get my head around it. Eddie said he needed money to live whatever stupid life he had in mind. He didn't even mention Kathleen. He didn't know about us.'

Roxanne frowned. 'I thought she died of a broken heart or some shit.'

'It's misnamed,' Dorothy said. 'It can be caused by any kind of stress.'

'Eddie was responsible,' Mike said. 'I couldn't get that out of my head. I went there to talk to him, I really did.'

'With a knife?' Thomas said.

Dorothy knew what Thomas was doing, taking a knife was premeditated.

'For defence,' Mike said, tears running down his cheeks.

'This is such bullshit,' Roxanne said. 'You went there to kill him out of revenge because of your sordid little fuckfest.'

'It wasn't like that.'

'Mike, don't you fucking dare.'

'You don't understand.' Mike looked at Roxanne for the first time since they'd all come in, deep sorrow on his face. 'When Eddie went missing, it was our chance. I could be with Kathleen. I know you have someone else, you could've been with him. We could've been happy. Then she died and I was lost, Roxy.'

Roxanne balled her fists. 'You slit his fucking throat. You murdered your own brother.'

Mike glanced out the window again, then turned back to the room.

Thomas stepped forward. 'You need to come with us.'

Dorothy saw the other officers move on the edge of her vision. Mike pushed his lips together and shook his head. 'No.'

He pulled open the desk drawer and took out a large, serrated knife. He looked at Roxanne and dragged it hard across his throat, dark blood spurting from the wound and down his shirt, pouring onto the floor as he wobbled in his chair, eyes unfocused.

Roxanne screamed and lunged at him. 'Mike! Jesus fucking Christ.'

Thomas was on him, pulled a handkerchief from his pocket and pressed it against his neck. The knife clattered to the floor, splashing in the blood. Mike slumped in the chair as Roxanne touched his cheek.

'You fucking idiot,' she said.

Thomas's hand was pressed hard at the gaping wound. He spoke to the police behind Dorothy, one of them already calling for an ambulance.

She looked at Mike then beyond him to the garden, wondering where the fox was now.

60
JENNY

The taxi bundled down Bonnington and across Canonmills into Warriston. They crossed Ferry Road into Trinity, Warriston Crem to their right in the darkness. Then the road turned towards Granton Harbour and they passed the turn-off for St Columba's Hospice. She hated that she knew all these places, the spider's web of death houses that lay underneath the living in the city. The dead amongst us and we never see them, never think about them. This was her life now.

She thought about Stella's phone call – come alone, me and you, ends tonight. She should call Thomas, get him to bring the police, but there was no crime here yet. And part of her agreed with Stella, this was between them now. They needed to finish things with Craig.

The taxi drove round Granton Square and onto the low road then pulled in at Wardie Bay. There wasn't much traffic and the pavement was empty. The taxi pulled away. She watched it go then realised she should've asked the driver to stay.

The tenements behind her had their lights on as she walked through the gap in the seafront embankment into the bay. The long, low breakwater was like a giant gangplank into the dark sea, splitting the beach from the harbour. Overhead, a sprinkle of stars were sprayed across a clear sky, and she could see lighthouses blinking in the distance.

She stumbled across the bare grass towards the sand, peering into the gloom. She walked over seaweed and flotsam at the high-tide line. She spotted something to her right and stopped. A shape, longer than it was high, near the water's edge. She remembered being here a week ago, forensic teams in white outfits, spot-lights and tented coverings, the cop who pushed her.

She looked around for the trap, waited for Stella to spring from somewhere, emerge from the sea like a selkie, run at her full of anger and vengeance. But there was nothing.

She stepped towards the shape, trying to instil her footfall with a confidence she didn't feel. As she got closer she saw more contours, light and shade. Her heart sank as she realised it was just a tree trunk, sodden and pockmarked from years at sea. She walked round it, checking.

She looked in each direction. To the east was the low road to Ocean Terminal. The harbour was quiet, a handful of yachts, occasional clank of masts and rigging. The breakwater was empty. The sea was quiet, waves rippling on the shore.

Stella wasn't here. Craig wasn't here.

She took her phone out and called Stella. No answer, no voice-mail.

What the fuck was this about?

She rang the number again. Nothing.

Again.

This time someone picked up.

'Fuck's sake,' Stella said.

Jenny looked around. 'Where are you?'

The sound of exertion down the line.

'Stella, what is this?'

'Are you there?' Stella said, out of breath.

'Where are you?'

'I'll be there soon, something came up.'

'Are you fucking joking?'

Engine noise down the line. 'I'd forgotten how fucking terrible the traffic is in this town.'

'What's your plan, Stella?'

Silence down the line.

'Why not just tell me?'

'Don't worry, you'll get your fucking closure.'

Something wasn't right. 'What do you mean?'

'That's what you want, right? Everything wrapped up in a neat bow so you can get on with your life.'

'I just want everyone to move on, I thought you wanted the same.'

'Move on. From my brother's putrid corpse.'

'You said—'

'I said your family would get closure and I meant it.'

Jenny felt sick. 'What's my family got to do with this?'

'I'll be there in five minutes. Just wait.'

She hung up.

Wait here. The family. Closure.

Jenny swallowed hard and looked at the empty beach.

Stella wasn't coming, she wasn't bringing Craig, it was all a distraction while she did something else.

Fuck.

Jenny called Dorothy, straight to voicemail.

'Mum, are you OK? I'm worried Stella is up to something. Call me.'

Hannah's phone went to voicemail too. 'Han, give me a call as soon as you get this.'

She called Indy then Thomas, both went to voicemail.

She put her phone away and kicked the driftwood. 'Fuck it.'

She ran up the beach towards the road. She wished she'd told that fucking taxi driver to wait.

61

Hannah

She was swimming in the Forth like a dolphin, Mum and Dad by her side, diving through the wash, under the bridges, leaping into the air and flipping. Suddenly her dad was on fire underwater, chunks of flesh peeling away and falling to the seafloor, impossible flames licking his face. He didn't panic, just frowned as his body decomposed and slid away. She realised she was swimming through a soup made of him and felt sick. He sank to the bottom, waving sadly, flames consuming him. When he was out of sight, she turned to Mum.

'Tough break,' Jenny said and swam away.

Her head pounded and a shiver ran through her. She heard singing, a tune she recognised. She opened her eyes and winced at the light, felt the breeze of the air con, realised she was still in the embalming room. She felt the metal table under her and moved her head to see. She was still clothed, hands restrained with cable ties through the sluice holes at the edge of the table. Her feet were the same. Her head hammered with pain.

The singing got louder, 'The Winner Takes It All' by ABBA, just the melody, no words.

Laura came into view. 'Hey, sleepy.'

'Laura, please.' Hannah's tongue felt swollen. 'Don't do this.'

'I'm not going to harm you, silly. I just need time to take Mum home.'

Hannah pulled at her restraints and Laura tutted.

'Laura, your mum's dead, you have to accept that.'

'I *know* that,' Laura said in a sing-song voice.

'Then what are you doing?'

Laura walked around the bottom of the table humming to herself.

'Mum and I love *Mamma Mia*. We must've watched it a hundred times, singing along. We laugh at the jokes, at Piers Brosnan's voice. He's lovely and tries his best. We always cry at the end.'

She walked to the other table. Elizabeth was still there, now tucked into her body bag, just her head showing. Laura picked up a hairbrush and ran it through her mum's hair.

'She loves it when I brush her hair.'

Hannah's stomach lurched. 'Where's Indy?'

Laura kept brushing.

'Laura.' Hannah made her voice more forceful, tried to hide her panic. 'What have you done with Indy.'

Laura turned. 'She's very beautiful, you're lucky to have each other, like me and Mum.'

She returned to brushing Elizabeth's hair and started humming another ABBA song, 'Slipping through My Fingers'. Hannah remembered watching *Mamma Mia* with Indy, snuggling on the sofa and laughing through the cringe. Then getting sucker-punched by this song, Meryl Streep singing it to her daughter on her wedding day about how she's grown up and left.

'Where's Indy?' Hannah shouted.

Laura stopped brushing, angled her head like she was telling off a toddler. 'You're very rude, you know that? Sometimes I wonder why we're friends.'

Hannah tried to keep calm. 'We're not friends, I never met you until a week ago and you've got me tied to a table. Now where the hell is Indy.'

'She's safe.'

'Safe?'

Laura glanced at the fridges along the wall.

Hannah took a moment to get it. 'She's in a fridge?'

Laura waved the hairbrush. 'I had to put her somewhere, I was running out of space. Did you want me to put her in a coffin?'

Hannah strained at her wrist and ankle ties. 'Laura, she's unconscious. She could get hypothermia or die.'

'She won't die, silly, she's just sleeping like Mum.'

'You'll be a murderer, is that what you want?'

Laura brushed her mum's hair a few more times, still humming under her breath, then leaned forward and kissed Elizabeth's blue lips for a long time. Then she zipped up the body bag, unlocked the wheels on the table and pushed it to the loading entrance.

Hannah craned her neck. 'Laura, untie me, please.'

Laura pressed the release and the corrugated-iron door rolled upwards. Hannah saw a hire van outside, anonymous white, parked with its rear facing them.

'Help,' Hannah yelled at the top of her voice.

Laura strode over and belted Hannah hard on the cheek with the back of the hairbrush. Hannah tried to blink the pain away as tears came to her eyes.

'Shoosh,' Laura said.

She walked back across the room, opened the van doors and slid the tray from the table into the back of the van, closed up. She shoved the table back into the room then turned, placed her finger on the door release.

'See you soon.'

She pressed the door to close it and ducked underneath.

Hannah yelled again, voice hoarse, mouth dry. She heard the engine start, the crunch of gravel as Laura drove away.

Then a thud from inside one of the fridges.

'Indy,' she shouted.

'Han?'

'Can you get out?'

More thuds. 'I can't budge it.'

'Hold on. I'm tied up, but I'll work something out.'

'It's cold.' Something in Indy's voice made Hannah feel sick. 'What happened?'

'Laura, but she's gone now.'

She waited for a reply.

'Indy?'

'Babe?' Weak and quiet.

'I'm coming.'

She felt in her pockets, nothing. She looked at the workbench, bottles of fluid, brushes, makeup and cloths. And a scalpel. She remembered Laura wheeling her mum to the door. She craned over the side of the table, saw the wheels, the brakes were on. She heaved her body up, tried to shift her weight to the right. The table scuffed along the tiles, the wheels locked in position. But it did move.

'Hang on, Indy,' she yelled.

She tried to ignore the pain as she heaved her body to the right again and again. The table moved a few more inches. She got into the rhythm of it, the table inching closer to the workbench. A few more heaves, her back arching, sinews singing in pain, and she was almost there. She stretched out her fingers but the scalpel was still out of reach. She threw herself to the side again and again and the table shuffled across.

She spread her fingers out carefully and managed to touch the handle. She wrapped her fingers under and lifted it from the bench. The cable tie was at her wrist so she had to slowly turn the scalpel upside down, angle the blade against the plastic.

She heard a muffled knock from inside the fridge, quieter than before.

She gently sawed the scalpel against the plastic, but the angle wasn't quite right. She readjusted, her hands sweating, then moved it back and forth. She looked down, saw plastic shavings stuck to her moist skin. She kept going but the scalpel was slippery in her hand. She sawed some more then felt it catch against the plastic, flip out of her grasp and clatter to the floor.

She tried not to cry. She heaved her arm hoping she'd done enough, but it didn't break. She kept pulling, the ragged plastic cutting a bleeding line into her wrist. She yanked and yanked, the table legs bumping on the floor.

She looked down, saw the scalpel shining against the floor tiles. 'Fuck,' she said, then raised her voice. 'Hang on, I'm coming.'

62

JENNY

She spent the taxi ride trying to call people. The driver took a stupid route, hit roadworks at the top of The Mound. Jenny sat forward tapping her phone against her leg until they got a green light, her body tense as they went through it. She kept chewing over what Stella had said on the phone. Wardie Bay was a decoy, Stella wanted her on a deserted beach out of the way.

The taxi finally ran up Bruntsfield Place. Jenny peered through the park at the house. She couldn't see any lights on the top two floors, just their pine tree standing tall.

'Here.' She tapped her card against the reader and jumped out into the street. She stood for a moment and listened. Smelled the air and caught the scent of burning.

She turned into the driveway and saw the fire. Low flames licked from the smashed glass of the front door, the doorframe blackening. There was another fire to the left, one of the viewing rooms, orange flickering around the broken window. A trail of burning grass went from window to door and spread to the right, nearly at the embalming room loading door.

She pulled out her phone as she ran to the house.

There was a dark van parked near the hedge she didn't recognise.

Her phone connected. 'Fire service, quick.'

She walked to the front door and the heat pushed her back.

A voice in her ear. She interrupted.

'Our house is on fire, 0 Greenhill Gardens in Bruntsfield, please hurry.'

She heard a crunch of gravel and felt a thud of blinding pain on the back of her head, knocking her to the ground, her phone spinning out of her hand.

She turned on her knees and saw Stella, long-handled torch in one hand, can of petrol in the other.

'You should've stayed at the seaside.'

'You've lost your fucking mind.'

Stella was manic, her face lit by the flames. They were spreading upward, black smoke billowing out. Jenny felt the heat on her face.

'No.' Stella waved the petrol about. 'Just a little bit of payback. You set fire to someone I love, I'm setting fire to something you love. Seems fair.'

Jenny glanced at the van behind her, rear doors open.

'Is Craig in there?'

Stella stepped forward and swung the torch at Jenny's head. She managed to get her arm up and felt the brunt of the strike against her elbow, pain down her body. She tried to catch her breath, heard glugging and looked up.

Stella was spreading petrol along the grass towards the embalming room and workshop. If the coffins caught, they would go up like kindling. And what about the bodies in the fridges? Jesus Christ. Jenny looked for her phone, couldn't see it.

She struggled to her feet and staggered towards Stella. Stella turned and swung the torch at her again, connecting with her jaw, but Jenny still barrelled into her, splashing petrol over them both. She had a flash of being covered in the same shit with Craig a year ago and wondered if this was all some sick déjà vu.

She felt something in her mouth and spat out a tooth. The pain in her jaw was excruciating. Stella stepped back and hit her again with the torch, this time flooring her.

Jenny felt the gravel under her fingers as she knelt on all fours, blood dripping from her mouth. She was dizzy as she looked up. Stella ran a line of petrol from the viewing room window to the old pine tree, which took light immediately, orange and blue flames dancing around its thick trunk, bark curling, needles fizzling and disappearing in the heat.

'That'll do it.' Stella emptied the dregs of the can and threw it through the broken front-door glass. The whole ground floor was now dancing in flames, smoke thrusting into the air. Jenny remembered standing in this garden at her dad's funeral pyre, the smell of him on the wind.

She tried to get up and felt another thump from the torch on her back, knocking her to the ground, face in the gravel.

'Don't try to find me.' Stella strode across the driveway and closed the van doors. She stopped at the driver's door and turned back, surveying the carnage and nodding at Jenny. She got in the van and drove off, tyres chewing the gravel as she left.

Jenny stumbled across to look for her phone. The flames had spread to the embalming-room door, the metal charring along the bottom. She wondered how far the fire had spread inside. She looked up, the top two floors were still in darkness, still intact. Where the fuck were the fire engines? She listened for sirens but didn't hear any.

'Help.' A faint voice.

She stopped and listened. 'Hello?'

Just the crack and rumble of flames. The tree behind her was an inferno now, a beacon. Surely someone would come soon.

'Hello?' she shouted.

'Mum?'

'Hannah, where are you?'

She moved towards the embalming-room door, angled her head.

'There's smoke.'

Jenny felt sick. 'Hannah, wait. I'll get you out.'

The fire was all along the bottom of the loading door. She moved to the far corner, touched the metal, which burned her hand. There was no release button on the outside. Fuck.

'I'll be there in a minute,' she shouted. 'Hang on.'

She ran around the back, blinking her eyes to get used to the darkness. There was a fire exit beyond the storeroom. She tried it, locked. She threw herself against it, a judder of pain in her shoulder. She turned and looked around. A pile of rocks leftover from some wall renovation, green with moss. She sifted through, found one with an edge. She slammed it down on the round metal handle, pain up her arm. Did it again, felt a surge of power through her body despite the pain. Switched to holding the rock in both hands, bringing it down from above her head onto the handle, over and over, screaming with each smash.

The metal buckled and crumpled under the weight then finally broke away from the door, leaving an exposed hole.

Jenny reached her fingers in and scrabbled around, felt the release bar and pulled it. The door swung open. She ran in past the storeroom and workshop into the embalming room, full of black smoke.

Hannah was on a metal table by the workbench, coughing, tears in her eyes.

Jenny tried to lift her but she was tied to it. 'What the fuck?'

Hannah opened her eyes. 'You came.'

Jenny's eyes stung from the smoke. The heat from the doorway was intense, flames licking along the base.

Hannah angled her head at the floor. 'Scalpel.'

Jenny scoured the floor under the table, tears in her eyes, and spotted it. She drew it hard across the first cable tie, sawed until it was cut, then did the other wrist.

'Indy.' Hannah rubbed her wrists and tried to sit up. She pointed at the fridges. 'In there.'

'OK.' Jenny cut Hannah's ankle ties and helped her up. The smoke was everywhere now, curling in billows across the ceiling.

'Is Mum here?' Jenny said.

'What?'

'Mum, is she in the house?'

Hannah shook her head. 'She's with Thomas.'

'You're sure?'

A nod.

She helped Hannah stand then grabbed two ragged cloths from the worktop, wrapped one around her nose and mouth, did the same for Hannah. It smelled of embalming fluid. She went to the fridges, began opening doors. The first four were corpses. The fifth one had Indy in it. Jenny checked for a pulse, weak but there. Her skin was icy. Jenny tried to rouse her. Nothing. She shoved her hands into Indy's armpits and heaved her off the tray, staggering backwards with the weight, the smoke making her blind with tears. Hannah reached out a hand for Indy's feet but Jenny pushed her towards the doorway.

'Go.'

Hannah staggered to the door, looking behind. Jenny dragged Indy, back aching, eyes stinging, lungs on fire. They stumbled out of the room, down the corridor and out of the fire exit.

Hannah took one side of Indy and helped Jenny drag her to the front of the house, along the driveway to a safe distance.

Hannah looked at the flames licking the ground floor, the pine tree blazing in the dark. 'What the hell?'

They slumped on the grass near the gateposts. Hannah touched Indy's face, pushed the hair from her eyes. Jenny watched them for a moment then turned to the burning house and listened for sirens.

63

DOROTHY

Dorothy watched Archie manoeuvre the van through the morning traffic and swallowed back tears. In the row of seats behind her were Jenny, Hannah and Indy, all silent after a night at the hospital. Minor smoke inhalation, cuts and bruises from the beating Jenny got, residual grogginess for the others from whatever date-rape drug Laura used. No sign of hypothermia for Indy. Battered, but still alive. They were told to go home and rest but Dorothy wasn't sure they had a home to go to.

The van passed Cameron Toll, stopped at the King's Buildings lights. Archie threw her a smile full of sorrow. She'd had Thomas on the phone while she was at the hospital, keeping her updated about the house. He even put the chief firefighter on the call at one point. They'd reassured her as much as they could, but she had to see it for herself. Traffic was slow through Blackford and The Grange. Dorothy looked at the sky for traces of smoke as they approached Greenhill. Just blue skies and a sharp sun.

As they reached the street, Archie leaned over and gripped her hand.

Her breath caught in her throat when she saw the house and the remains of the tree. Archie parked alongside the one remaining fire engine. Two firefighters were sitting on the back, gear off, eating bacon rolls, swinging their legs like little kids. Behind the ambulance was a police car.

'Jesus,' Hannah said behind her.

Dorothy got out, damp smoke sticking in her throat. Thomas emerged from the police car with his arms out. She received a hug but kept her eyes on the house. It wasn't as bad as she'd feared, but still pretty terrible.

She untangled herself from Thomas, touched his cheek then walked closer to the house. She was aware of the others climbing out of the van behind her.

Through the shattered window she could see that the viewing room was gutted, furniture torched, rags of wallpaper bubbled and scorched. Curtains gone. On the right-hand side of the house the damage was less severe. The embalming room door was up and Archie was already there, talking to a firefighter who'd come over. Dorothy knew the most important thing from Thomas on the phone, all their deceased were OK. The flames didn't reach as far as the fridges, and the bodies inside were protected from the smoke.

Dorothy heard a purr and turned to see Schrödinger emerge from the hedge. She laughed with relief as he padded towards her, then noticed something in his mouth. A sparrow. He dropped it at her feet. She knelt down, picked him up and squeezed hard until he wriggled free and leapt from her grasp.

She looked at Thomas and pointed at the front door. 'Is it safe?'

He nodded. 'But be careful.'

She walked inside and tears filled her eyes. The reception was blackened and scorched, the carpet in ragged black threads, floorboards buckled from the heat. The walls were streaked with smoke and burnt in places, the desk torched, collapsed in the middle. There had been bouquets of flowers in the corner of reception for their next funeral services, gone. She looked at the charred ceiling. The cornicing was intact but discoloured. The stench was strong, burnt wood and carpet, plastic and wallpaper, toxic chemicals drifting into her lungs as she breathed with a shudder. She imagined those atoms of the house making their way into her bloodstream and she felt happy about that, at least. Becoming a part of her.

She looked at the stairs. The bannister was blackened but seemed solid.

The other women and Thomas had come in behind her.

'Fuck,' Jenny said under her breath.

'Indeed,' Dorothy said.

Indy leaned on Hannah.

'Upstairs?' Dorothy said.

Thomas raised his eyebrows. 'Mostly fine, thanks to those guys.' He pointed towards the fire engine outside. 'Some smoke damage, but basically OK.'

Dorothy wiped away tears. Her hands were grey with soot and she remembered her husband's ashes, dipping her finger in.

'Cup of tea, then?'

64

JENNY

Jenny took a big hit of Highland Park and looked out of the window over Bruntsfield Links. The burn of the whisky matched the smell of torched house. It turned out the firefighters had shut off the fuses to the whole house until they could get an electrician to check things over. So there was no tea but Dorothy had upgraded them all to a large dram. Jenny wasn't complaining.

She looked to the left, saw the burnt remains of their pine tree. She'd climbed it as a kid, it had been here as long as the house. She felt stupid, sentimental about a tree. Maybe it didn't matter.

She turned back to the room. 'So.'

They were all sitting around the kitchen table like a normal family, like the world hadn't gone up in flames.

Dorothy pulled out a chair. 'Please sit.'

'I'm OK.' Her voice sounded petulant. She swallowed and sat with a sheepish look. 'Where's Stella?'

'And Laura,' Hannah said, rubbing Indy's hand on the table.

'One at a time,' Dorothy said, looking at Thomas.

Imagine being this guy, Jenny thought, suddenly having to deal with all this. The Skelfs were magnets for weird shit and Thomas had to handle the aftermath.

'Laura is easy,' Thomas said. 'We have her in custody. I sent officers to her house.'

'And?' Hannah looked pale and fragile.

'She was there.' Thomas held his palms upward. 'With her mum.'

Indy frowned. 'What?'

'She just took Elizabeth home, dragged her inside and put her to bed. She told the officers she wasn't ready to say goodbye.'

'Fucking hell,' Jenny said. 'All because she loves her mum? How very *Psycho*.'

'Jenny.' The tone of Dorothy's voice took Jenny back to being a kid and her cheeks flushed.

'I know, we all deal with grief differently, blah blah blah, but come on, that's crazy. This girl steals her mum's body, moments later, Stella, with Craig's body in the back of a van, tries to set us on fire.'

'Stella didn't know anyone was in the house,' Dorothy said.

Jenny turned to her. 'How the hell do you know? Why are you defending these lunatics?'

'I'm not.'

Dorothy lowered her head and Jenny felt her cheeks again. None of this was Dorothy's fault. All she did was try to help people and now half their house was burnt down.

Jenny turned to Thomas. 'So where's Stella?'

She knew the look on his face. She'd had bad news from him before and she felt sick.

'We're not sure.' Thomas held his hands together like he was praying. 'We have your description of the van, patrol cars are looking, and there's a nationwide alert. She won't get far.'

'Jesus Christ. An insane arsonist is just driving around with her decomposed brother in the back, whistling a merry fucking tune?'

She glugged her whisky. She'd sucked all the life out of the room and she didn't care. Hannah and Indy could've died and she couldn't shake her anger about that. The terror of losing her daughter. She turned away from the table, wiping at her wet eyes. She cleared her throat and finished her whisky, felt the heat through her body. She thunked her glass on the table and turned to Thomas. 'Find her.'

She started to walk away, scared she might collapse.

'Where are you going?' Hannah said.

At the doorway, she swallowed down the stench of smoke then ran downstairs. In the burnt-out reception she broke down crying.

A weight pressed on her chest and she struggled to get air in as sobs shook her body and her hair fell over her face.

It was too much. Hannah almost died, Indy too. This stupid fucking damaged house. Stella and Craig, Laura and her mum. Why did the Skelfs deal with the dead if this was the shit that came to their door?

She leaned against the wall and started to breathe, raggedly at first, then more cleanly. She didn't want the others to see her like this, and she was ashamed that she couldn't show them.

'Jenny?'

She jumped at Archie's voice. She expected pity in his eyes when she looked up, but his face was full of kindness.

She shook her head. She was scared to speak, scared of what would come out.

'I know.' Archie looked around at the damage. 'It's all too much. But you have to cling to the positives – we're all still here.'

'We almost weren't.'

'Thanks to you.'

'No.'

'You saved Hannah and Indy. Why can't you let yourself—'

'No.' Jenny's body shook as she breathed in smoky air.

Archie stayed silent for a while, then stepped forward and held his hand out. 'I want you to have this.'

He opened his fist. It was the little fox netsuke he was carving in the workshop that night. There was a sinuous curve to the animal's body, contented smile on its sleeping face. Jenny wondered what that felt like.

Archie pressed it into her hand. 'Think of it as a lucky charm.'

Jenny laughed. 'Lucky?'

Archie looked dead serious. 'We're all very lucky to have each other.'

She examined his face for meaning, then turned the fox over in her hand. It was so beautiful. That he had made it for her was overwhelming. 'Thank you, Archie.'

She held her arms out self-consciously, pushed herself into his solid body, hugged him for a long time. She felt his warmth, smelled the smoke, wondered what her fox was dreaming about.

❧

A cold wind blew across Bruntsfield Links. She blew her nose and wiped her face, felt heartburn from the whisky. Her legs were trembling as she walked. She pictured Stella out there with Craig's remains. What must Violet think? She rubbed at the netsuke in her palm, her lucky talisman.

She was almost at Chalmers Street before she admitted to herself she was going to see Brandon. Someone held the building door open and she went upstairs trying to breathe normally, wafting her face, whisky on her breath. She went to his office, cleared her throat and knocked.

'Come in.'

She opened the door and stood there.

Brandon flinched when he saw her. 'I told you, I can't see you.'

'I need help.'

'I don't doubt it.'

She felt tears coming again, covered her face with her hands, leaned against the doorframe. She heard him get up and come over.

'Hey.'

She looked up. He had kind eyes, concern on his face. She didn't deserve it.

'You smell of whisky,' he said.

'I know.'

'It's ten past nine in the morning.'

'I know.'

He sighed, looked into the corridor behind her.

She lowered her hands and straightened her shoulders, totally failing to convey any confidence. 'Please, I'm a fucking mess.'

He stared at her for a long time. Eventually he waved her into the office.

'You'd better come in.'

65

HANNAH

She sat on the bench with Indy's head on her shoulder, their breathing in synch. They were in the front garden staring at the house. The fire engine and police car were gone. Dorothy was away too, to speak to Danny. She could hear Archie inside doing an inventory of the embalming room and workshop.

Schrödinger padded across the gravel. He looked at the blackened house and the charred tree then disappeared into the bushes.

She and Indy had hardly spoken since last night. It felt like words weren't enough. What could they say that wouldn't seem trite? They were both alive and safe. She imagined she was the Milky Way, a giant black hole at her core. But she wasn't empty, she had Indy, her family, this life.

She jumped at the sound of a van and felt Indy flinch. She saw Willow in the driver's seat, Udo next to her. She'd forgotten all about them, with everything here.

Willow pulled up alongside them and jumped out with a crunch of gravel. She didn't have the bandage on her head anymore but Hannah could see the cut.

She stared at the house. 'What in the Jesus Christ of fuck happened here?'

Hannah didn't have words.

Indy sat up. 'A confused client.'

'Holy shit, that is some confusion.'

Indy brushed at her trousers. 'She didn't handle grief very well.'

'So she burnt your house down,' Willow said.

Udo came around from the other side of the van, stood with his hands on his back.

They all looked at the house for a long time.

Eventually Willow nodded at Udo. 'Makes our little run-in seem amateur.'

She waited for a response, didn't get one. Hannah felt tired, eyelids heavy, the drugs from last night still in her veins.

'Anyway,' Willow said. 'That why we're here, right Jiji?'

Udo put his hands together and bowed. 'Is your grandmother home?'

Hannah shook her head. 'She had to deal with something.'

Willow's eyebrows went up. 'Seems like she's dealing with a lot.'

Hannah stuck her bottom lip out, worried she would start crying.

Willow seemed to realise. 'Sorry, I'm an ass, ignore me.'

Udo walked to the van. 'We have a present for Dorothy, for all of you. To say thank you.'

Indy stood up. 'And you needed a van?'

Willow nodded. 'It's a big present.'

Udo opened the doors. Hannah half expected to see Laura's mum, or her own dad. Instead, lying on its side was a red phone box.

'A wind phone,' Udo said.

'It was Jiji's idea,' Willow said. 'I sourced a phone box on eBay. Sorry we haven't had time to paint it white.'

Udo bowed again. 'I know how useful I find my phone. And my neighbours. I saw how your grandmother looked at it.'

He lowered his head and Hannah wondered about the shame and guilt he talked about. How Dorothy always understood, tried to see things from all angles. He turned and examined the box on its side in the van.

Willow leaned towards Hannah and spoke quietly. 'Jiji and I sat and talked for a long time yesterday. It was good to get it all out in the open. He's still upset and feels guilty, but I told him I'd stick around for a bit, keep him company. Help him. He had his first good night's sleep in forever. Things feel a lot better.'

Udo turned and smiled. 'It seems to me that a funeral home is a good place to have a wind phone. You have many bereaved people here. Maybe they want to speak to their loved ones.'

Hannah nodded.

'Are you sure about this?' Indy said.

Udo and Willow shared a smile.

'Then that's very kind, thank you.'

She called Archie over from the embalming room, and between them and Willow, the three of them cajoled the wind phone out of the van and over to the corner of the garden. Once it was upright, Udo fussed a little inside, making sure everything was right.

Indy wiped her hands free of dust. 'Thank you so much.'

Hannah couldn't understand how Indy was managing, as if they hadn't almost died. But she'd always been the strong one.

Hannah walked to the phone box, rested her hand against the door, tried to feel something. She went inside, waited as the door closed behind her. She picked up the handset and looked at it. Put it to her mouth and turned round.

They were all looking at her. Gran was away in a cemetery, Mum was God knows where. She was alive, they were all still alive.

She looked at the phone but didn't speak. She had no words.

66

DOROTHY

Liberton Cemetery felt more hopeful in the sunshine, blue skies overhead, sparrows flitting between the trees. Dorothy couldn't get the smell of burning out of her nose. She walked down the row of tombstones, saw Danny at his mother's grave. He took a moment to turn. He was pale and tired, but who wasn't? And he had every reason. He seemed sober.

'Thanks for meeting me,' he said.

'My pleasure.' She wondered if she should've used that word. Good to know she was still doubting herself. If anyone ever told you they had life sorted, they were delusional. 'I'm so sorry.'

He rubbed at his chin, a few days of stubble. 'You have nothing to be sorry for. I asked you to find my dad and you did. You did much more besides.'

Dorothy couldn't imagine how he felt. Kathleen was dead, Eddie was dead. Mike had survived the suicide attempt, would face trial for murder.

'Some fucking mess,' Danny said, reading her mind.

Dorothy touched his shoulder. She remembered seeing him here with Jenny on the gravecam. She'd never asked about that. Some things are best left alone.

He waved a hand around the cemetery. 'Now I'm alone all over again.'

'You're not alone, I'm here. That sounds like empty words, I know. But I mean it.'

Danny looked at Kathleen's headstone and Dorothy followed his gaze. Read the name and dates, something she'd done thousands of times. All those lives, all that energy. All the endless sorrow and loss.

'There is something.' Danny looked up. 'Could you do Dad's funeral?'

Dorothy could see he was only just holding on.

'Of course.'

❧

She stepped around the wind phone, gazed at it, ran her hand across the surface making sure it was real. She smiled as she reached the door, Hannah standing alongside.

'Udo just brought it round?'

'With Willow's help.'

'Are they both OK?'

Hannah nodded. 'They will be.'

Dorothy's eyes went up and down the box. It was a lovely gesture and a perfect gift. A funeral director with a hotline to the afterlife. She was sure it would get plenty of use.

She heard the crunch of gravel and turned to see Jenny walking up the drive. She raised her eyebrows and came over when she saw the wind phone. Dorothy's heart sang to see her. Despite everything, she seemed clear-eyed, determined. Less angry than earlier. Maybe she would be OK. Maybe they all would be.

Jenny peered inside the box.

'A wind phone,' Hannah said. 'For speaking to the deceased.'

Jenny nodded as if that was completely normal.

Dorothy looked at the blackened ground floor of their house. Damaged, but not destroyed. They would rebuild. She looked at the burnt-out tree and wondered if it was still alive underground, sap still in the roots, waiting to grow again. She looked at Hannah and Jenny, thought about the three of them, their roots and branches intertwining with each other, supporting and nurturing, forever interlinked.

She breathed deeply, smelled the smoke of their past, and set her mind to the future.

ACKNOWLEDGEMENTS

Massive thanks to Karen Sullivan and everyone at Orenda Books for all their hard work and dedication. Thanks to Phil Patterson and all at Marjacq for their constant support. Thanks to everyone who has championed my books over the years, it means so much. Huge love to Tricia, Aidan and Amber, always.